The Sword in the Sea

Jerry Carpenter

Published by Jerry Carpenter at Smashwords

This is a work of fiction. Similarities to real people, places, or events are entirely coincidental.

THE SWORD IN THE SEA

First edition. June 20, 2013.

ISBN: 979-8230820994

Written by Jerry Carpenter.

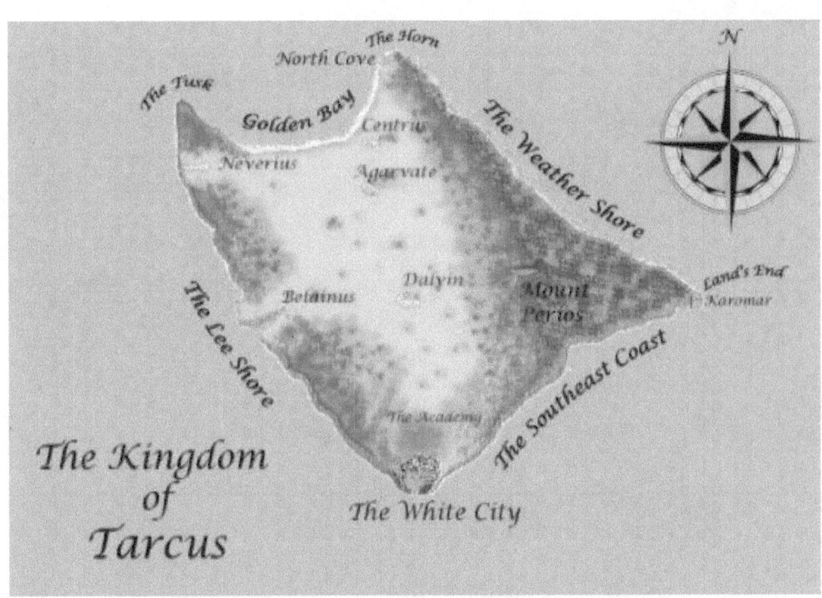
The Horn
North Cove
The Tusk
Golden Bay
Neverius
Agarvate
The Weather Shore
N
Land's End
Karomar
Dalyin
Belainus
Mount Perios
The Lee Shore
The Southeast Coast
The Academy
The Kingdom of Tarcus
The White City

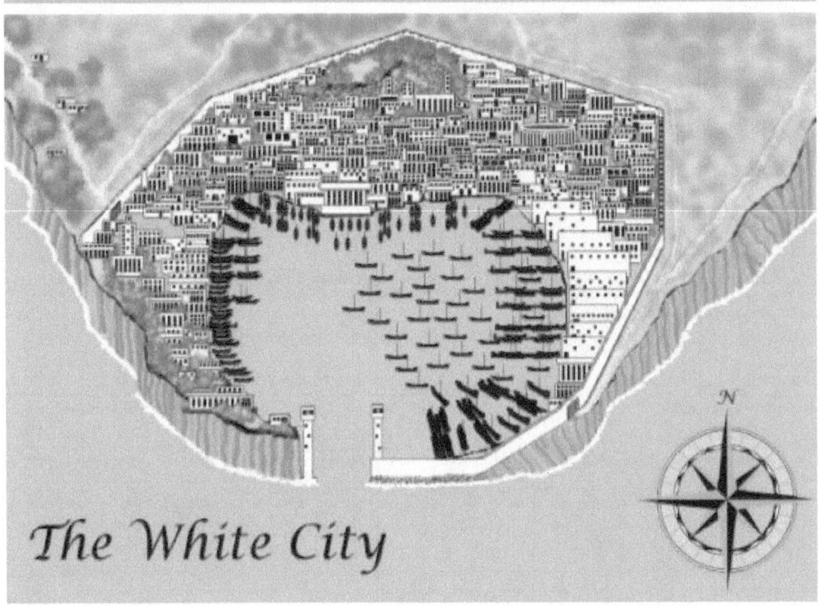
N
The White City

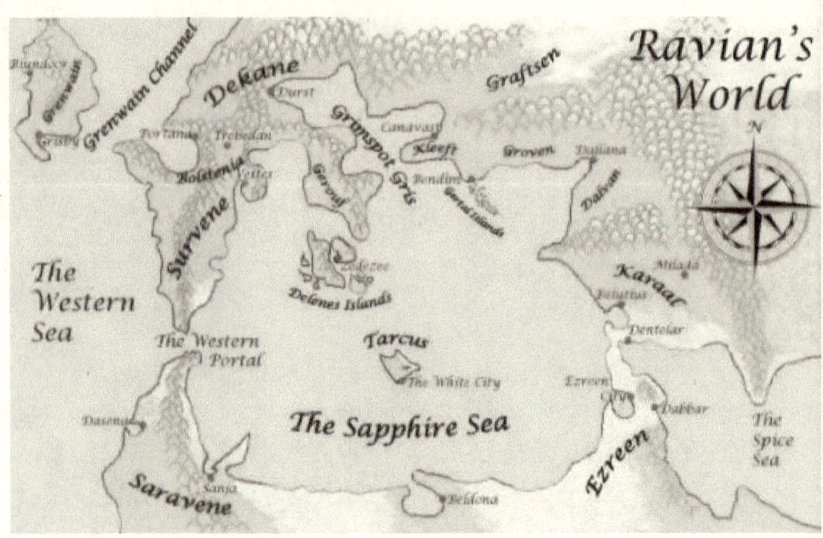
Ravian's World
N
Grenwain
Grenwain Channel
Dekane
Durst
Trebedan
Grimspot Gris
Geroud
Canavar
Kleeft
Graftsen
Groven
Bendim
Dalvan
Bolstenia
Survene
Delenes Islands
The Western Sea
The Western Portal
Tarcus
The White City
The Sapphire Sea
Karaal
Dentolar
Ezreen
Dabbar
The Spice Sea
Saravene
Sanja
Beldona

Chapter One

King Jabacus and Prince Ravian rode out alone onto the arid, almost treeless plain beyond the White City's northern walls. Even though the times were settled and the rule of law was strong throughout Tarcus, it was unusual for the king and the second in line to the throne to travel without an escort. The Academy however, was only three miles distance from the North Gate and both father and son knew that it would be the last private moment they would have for a long time.

In the distance ahead, the white walls of the military school gleamed in the harsh, early afternoon sun. Clouds of red dust rose from the several points about the surrounding countryside and Ravian could just make out the groups of tiny figures that were the cause – young male Tarcuns practicing the craft of war. Ravian knew that, like him, those boys would have looked forward to the day when they reached fourteen years of age and commenced their two-year term of basic military training. For the young prince however, there was an extra dimension to this new beginning, his father having ordained his destiny – and that of his two brothers – four years' beforehand.

Jabacus had summoned the three princes to the Hunting Room, a favourite reception chamber of the king's, located high in the palace's western wing. The room was comfortable and masculine – its floors covered with beautiful animal skins and its walls hung with tapestries depicting deeds of the hunt. Outside the tall, column-framed windows that ran the length of its southern wall, the rooftops of the thousands of gleaming white houses that gave the city its name swept down towards the distant, deep blue circle of the harbour. Still more dwellings to east and west of the palace clung to the steep-sided, curving arms of land that embraced the bay without quite meeting at its southern extremity. At the narrow entrance there, the white sentinels of the two watchtowers guarded the finest natural anchorage in the world – a haven where all manner and size of vessel scurried in a constant frenzy of mercantile activity.

Jeniel, Ravian and Ramus gave scant regard to this magnificent panorama – it was something that they had grown up with and took for granted. Besides, this was the first time their father had assembled the three waiting princes in such a formal manner and they were anticipating a momentous announcement.

They were not to be disappointed.

Jabacus, king of Tarcus, strode into the chamber alone. He was a powerfully built, energetic man whose productive, enlightened reign had endeared him to his nation. He was also a loving father to his three sons and Ravian felt a strange pang as he and his brothers came to their feet and bowed the king to his throne. Their lives, he realised, were about to move forward in a way that could never be reversed.

Jabacus settled into his seat and waved the boys to their own chairs.

'My Sons,' Jabacus began, 'Jeniel has now reached the age where he must begin his formal training as my successor.'

Ravian stole a glance sideways at his older sibling. Now approaching his fourteenth year, Jeniel already had Jabacus's dark complexion and the beginnings of his broad build. Ravian, fair-haired and slender in the way of his mother's family, had often wished that he were more like the two of them.

'As king, your brother will have something that I never had,' Jabacus continued, 'two loyal and loving brothers to support him.'

The three boys nodded their understanding – their father had been an only child.

'Ravian,' Jabacus said, 'on your brother's accession, you become next in line to the throne until such time as Jeniel has his own children. When you turn fourteen you will go into the Academy like any other Tarcun lad but, from this moment on, you are to focus on becoming the protector of your brother's throne and of this kingdom. After you complete your two years' basic training, you'll spend the usual two-year break receiving further instruction here at the Palace before you go on to your naval training. Ultimately, when the time is right and you have accumulated sufficient experience, you will be given the title of Defender of the Nation – and the overall command of the army and navy.'

'Yes, Father,' Ravian replied, his heart singing.

A full-time military career! The young prince could barely believe his good fortune.

'Ramus,' the king said, turning to the youngest of the brothers, 'you must learn the ways of commerce and diplomacy.'

Ramus made a face. At nine years' age, the freckle-faced prince was already a cheeky and irrepressible handful.

'None of that, Ramus!' the king admonished him sharply. 'I have already instructed your tutors to school you thus. When you turn twelve, you will enter the House of Bomma, your mother's house, where you will learn first-hand the ways of trade that have made Tarcus the great nation that she is today. Our swords and our longships exist only to protect this nation's trading interests and it is vital that you learn to understand and foster the interests of the Nine Houses.'

Ravian and Jeniel exchanged looks.

Poor Ramus – no military training for him!

The king turned back to his first-born son.

'And you, Jeniel, will learn all that these two will and more. As ruler, you will need to know everything that goes on in your kingdom. From the lofty towers of this palace to the sweat of a Belainian furnace – everything will be your concern. Moreover, you will need to know what is happening on every shore of the Sapphire Sea. You will need spies, you will need diplomats and you will need allies. But none of these, Jeniel, will you need more than the love and loyalty of your own brothers.'

Ravian remembered that day now as he rode beside his father.

He had never felt envious of his brother – far from it. The responsibility of kingship seemed far too weighty a thing and, privately, Ravian hoped that Jeniel would be prompt in siring many children. The more princesses and princes between him and the throne the better, he thought.

'Nervous, Son?' Jabacus asked, interrupting his reverie.

Ravian realised that, although he had longed for this day, he felt slightly apprehensive now that it had arrived.

'A little, Father,' he admitted.

The king gave him a searching look.

'I understand,' he said. 'You must feel as though your mother and I are abandoning you for the next two years – but you know why, don't you?'

Ravian nodded. His parents had discussed this with him on a number of occasions.

'Because I need to learn to stand on my own two feet among the common people,' he replied.

Jabacus frowned. Until now, his sons had been sole companions to each other, used to everyone beyond their immediate family being their servants and their subjects.

'Ravian,' he said gently, 'this is the last time that I can remind you that, for the next two years, you must forget that you are of the royal line. The only hierarchy that is going to matter to you while you are at the Academy is the army's – and none of your fellow trainees are going to take it too kindly if you use terms like "common people".'

Ravian's ears reddened.

'Yes, Father,' said, acknowledging the king's advice and embarrassed that he had made the mistake.

His father sighed.

'It's alright, Son,' he said. 'I went through the same thing at your age. It was very difficult for me, being the crown prince. That's why I decided to give your older brother his military training at the palace.'

Ravian was silent – he knew how deeply both his brothers resented being denied their terms at the Academy. Normally, the only able-bodied Tarcun boys who received exemption from basic training did so for specific and exceptional reasons that only the Citizen's Council could approve. The same applied for the traditional recall to naval training after the two-year hiatus although, by then, some of the Nine Houses' eighteen year-olds would already be so involved in their families' business empires that the council would be forced to grant them exemptions.

This system of compulsory military training for all, creating a large citizens' reserve to support the core military establishment, served the island nation's strategic needs well. A military career might not offer the same potential for the accumulation of wealth as that of a merchant, but the tax system of the country funded secure, adequate incomes for its soldiers and sailors and permanent positions in the forces, particularly in the navy, were highly sought after.

Ravian was proud that he would one day command Tarcus' battle fleet of over fifty longships, as well as the nation's full-time land army of some fifteen hundred soldiers and five hundred cavalrymen. This military capability, along with Tarcus's relatively remote position in the centre of the Sapphire Sea, had long presented an effective deterrent to any neighbouring nations covetous of the island kingdom's wealth.

'For you, it will be very different,' the king continued. 'Some of the boys you are about to meet will be your comrades for life. You'll command all of them one day, of course, but to do that with any real authority you must first earn their respect and trust. They are two of the cornerstones of leadership, Ravian – Tarcuns don't like taking orders, but they'll follow a leader they believe in to the ends of the earth and beyond.'

No one was better qualified to give that advice than his father was, Ravian reflected. The king had the Citizen's Council wrapped around his little finger and enjoyed the absolute loyalty of the army and navy.

'Ah,' said Jabacus, as a lone horseman galloped out from the Academy's gates to meet them, 'here comes General Grabbus.'

The fast-closing rider, wearing a crested helmet and armour that flashed in the afternoon sun, sat rigidly upright on his galloping steed. A few paces short of the royal pair, he stood in the stirrups and hauled back on the reins, muscling his mount to a dusty halt in a spectacular exhibition of strength and horsemanship. Grabbus removed his helmet to reveal a lined, sun-darkened face topped by a mane of white hair.

'Welcome, Your Majesty!' he boomed, surprising Ravian by giving the king the military salute – right fist clenched over heart – instead of the bow that was his father's usual due.

'It's good to see you, General,' Jabacus replied, dismounting.

Grabbus followed suite and then, to Ravian's utter astonishment, the two men embraced each other.

'I did my military service alongside this old lion,' Jabacus explained, as Ravian swung down off his own horse. 'I fancy we saved each other's necks a few times during those days, eh Grabbus?'

'Aye, Your Majesty,' Grabbus growled, 'especially when we had to flush out those pirates around the Gertals.'

'Almost as risky as those expeditions through the fleshpots of Ezreen, eh, Old Friend?' the king boomed.

Grabbus looked vaguely uncomfortable at this and Ravian blushed. Jabacus seemed to realise he had gone too far and cleared his throat.

'Yes, well,' the King said. 'I have come to deliver this young man into your charge for the next two years – he understands that there will be no special favours on account of his lineage. Prepare him well to defend his brother and the kingdom.'

'It will be my honour, Your Majesty,' Grabbus growled.

Father and son embraced quickly and awkwardly under the eye of the Academy's commander.

'Goodbye, Son,' Jabacus said in a low voice. 'The love of your mother and I will be with you.'

Ravian was unable to reply. His throat felt tight and his eyes burned. He loved his family dearly and the two years that he had anticipated so keenly suddenly yawned before him like a huge chasm.

With no further words, his father released his son and, taking up the reins of the prince's horse, remounted his own stallion. Without a backward glance, the king kicked his steed into a gallop in the direction of the White City, quickly disappearing from sight behind his own dust cloud.

Ravian would always remember how hurt and abandoned he had felt at his father's brusque departure. Many years later though, when he had children himself, it would occur to him that Jabacus had probably kept his back turned on that day to hide the tears in his own eyes.

'Ravian,' Grabbus' voice broke into his misery, 'report to the main courtyard and ask for Delanion – he's to be your training officer.'

Ravian's head snapped around. Grabbus had forgotten to address him by his title.

Grabbus glared at him.

'You heard His Majesty,' the old soldier said firmly. 'There are no titles here – you are all trainees the same.'

Then the Academy Commander's eyes and voice softened a little.

'And the sooner you understand that, the easier it will be for you,' he said, 'although it can never be that easy for a prince of the realm. I fancy that your father found it very hard at your age.'

Then the hardness returned and, with the fluid grace of a much younger man, Grabbus swung himself up into his saddle.

'Now,' he ordered, towering above the young prince, 'give me your best salute and carry on!'

Ravian did as he was ordered and Grabbus wheeled his horse and galloped back towards the academy gates. The young prince stared after the departing figure for a few moments, then straightened his shoulders and marched forward into commander's lingering dust cloud.

His destiny now lay within the walls of the Academy – he might as well get on with it!

Delanion was the first person Ravian encountered as he marched in through the open gates of the Academy and onto its main courtyard. This was partly because the training officer had been standing at the centre of the baking expanse of cobblestones awaiting his latest recruit's arrival for some time, and partly because, at that time of day, the two young men were the sole occupants of the inner parade ground. The encounter began badly for Ravian who, yet to receive his training in such things, was unaware of the significance of the red shoulder flashes worn by the lean, dour-faced young man who stood awaiting his approach.

'You!' Delanion barked when the prince was still ten paces from him. 'Don't you salute a senior rank?'

Ravian quickly came to attention and saluted the glowering youth who was to be his immediate superior for the next two years.

'Very well!' Delanion snapped. 'Report inside that building to the Stores Master and he will issue you your kit. Report back to me here as soon as you have done that!'

Sensing that it was the appropriate thing to do, Ravian saluted and moved off in the direction of the building Delanion had indicated.

'Stand still!' the training officer bellowed at him.

Ravian came rigidly to attention and Delanion was in front of him in two strides, disdain and dislike etched on his face.

'When you receive an order from a superior,' he snarled, 'you will salute and reply, "Yes Sir!" loudly and clearly. Do you understand?'

'Yes, Sir!' Ravian barked.

'Very well,' Delanion growled. 'Now carry on!'

'Yes, Sir!' Ravian bellowed again, saluting the stiff-backed youth before stepping around him and continuing on his way.

'At the double!' Delanion thundered after him. 'I don't intend to wait any longer out here in this heat than I have to!'

'Yes, Sir!' Ravian roared, correctly surmising the meaning of "at the double" and breaking into a run.

Shortly thereafter, weighed down by an armload of armour, military tunics and a bedroll, Ravian trotted back to the centre of the shimmering courtyard to report to his superior.

'Follow me,' barked Delanion and set off in a fast, long stride – his sword clinking at his side.

Ravian almost had to run to keep up as they headed toward a group of identical, single-storey buildings set against the back wall of the institution. Entering the one in the furthest corner, Delanion led him into a long, open hall down both sides of which ran a line of rough, wooden beds.

'This is your bed here,' the training officer growled. 'Stow your gear underneath it for the moment – your fellow trainees will show you how to do it properly when they get back. There's no point in you joining them now – they'll be halfway through their afternoon evolutions. Wait for them to return and then come with them to the mess hall for dinner. Understand?'

'Yes, Sir!' Ravian replied, snapping to attention but unable to salute because of his armload.

Delanion glared at him silently for a few seconds and Ravian waited helplessly for the next reprimand. Delanion however, seemed to have tired of harassing his new charge for the moment.

'Very well!' he snapped and stalked out of the hall.

Ravian looked around and saw little to add to his first impression. Apart from the beds, the walls and the windows, the hall was almost featureless. A lingering odour of young, unwashed, male bodies assailed his nostrils as he changed into his coarse military tunic, pushed his gear under his bed and sat down to wait.

After two hours, feeling very alone and increasingly anxious about his first meeting with his year mates, he heard the sounds of clanking armour and young voices approaching. As he rose to his feet, about twenty sweaty youths exploded noisily into the hall – only to come to halt in surprised silence when they saw the new arrival. One of their number, a dark-haired boy taller and more powerfully built than the rest, shouldered his fellows aside and advanced towards the prince. Somehow, despite still wearing full armour, he moved with cat-like silence, his glittering green eyes radiating malice.

Later in life, Ravian would reflect on how one could occasionally meet a complete stranger for the first time and instantly, instinctively know a life-long friend, a love about to be...or an eternal enemy.

The tall boy's lower lip curled.

'Look!' he announced loudly, drawing himself up into a swagger. 'We have a new arrival. What's your name, little boy? Does your mummy know you're here?'

'My name is Ravian,' the prince answered.

'Well, well, well,' the other boy said, coming to a halt before him with his hands on his hips. 'Surely not Prince Ravian? Don't tell me we are to be nursemaids to the king's royal puppy?'

Ravian heard couple of sniggers and saw the rest of the boys edging forward behind their leader.

'I've never had a nursemaid,' replied Ravian, 'and I can look after myself.'

'Ha! You hear that boys?' the green-eyed boy said, looking around the young faces behind him. 'The little prince can look after himself.'

There were more sniggers at this. Then the larger youth leaned menacingly forward, clenching his fists as he towering over Ravian.

'You'll need to, Blue Eyes,' he hissed menacingly. 'There's no room here for sissies.'

'Oh, leave him alone, Graticus,' a stocky, fair-haired boy behind him said. 'He's only just got here.'

Graticus spun and lashed out a fist in a sinuous blur of movement. The shorter boy's head snapped back and he tumbled backwards onto the floor with a crash of armour.

Graticus took a pace forward and leaned over the fallen boy.

'I've told you before to hold your tongue, Billus!' he snarled. 'You've got a big mouth for such a short arse!'

'And you!' he ground out, wheeling around to face Ravian. 'If you know what's good for you, you'll stay out of my way!'

With that, he stalked past Ravian's bed to his own place at the end of the hall. The rest of the boys filed silently past, watching the prince to see what his reaction would be.

Ravian bent to help Billus to his feet. The boy's lips were already swelling where they had burst against his teeth and small stream of blood ran down his chin.

'It's alright,' Billus said bravely, shrugging away the prince's helping hand. 'I've had worse in weapons training.'

'You should complain to the Training Officer,' Ravian said in a low voice.

'To Delanion?' Billus queried – and then began to smile before his split lip stopped him with a frown of pain.

'You don't seem to understand, Your Highness,' he said after a moment. 'The Academy has its rules but, in here...well, this hall makes its own laws and Graticus makes most of them.'

By chance, Billus's bed was next to Ravian's and, as they waited for the sound of the dinner gong, he showed the prince how to stow his gear tidily and correctly beneath it. The penalty for not doing so properly, he explained, was ten laps around the outside walls of the Academy in full armour.

At the other end of the hall, surrounded by most of the other boys, Graticus held court over a game of dice. He looked up occasionally to glower in their direction.

'What's the story with Graticus?' Ravian asked.

'He's the oldest son of Granius, master of the House of Palin, Your Highness,' explained Billus. 'Ever since he's been here he's made life a misery for anyone who's dared to stand up to him.'

'Look, Billus,' Ravian said to his companion. 'I don't think calling me "Your Highness" is going to make my life any easier while I'm here – just "Ravian" will do. I must agree though, this Graticus character certainly seems like a bit of a bully.'

'He's more than a bully, Ravian,' Billus replied matter-of-factly. 'He's dangerous.'

That evening, after a simple, nourishing dinner in the mess hall, the young students of war returned straight to their quarters. Almost immediately, Delanion stalked into the hall and ordered the torches extinguished and his charges to bed, even though dusk still glowed faintly outside the windows. This early bedtime made little difference to the other boys, Ravian noticed, as they all seemed to quickly fall asleep. The prince lay awake for sometime in the snore-filled darkness, reliving his encounter with Graticus and wondering what the morning would bring.

The need for such an early night became apparent the next morning, as it was still dark when Delanion, carrying a flaming torch, marched into the hall to wake them.

'All right, you Little Toads!' he bellowed. 'It's time to rise and Greet the Dawn!'

"Greeting the Dawn", Ravian discovered, was the name given to their daily run from the Academy gates out to a prominent rise, crowned with a single tree, some three miles northeast across the plains. This, ominously-named, "Heartbreak Hill" was, in fact, the first of a series of foothills that were the beginning of the land's rise eastwards towards the distant, towering shadow of Mount Perios, the highest point of the island. The journey around the tree and back neatly filled in the time between the rising of the Academy's students and the sun's first appearance over Mount Perios's shoulder.

As the boys from Ravian's hall set out, the other trainees of the establishment joined them and the youths fanned out across the shadowy plain like a stampede of wild horses. Ravian was pleased to find that he was able to keep up with the leading pack although, ahead of him, the broad-shouldered figure of Graticus soon pulled away – the bully easily stretching out to and holding a lead of a hundred paces over the rest of his fellows. Somehow, despite his stout frame and short legs, Billus managed to keep up beside Ravian in the leading group.

'Do you do this every morning?' Ravian gasped, as they wound their way up the hill to their turning point around the lone tree.

'Every morning – rain or shine,' Billus panted.

'Where are Delanion or the rest of the training officers?' Ravian asked. 'Does no one ever cheat?'

'Someone would be bound to tell,' Billus huffed. 'Then everyone would have to do the run all over again. I wouldn't want to be the boy responsible for that.'

On their return to the Academy, they went straight to a hurried breakfast in the mess hall, surrounded by perhaps three hundred other noisy, perspiring boys of around their own age. The last stragglers from the run had barely had time to stagger in and take a couple of mouthfuls before a loud horn blast came from the direction of the gates.

'Assemble!' bellowed Delanion, stalking into the hall with a group of older youths, who Ravian recognised by their insignia as being the other training officers.

'If you haven't had time to eat your breakfast – too bad!' Delanion snarled. 'Some of you slow pokes could stand to lose some weight anyway!'

The boys cleared the tables quickly, helped along by some of the training officers producing short lengths of rope with knotted ends with which they lashed out at tardy behinds. The trainees hurriedly poured out the main gates and onto the plain, assembling into groups as their breath steamed in the crisp morning air. These groups were, Ravian learned, "Divisions" and his own group, the boys in whose company he had just spent his first night, was the "Lizard Division".

The youthful prince felt a prick of envy for the young Tarcuns who had been lucky enough to join other, more imposingly named entities such as the "Hawk" or "Lion" divisions.

Each division quickly formed into two rows and, as the training officers ordered them to silence, three figures – two in armour and one in the bright red robes of the priesthood – strode out of the shadows of the gates and into the morning light. Ravian recognised the soldier in the centre of the group as Grabbus and he deduced that the other armoured man was the Chief Training Officer and Second in Command. In a booming voice, Grabbus proceeded to address them with what, it was to turn out, was one of his daily morning servings of advice to the trainees.

This morning's subject was brutally down to earth.

'Self-abuse will only weaken you!' Grabbus thundered. 'Besides, you young men should not have the time or the energy for any such carrying on while you are here. Save your strength for your training and you will always do better. Grasp yourself in the night and you risk inflaming your fellow trainees to an abominable act!'

The sniggering of several boys in the division confirmed the implication of the last sentence and Ravian blushed. What sort of life had he come to?

Having completed his mercifully brief sermon, Grabbus stepped back and motioned the priest forward to lead the assembly in the Morning Prayer to Delikas. This duty also swiftly despatched, Grabbus ordered, 'Carry on, Chief Training Officer', and after returning the salute of his second in command, the commander and priest marched back into the Academy.

The chief training officer then stepped forward and began detailing the day's activities for the various divisions.

'Eagle Division – marching this morning, and archery this afternoon.'

'Wolf Division – construction this morning, and sea knowledge this afternoon.'

'Lizard Division – archery this morning, and sword drill this afternoon.'

Beside him, Ravian heard Billus quietly groan and, as soon as the officer had completed reading the detail and the assembly had been dismissed, he asked him the reason.

'First year trainees always train with lead swords,' Billus explained. 'It's going to be a stinking hot day today and we are going to be spending the afternoon swinging lead!'

The temperature at the archery range, situated at the rear of the Academy, was pleasant enough, thanks to a line of trees on each side of the ground that afforded some shade from the relentlessly rising sun. Snatching covert glances away from Delanion's instruction however, Ravian could see the other divisions carrying out their training amidst clouds of dust further out on the plain and he reflected that Billus was right – it was going to be a long, hot, afternoon.

Delanion had lined his charges up in front of him to demonstrate the use of the bow and arrow. He showed them a typical Tarcun bow constructed of several laminations of wood and bone and explained that, at close range, it had the power to punch an arrow through all but the heaviest armour.

Ravian's eyes strayed towards the stand of bows and the pyramid of arrow-filled quivers behind Delanion and he flexed his fingers in anticipation. In the courtyards of the palace, he and Jeniel had spent many hours competing against each other with their father's hunting bows, and he knew that he had a good eye. When Delanion finally finished his demonstration and issued the boys their bows and quivers however, the prince noticed that the weight of the practice weapons were a lot lighter than he was used to – a concession to the age and strength of the trainees, he suspected.

Delanion assembled the boys into a line thirty paces opposite a row of round, upright targets and, despite the lightness of his bow, Ravian had little doubt he would be able to find the red-painted bull's-eye from such a close range. Delanion ordered his charges to fire five arrows at the target directly in front of each of them and, with calm deliberation, Ravian clustered his missiles within the red centre. Most of the boys at least hit their targets at this distance – although the occasional arrow sailed past to land out in the field behind. Delanion prudently ordered his division to lay their weapons on the ground and then stalked out to the line of targets, inspecting it from end to end without comment. Then, he ordered the boys to retrieve their arrows and withdraw to a distance of fifty paces from the target line.

Once they were in position, Delanion again gave the order to fire and, again, Ravian neatly clustered his shots in the centre of the target.

This time, as Delanion inspected each target, he passed a comment – usually scathing – on the accuracy of each archer. Coming to Ravian's target, he paused and looked around to confirm the identity of the sharpshooter.

'Ravian,' he said, a hint of surprise in his voice. 'Good shooting.'

Again, they retrieved their arrows and, this time, Delanion ordered a withdrawal to seventy paces.

At this range, Ravian had to use all his concentration – but he was rewarded by a grouping of arrows spread no wider than two hand-spans. Looking about, he saw that only one other archer had managed to put all five arrows on his target – and that some of his classmates had failed to hit their marks at all.

As Delanion again stalked the target line, this time in silence, Ravian looked along the row of boys, trying to make out which marksman had also found the target with all five arrows. With a feeling of foreboding, he realised that Graticus must be very close to the point where the accurate shooting had come from.

'Very well!' boomed Delanion. 'Retrieve your arrows!'

Then, 'All of you except Ravian and Graticus, stand to the side of the field! You two – retire to one hundred paces!'

Keeping a careful distance from each other, the two adversaries silently paced out the distance. Only when they turned did they look at each other directly and Ravian was, again, surprised by the reptilian, glittering coldness of his opponent's eyes.

'Fire when ready!' Delanion bellowed from the side of the range.

Ravian watched Graticus closely as he drew back his bow for his first shot, observing the muscular arms and stiff, hunched stance of the other boy. His arrow flew, landing just wide of the centre of the target and raising a cheer from the watching division.

Graticus lowered his bow and looked across at Ravian.

'Beat that!' his expression clearly said.

Ravian wished that his bow was more powerful, the training weapon's soft action not lending itself to shooting at such a long range. He loosed his first arrow and, even though he had compensated for the distance by aiming high, he saw it drop more than he had expected, hitting the target two hand-spans below the bull.

'Weak as water,' he heard Graticus sneer beside him.

At least his aim had been correct for line, Ravian consoled himself as his opponent lined up his second shot.

Graticus's arrow flew across the distance but, perhaps thinking too much about his comment to Ravian, he had aimed too high and his arrow only just caught the top of the target. There were more cheers from the other boys – although Ravian thought he heard a 'boo' mixed in with them.

Having ranged-in his weapon, Ravian then placed his second arrow in the central ring of the bulls-eye, the applause that followed this increasing in volume as, in quick succession, he clustered his three remaining shots within the same red circle.

In the face of this display, Graticus seemed to become flustered, landing his next two arrows wide on his target and, as a final humiliation, missing the mark completely with his last. Some brave souls amongst the division laughed and Graticus flushed angrily.

'Well done, Ravian,' Delanion bellowed. 'We seem to have a new champion archer in our midst.'

Ravian turned to speak to Graticus but the other boy was already walking back to the group, his back rigid with anger.

Sword drill, after a brief lunch in the welcome cool of the mess hall, took place in a dust bowl that seemed designed to trap the full heat of the afternoon sun. Their dress for the exercise was full armour – bronze helmet, chest plate, back plate and greaves – and each boy carried a large, round, shield and a short lead sword.

Delanion drilled the sweating boys in the basics movements of swordsmanship for a full, relentless hour. Ravian – who had never wielded anything but a toy wooden sword – enjoyed the lesson but, like the rest of the boys, found it hard toil under the hot sun. Indeed, by the end of the hour, the prince felt as though his lead weapon had trebled in weight and he was struggling to keep his bronze shield up in the proper guard position. At this point, one of the smaller boys in their group fainted and Delanion took this as a signal to rest his charges. The training officer despatched two trainees to the Academy and they returned with skins of cool water that the boys shared in exhausted silence.

After they had regained some energy – and the boy who had collapsed had been revived and sent back to the sleeping quarters – Delanion addressed them.

'All right you lot,' he announced. 'Now comes the part you've been waiting for! I'm going to pair you off against each other to practice what I've just taught you.'

With that, he proceeded to match the trainees into pairs of roughly equal size, lining them up in two opposing columns. As Delanion reeled off the names of the pairs, Ravian saw the training officer's eyes alight on him with an odd gleam.

'Ravian, you did well against Graticus in the archery this morning,' he said. 'Let's see how you go against each other in swordplay.'

Wearing a wolfish grin, Graticus promptly strode into position opposite the prince and Ravian felt a flash of fear. He had discreetly observed Graticus during the sword drill and it was evident that his much taller and heavier opponent was already an accomplished swordsman. The unfairness of the match was obvious to all and, suddenly, Ravian's trepidation was replaced by a surge of anger and determination.

'So be it,' he thought.

He had no doubt that Graticus would try to make him look like a fool but he was not going to make it easy for the green-eyed bully.

Delanion took up a position at the head of the two lines of opponents.

'Very well!' the training officer bellowed. 'The Division will prepare to engage. Division ready...'

Ravian had his eyes on Delanion, still wondering why the officer had matched him so unfairly. In later years, he would learn to read the small noises made by an adversary as though announced by thunder but on this, his first day with a sword in his hand, he missed the soft warning sounds of attack.

The sharp intake of breath.

The creak of leather bindings.

The whirr of a sword through the hot afternoon air.

'...engage!'

As the order left Delanion's lips, the flat of Graticus's blade crashed against the side of Ravian's helmet, knocking him to the ground and sending his sword and shield flying. The prince lay stunned, fighting off waves of darkness and, for a moment, he was sure that the force of the blow had broken his neck. He was vaguely aware of Graticus towering above him, yelling insults down at him – but he couldn't make out the words. As the world spun about him, he managed to get to his hands and knees – whereupon Graticus seized the opportunity to direct a kick to his backside that sent him sprawling in the dust again.

The next thing he knew, Graticus had withdrawn a couple of paces and Delanion was pulling him to his feet.

'Come on, Lizard Spawn!' the Training Officer snarled at him. 'You can't afford to go to sleep when you are facing a man with a sword in his hand – even a practice sword! Now, let's see you start using some of those skills I've just taught you!'

Still groggy, Ravian gathered up his sword and shield – barely having time to take up his guard before a triumphantly grinning Graticus bore in on him with a barrage of wild, savage blows. All Ravian could do was to protect his head with sword and shield – the strength and savagery of Graticus's assault driving him to down onto one knee.

Even as he defended himself though, the prince's mind had begun to clear and, as it did, his anger returned. Graticus's stance was wide as he stood over Ravian and hammered away at him – more like that of a blacksmith at the forge than that of a swordsman in combat. Unable to spare his own blade from its position defending his head, Ravian lashed upward with his right leg, and his instep connected with Graticus's genitals with significant force. The larger boy gasped, threw aside his sword and shield, and rolled backwards onto the ground with a squeal of agony as Ravian staggered upright.

Red-faced, Delanion stalked up to them and pushed the prince away from his writhing opponent.

'That's enough!' he roared. 'You are here to learn swordplay – not brawl like drunken sailors in a brothel! Ravian! Take your sword and shield for a jog around the tree on Heartbreak Hill! And you, Graticus! How many times have I told you that size and strength are no substitute for a sound defence?!'

Graticus ignored his instructor and continued to groan upon the ground as Ravian set off on the long run.

The prince's armour clanked and chafed with every pace and the weight of his sword and shield threatened to drag him to earth. He knew now that he had made an implacable enemy of Graticus but he consoled himself with the knowledge that there had been no alternative. At least the bully now knew that he would stand up to him.

Somehow, Ravian made it to the crest of the hill and the turning point around the tree. As he tottered back across the hot plain, heart pounding and almost blinded by sweat, he was both surprised and relieved to realise that he was almost back to the drill field. He had just begun to make out the individual faces of the other boys when a black fog suddenly swept around him and he pitched forward into darkness.

He awoke on his bed, the noise of the Lizard Division barracks around him. Billus sat on the edge of the bunk, a bowl of water on his knee and a wet cloth in his hands, and Ravian realised that he had been stripped and that his friend had been bathing him.

'Well,' said Billus, 'you've certainly had a mixed day.'

Ravian tried to say something but only managed a feeble croak. Billus handed him a smaller bowl of water to drink. The water was tepid but clean and it soothed the young prince's throat. His head ached mightily from Graticus's sneak attack and the muscles in the side of his neck felt wrenched and torn.

'I think that you might have given Delanion a fright,' his friend said quietly as Ravian drank. 'He's not the most pleasant piece of work, but I think he saw his military career flash before his eyes when you collapsed out there on the plain.'

'Why does he particularly dislike me?' whispered Ravian.

'He's from a very poor background,' said Billus. 'His father's a rough sort who's clawed his way up from the ranks to officer level – the rumour is that he met Delanion's mother when she was working as a cleaner in the barracks latrines. Delanion sinks his teeth into anyone who he thinks has had a more privileged upbringing than he has –

which is just about anybody. You, however, Your Highness, are as close to the top of his menu as anybody could get.'

'What about Graticus?' Ravian asked. 'Delanion doesn't seem to mind him too much.'

'Don't worry,' his friend replied with a wry smile. 'Until you came here, Graticus was Delanion' favourite target. How do you think you got back here? – Graticus had to carry you back. Delanion made him do it with both of you still in full armour and he had to carry both your swords and shields as well.'

Ravian turned his head and looked over towards the end of the dormitory where Graticus was holding his court of dice with his cronies. Their eyes locked briefly before the bigger boy looked away.

'I'd better go and say thank you, then,' said Ravian, painfully sitting up and putting his feet on the floor.

'You are wasting your breath, My Friend,' he heard Billus murmur behind him as he pulled on his tunic and tottered towards Graticus's group.

Graticus ignored his approach but, as the other boys stopped playing and stared up at Ravian, the green eyes finally lifted from the game and met the prince's.

'I understand that you carried me back,' Ravian said. 'I wanted to thank you.'

'You don't need to thank me, Your Highness,' Graticus sneered. 'I was just obeying orders.'

'Well, thank you anyway.'

'Just stay at your end of the dormitory, Baboon Bum, and I'll stay at mine,' Graticus muttered.

Ravian saw it then, and heard it in Graticus's voice. Not fear – but a tiny scrap of respect.

He knew that Graticus would never forgive him for the double humiliation of the day and that the heir to the House of Palin would always be his enemy. Nevertheless, the previously undisputed master of the dormitory had just made a small concession to the prince – an admission that Ravian had his own small piece of territory and would never be one of the bully's gang. The other boys saw it, and heard it too, and the eyes of some of them widened.

'Your choice, Graticus,' Ravian said clearly, as he turned and walked back to his end of the dormitory – to his own tiny kingdom.

Chapter Two

The mid-morning sun sparkled off the sea with an intensity that seemed to vibrate, as *Storm Bringer* drove towards Ezreen with the speed of a galloping horse. Sheets of spray burst from the vessel's leeward bow, streaking down the gunwale in blurred white lines and spotting the straining red sails. Dolphins raced ahead, leaping clear of the water in gymnastic twists and tumbles as though sharing the exhilaration of the ship's crew. Occasionally, as the *Storm Bringer* surged ahead with a particularly powerful burst of speed, a sailor would let out a whoop of excitement – the call almost drowned out by the roar of the ocean and the chattering of the rigging.

A Tarcun longship – in a stiff breeze and under full sail – was one of the fastest, most impressive sights that the hand of man could offer the world.

Ravian, however – retching over the quarterdeck's lee rail – was having difficulty in sharing the excitement. If this was what going to sea was about, he thought miserably, then he would have to ask his father that he be transferred to the army instead.

On completion of his two years' of basic military training, Ravian had returned to the palace whereupon his father had immediately pressed him into an intense regime of civil education.

'You are to be Defender of the Nation,' the king patiently explained when Ravian had mildly protested, 'but, believe me, you are not going to be able to do that through force of arms alone. You must strive to understand the power of this country's trade and learn the levers of her politics. Remember, when I'm gone, you'll be next in line to the throne until your brother produces a family. If something happened to Jeniel and you *did* have to take the throne, I'd like to think that I had given the people of this land something more than a sword-swinging lout as a ruler. Learn to understand your world, Ravian – everything is related to everything else.'

Indeed, when Ravian considered the plight of his brothers, he decided that his lot was not so bad.

Ramus, although the other boys of his age were now tramping the dusty parade grounds of the Academy, was receiving only a bare minimum of military training from the palace tutors – the scales and the abacus featuring in his lessons as much as the sword and the bow had in Ravian's. Fortunately, Ramus had a cheerful disposition and an agile mind and it was soon obvious that, while he was no mean hand with a sword, the world of trade was going to be one that he would be very much at home in.

Jeniel, on the other hand, was becoming an increasingly serious young man, his inevitable accession to the throne seeming to weigh heavily on his mind. Given to long and careful consideration of any decision, he appeared to spend all his waking hours studying – and worrying about his looming responsibility.

On returning from the Academy, Ravian had become concerned at the changes he found in his brother. One evening shortly after, as he and Jeniel sought a breath of cool air on a palace balcony, he asked him if he could help.

'You don't know what it's like, Ravian,' the older prince replied. 'For you it may never happen, but for me, well, all my life it's been "when you are King Jeniel" this and "when you are King Jeniel" that. I just can't escape the fact that, one day, everyone will look to me to rule them. I have so much to learn and sometimes I feel like I'll never be ready for the responsibility.'

Ravian felt truly sorry for his brother.

'Neither of us can change your destiny, Jeniel,' he said, 'but you know that I'll always be behind you – and so will Ramus. You're not alone.'

Jeniel nodded. Despite the darkening twilight, Ravian saw the sparkle of a tear in his brother's eye and glimpsed the huge burden that he felt.

'Thanks, Ravian,' he replied. 'I know that. I'll miss you when you go into the navy.'

Ravian's attitude to his continuing education at the palace changed after that conversation.

A study of the White City's water and sewerage systems, for instance, would not normally have interested him in the slightest, but, desiring to be a better support to his older brother, Ravian strove to become more informed about the subject. Thus, he learned that the White City's fresh water requirements were served by a perpetual spring that gushed from a point high on the walls of the drowned crater within which the Tarcun capital nestled, this precious water supply, allied with the splendid natural protection of the harbour, having been a key factor in Tarcus the Great establishing his settlement there centuries ago. Now, a complex system of pipes and aqueducts distributed clean water to most of the White City's households as well as to a number of public fountains. The same constant flow also powered a sewerage and drainage system that ducted the settlement's wastes to an outfall on the seaward side of the harbour's southern arm.

The strategic importance of this knowledge was not lost on Ravian. The secure fresh water supply meant that, once the chain guarding the harbour entrance was raised, and the three gates in the White City's walls closed and bolted, the metropolis could hold out against an attacking force for as long as its food supplies lasted.

His father was right, he saw – everything was related to everything else.

Ravian plunged into the sea of knowledge at his disposal in the form of the palace's advisers and ministers, often taking instruction alongside one or the other of his brothers and, sometimes, both.

He learned how the taxation system of the harbour functioned and how vital it was to the funding of the Royal House, the civil service and the military. He learned the rules and politics of the Citizens' Council and its subtle, if not always subservient, relationship to the

Tarcun throne. He learned about the Nine Houses, the great merchant dynasties of the White City, with their fleets of merchant ships and their giant warehouses on the eastern shores of the harbour. Especially though, Ravian studied the geography of Tarcus and, during his two years at the palace, he seized every opportunity to explore the island.

Thus, he joined with some palace priests in a pilgrimage to the summit of Mount Perios, praying with them there at the Oracle of Delikas before cleansing his soul in the brooding, sacred waters of the Heart Lake. He rode inland to Dalvin, the kingdom's second-largest settlement, and increased his knowledge of Tarcun agriculture by visiting the surrounding farms and vineyards and attending the thriving weekly market in the city. He journeyed to the harbour town of Belainus, centre for the manufacture of ceramics and, closer to his heart, home to the bronze smelters and the metalsmiths who kept the White City's armoury well stocked.

Finally, and shortly before he was due to go into the navy, he took two armed guards and headed out on the cliff-top trail that ran along the Southeast Coast to Land's End. After two days' rugged ride, he arrived at the craggy bluff with its two lighthouses, one black and one white, and the military garrison perched high above the tiny fishing port of Karomar.

'Why two lighthouses?' he asked the garrison commander whose overnight hospitality he had gratefully accepted.

The soldier was surprised that the prince did not know the story but seemed pleased at the opportunity to tell it.

'The Dark Tower is the oldest, Your Highness,' he explained. 'It was built over two centuries ago to guide fishing boats and naval vessels into Karomar from the Southeast Coast. Of course, that was long before anyone realised how rich the fishing grounds were to the north.'

Ravian had ridden the zigzag trail down the cliffs to the small, harbourside village that afternoon – a pretty enough place in weather-beaten sort of way, he had decided. Talking with some fishermen there, he learned that, sea conditions permitting, the boats would leave harbour, weather the point and tack northwest for the bountiful fishing grounds lying just off the dangerous, reef-dotted coastline of the Weather Shore. When they had filled their holds, they would set a course to run past Land's End and then down the Southeast Coast to the White City. Once they had sold their catch there, they would beat back home against the prevailing winds – savage northerlies in winter and gentle easterlies in summer – for a day or two of rest before doing it all over again. A hard life, Ravian had thought, but an honest one.

'The position of the old lighthouse meant that it was invisible in the northern arc,' the garrison commander continued. 'All very well for ships coming across from Ezreen, but useless for the returning fishing boats – not to mention the increased shipping we had begun to see from places like Kleeft or Dalvan. Vessels approaching Tarcus from the north at night had to run in blind and any poor devils that strayed too far to starboard would suddenly find themselves in amongst the reefs of the Weather Shore – and there aren't too many who've survived a shipwreck on that coast. Your ancestor, King Kombula, needed to protect both the fishing and trading fleets, so he ordered a new lighthouse, the White Tower, built further east and higher up on the headland, and that is where the beacon burns today.'

Leaving Land's End the next day, Ravian took the rough, rarely-travelled trail that ran northwest along the cliff edges of the Weather Shore. The garrison commander had warned him to expect a rocky, desolate coastline, completely devoid of fresh water and human habitation, and that he and his two guards would need to carry enough food and water to last the five-day ride. What no one could have prepared the prince for however, was the wild, untamed beauty of the wind-whipped edge of land that they discovered there. Ravian had thought the cliffs of the Southeast Coast impressive enough, but they were neither as tall nor as precipitous as the grey, forbidding bulwark that now unfolded, seemingly endlessly, before he and his men. Far below – too far for the sound to carry – mighty ocean swells crashed against the coast in angry explosions of spray. Further out from the coast, patches of boiling foam dotted with rocky black teeth marked where countless clusters of reef waited to snare unwary shipping. It was certainly a coast to give a wide berth to, Ravian thought and, by the time he arrived at The Horn, Tarcus's northernmost point, he was satisfied that nature had more than adequately provided the only defences required for that sector of the kingdom.

The land changed markedly as they arrived at the steep promontory of The Horn though, the gleaming sands that gave the vast Golden Bay its name prescribing an unbroken arc westwards to the far-off, towering silhouette of The Tusk. A bad place for a vessel to become embayed during the northerly gales of winter, Ravian knew, but an equally sheltered and welcoming coast during the gentle summer months. The smuggling trade it attracted at this time had necessitated a permanent garrison of both army and navy at North Cove, the small, summer-only harbour that nestled beneath the western cliffs of The Horn. When the first northerly storms signalled the end of Golden Bay's smuggling season, he learned, the five long ships based there would be hauled out and stored in giant boathouses well above the high tide mark and the crashing winter rollers.

It was immediately evident to Ravian that this was the kingdom's strategic weak point as, with the exception of the White City, Karomar and Belainus, Tarcus could rely on the almost unbroken cliffs that made up the rest of her coastline to repel any landing attempt by an enemy force. In summer though, Golden Bay posed an impossible defensive problem and offered any invading army easy access to the fertile, rolling farmland that lay behind it. The small rural city of Centrus lay barely two hours' ride from the coast and, from there, a busy, paved road ran almost due south to Agarvate, Dalvin and, ultimately, the White City itself. Ravian knew that he and his guards would make the ride in two days – and that an enemy army would be able to force march it in three.

The prince had turned his back on the Golden Bay and ridden inland with a sense of unease.

Shortly after Ravian's return from this expedition, his eighteenth birthday had arrived and, as custom dictated, he received his orders to report to his first ship. Not surprisingly, he had found himself posted to the longship of the senior officer of the Tarcun navy – the bearded and intimidating Admiral Acrusta, scourge of the pirates of the Sapphire Sea.

Now, only a few hours out from the calmer waters under the lee of Land's End, the prince felt the disdainful eye of the old sea dog upon him as he once more heaved into the foam that trailed astern.

Ravian felt ghastly. His skin was clammy, his knees were so weak that he could barely stand and, although it was a warm day, his hands shook violently as they gripped the rail. He felt the powerful presence of the admiral loom behind him and prepared to be denounced as a fop and a sissy.

'Young Man, I'm not as sharp of eye as I used to be,' the old admiral rumbled at his miserable royal recruit. 'Make yourself useful and get up to the port bow to keep a lookout for me. At this sort of speed, it's all too easy to catch another vessel broadside before we even know we're upon them.'

'Aye, aye, Sir!' Ravian responded in a shaky voice – having quickly established that, in the navy, these words were the only allowable response to a direct order.

He made his way unsteadily down the short flight of steps and onto the raised platform that ran forward between the twenty rowing thwarts on each side of the ship. As he passed the straining, creaking mast, he was painfully aware of the amused grins of the crew, positioned along the weather rail of the longship so that their weight helped to offset the heel of the vessel.

'Lovely day for a sail, Young Sir,' one of them called out cheerfully.

Ravian smiled back weakly and nodded – he has heard people described as being green with seasickness and had no doubt that his face was the colour of grass. Somehow, he made it up to the forecastle – the raised section of deck inside the bow – where he took up a position on the rail and braced himself against the humming forestay. Here, the wind seemed to come directly over the ship's bow and his eyes streamed as he dutifully searched the horizon for any other vessels.

After a time, he realised that he no longer felt quite as ill as he had.

The view of the horizon and the breeze in his face, while not totally curing his seasickness, had at least forced it to retreat far enough for him to be able to start thinking again, and he had the sudden realisation that the admiral had sent him forward for this very reason.

Looking aft, he met Acrusta's eyes and saw the barely perceptible nod the old sailor gave him before bellowing, 'Keep your eye out forward, Young Sir! There'll be no ships overtaking us from astern today!'

Ravian turned back towards the horizon and allowed himself a smile. The navy, he suspected, might not be so bad after all.

Ravian quickly learned that life aboard a longship on an extended patrol had its own rules and structure.

Unlike the slave oarsmen on the war-vessels of many other nations, Tarcun longships were manned entirely by free citizens. At the same time, the captain of a longship had supreme power over all who sailed on her and this power extended down through the first lieutenant, the two second-lieutenants and the bosun. Usually, these officers and about half of the crew were career sailors – the remainder being young citizens at various stages of their naval training.

Tarcun naval officers earned their promotion purely on merit and it was a tradition that, once on board a longship, its crewmembers forewent any claim to authority through family connection. Ravian found himself detailed for cooking and cleaning duties along with the other three new recruits on board – the only concession to his royal status being that everyone from Admiral Acrusta down addressed him as "Young Sir".

Ravian hated the title as much as those on board seemed to relish using it.

There was something utterly humiliating in being told, "Young Sir, scrub out that cooking pot" or "Young Sir, bail out the scuppers" but Ravian knew that he would be "Young Sir" until he made lieutenant's rank. Consequently, he resolved to be the best candidate for promotion that Acrusta had ever seen.

Admiral Acrusta – "Old Crusty" behind his back – was a hard but fair man, much loved and respected throughout the navy. Although he was careful not to show any favouritism to Ravian, it soon became obvious that his mission – whether he had been briefed to it or not – was to develop the prince's seamanship as rapidly as he could.

It was customary that, at least once a day, each new recruit would be taken aside by his longship's commander for what was known as a "Captain's Beating". While, on some ships, these Captain's Beatings may indeed have involved physical discipline, the usual practice was for the commanding officer to subject the new recruit to an intensive quiz of their knowledge of their ship and of the sea.

'Show me where northeast is!'

'How many oarsmen in a Survenian galley?'

'Show me an eye-splice!'

'What happens when a ship is "flat aback" and how do you get her out of it?'

'Tell me how you would board and inspect an Ezrenian trading vessel.'

'What is the purpose of a leeboard?'

These sessions were the bane of every new recruit's life – universally detested, and sometimes feared. Acrusta subjected Ravian to this daily harassment for sessions lasting at least twice as long as those he dished out to the three other new recruits – Petrus, Capernal and, to Ravian's delighted surprise, Billus, his friend from the Academy.

'It's not fair on you, Ravian,' grumbled Billus, as the four of them bunked down one evening in their cramped quarters beneath the forecastle. 'You're as good sailor as any of us – but Old Crusty still gives you a longer beating than we three put together'.

Ravian smiled in the darkness. Billus, he knew, was eager to follow his father's example and make the navy a career. He was as stout of heart as he was stout of form and, as the saying went, saw things very much with the "Eye of the Cyclops". He liked people or he didn't, accepted ideas or rejected them out of hand and was utterly loyal to his friends and his principles. Ravian knew that he was someone he could trust with his life.

'It goes with the blood, Billus,' Ravian replied. 'I don't mind.'

'Rather you than me,' said Capernal, laying out his sleeping mat. 'I'm quite satisfied with the amount of attention I get from our admiral as it is, thank you.'

Ravian had observed that Capernal, the son of a Belanian coppersmith, also seemed to be the subject of some extra focus from the admiral, although he suspected that this was more to do with Acrusta seeing potential in the pleasant, confident young man than any personal dislike on Old Crusty's behalf.

Petrus made no comment from his blankets. A tall, morose youth from Karomar, he seemed to have a grudge against life in general, facing it with a surly glare and cynical curl of the lip, and Ravian was finding him a hard shipmate to like.

It was during a Captain's Beating early on Ravian's first voyage, after the prince had failed to correctly name all the parts of a longship's standing rigging, that Acrusta handed down the first of many lessons in leadership. After briskly reeling off the correct names himself, the Admiral paused and then softened his voice.

'Young Sir,' he began, 'everyone enters the navy as an equal – there are no slaves here and rank is something that has to be earned. You must become a leader and there are, I believe, two ways that a man becomes one.'

Ravian gave the master mariner his complete attention – Old Crusty was an admirable example of the sort of leader he hoped to be himself one day.

'Some have it born in them,' Acrusta continued, 'and – if you are the sort of man that shines out amongst his fellows, the sort of man that draws people to him without even trying – that is one sort of leader. I look at young Capernal and see that he might be that sort of man.'

Ravian could only agree – Capernal emanated a quiet assurance that belied his youth.

'As for the rest of us,' Acrusta went on – and Ravian didn't miss the implications of the word "us" – 'we have to work at it. The men have to be able to trust that we have a complete knowledge of what we are doing. Knowledge is authority, Prince Ravian! Knowledge breeds competence – and competence breeds confidence. If the men believe their captain knows what he is doing, they will follow him anywhere!'

The Admiral's words seemed to echo his father's advice on the day that Ravian had entered the Academy and he determined to remember them.

Although he hated to admit it to himself, he already knew that he didn't have the easy authority that Capernal – or, irksomely, the Academy bully, Graticus – seemed to possess naturally. At the same time, he realised that the respect he had for *Storm Bringer's* officers came largely from his assumption that, when decisions needed to be made, they were competent to make the right ones – regardless of their personal charisma.

People didn't have to like somebody to follow them, Ravian realised – they just had to trust them. Even further, this knowledge strengthened his resolve to excel as a seaman.

The wind stayed fair from the northeast and, only five days out from the White City, a giant head and shoulders slowly began to rise from the horizon ahead. This was Kaddal, guardian of the City of Ezreen and, as they sailed towards the colossal statue, the towers and minarets of their destination began to grow from the sea behind the figure.

Ezreen was the wealthiest city in the world, founded at a point on the east coast of the Sapphire Sea only two days' camel journey across an isthmus from the port of Dabbar and the infinite reaches of the Spice Sea. It also lay on the meeting point of the land trade routes between the vast continents to the north and south and, thus, had become a commercial powerhouse.

Despite the nation's enormous fleet of merchant vessels on the Sapphire Sea however, Ezreen maintained only a small, ceremonial, navy on that ocean. The reason for this, as every Tarcun well knew, was the alliance between the eastern kingdom and their island nation dating back to the rule of King Phytus, grandson of King Tarcus. King Edron, the Ezrenian ruler of the time, had become tired of losing increasing amounts of shipping to piracy and, recognising that the superior speed and fighting abilities of the Tarcun longships had made the island's own merchant fleet virtually immune from the plague, he had sent emissaries to Phytus with a proposition. If Ezrenian vessels entering the White City were to pay double the usual taxation rate, would Phytus extend the protection of the Tarcun Navy to those vessels plying the Sapphire Sea?

Phytus had agreed – but only so far as to offer protection against piracy. The wise king had no wish to be dragged into any wars in which Ezreen might become involved.

The arrangement had worked well – so well, in fact, that within a few years Tarcus was also providing protection on the same basis for the vessels of that other major eastern kingdom, Karaal. The northern nations regarded this development with disdain, preferring to guard their own trading routes – albeit with more limited success. Karaal and Ezreen, however, were able to turn more and more of their vessels in the Sapphire Sea over to the business of trade, speeding the development of their economies. Tarcus found that, although these alliances slightly diminished the demand for the services of its own trading fleet, this loss was more than offset by the substantial increase in tax revenue and the additional foreign traffic through the White City's harbour.

Storm Bringer tacked between Kaddal's legs – one giant stone foot planted on each end of two long breakwaters protecting an anchorage at least three times the size of the White City's harbour. As the longship foamed through the entrance, Ravian, who, until now, had regarded Tarcus as the civilised centre of the universe, gasped at the forest of masts that almost obscured the harbour's shoreline. Above and beyond the mastheads, the City of Ezreen – its lights beginning to twinkle beneath the deepening purple of the eastern sky – covered the low, rolling hills to the very horizon, and Ravian and the rest of the crew began to smell tantalising, exotic aromas from the shore as the Tarcun ship shortened sail and threaded its way carefully through the press of merchant vessels. As they neared the dockside, they could hear the holy men of the city singing out their call to the evening devotions from the minarets of the temples and yet, despite the longship's arrival at prayer time, the jetty blazed with torchlight and jostled with a throng of people from many lands. Ezrenians in flowing white robes and turbans strode the same cobblestones as shining black tribesmen from the south and fair, hairy, barbarians from the north. Ravian was particularly intrigued by the veiled women who also walked the quayside, their direct, dark-eyed stares belying the modesty of their gowns and veils.

Two Ezrenian officials waved from the shore and, having caught Acrusta's attention, directed him to a clear section of the wharf where a small welcome party waited. The Tarcun admiral brought the longship smoothly alongside and, as the berthing lines were made fast, a sweating team of slaves lifted a gangway into place. Immediately, the waiting shore party boarded *Storm Bringer*, led by a man whom Ravian thought the most impressive individual he had ever seen.

The visitor's beard, turban and clothing were jet black and he wore a shining black breastplate with delicate golden inlays that gleamed in the torchlight. As he bowed to the waiting Acrusta with a flourish of his cape, Ravian did not fail to notice the enormous curved sword he carried at his waist – nor the easy, familiar way the man moved it aside as he bent.

To his surprise, Acrusta bowed just as deeply in return.

'Admiral Acrusta,' their visitor said smoothly, 'in the name of King Saravar of Ezreen, I bid you welcome'.

Their visitor spoke in Chesa, the mother tongue of Tarcus, with only the barest hint of an accent.

'Admiral Dirmar, this is a most unexpected pleasure,' the old Tarcun replied with a smile of genuine warmth. 'I understood you to be in the far reaches of the Spice Sea.'

The Ezrenian returned a smile of dazzling whiteness, his dark eyes twinkling.

'I have been recalled to attend upon the king,' he said, his eyes briefly meeting Ravian's before turning back to the Admiral. 'Out of respect for the royal presence you honour our city with and, of course, your own highly-esteemed self, His Majesty has invited me to welcome you personally.'

Acrusta nodded and motioned Ravian to join them.

'I must say, Admiral Dirmar, that the speed and accuracy with which you have been informed as to the identity of my newest recruit is truly impressive,' he said with a wry smile. 'Anyway, allow me to introduce Prince Ravian, second in line to the throne of Tarcus.'

Ravian stepped forward and saluted the Ezrenian admiral. Dirmar returned the courtesy with a surprised laugh and a nod of his head.

'Forgive my amusement, Your Highness,' he said, 'but, in Ezreen, princes do not usually salute humble sailors.'

'Perhaps not, Sir,' Ravian replied, 'but we are on a Tarcun longship – and I am just a recruit like any other.'

Over the Ezrenian's shoulder, he noticed a barely perceptible nod of approval from Acrusta.

'Well said, Prince Ravian,' Dirmar acknowledged. 'Indeed, our own crown prince is also undergoing his naval training – you are, as I'm sure you know, of a similar age. You will have something in common to talk about when you meet him.'

Ravian knew that Ezreen's sole heir to the throne was Prince Beneen.

'I look forward to meeting Prince Beneen,' said Ravian, 'but I doubt that *Storm Bringer* will be in Ezreen long enough for me to journey to Dabbar.'

Dirmar smiled. While Ezreen's naval presence in the Sapphire Sea was limited to a couple of galleys, Dabbar was home to the country's substantial fleet of war galleys on the Spice Sea.

'As chance would have it,' he said, 'I have recently shifted my flag to a vessel on the Sapphire Sea – and Prince Beneen has accompanied me.'

'In fact,' Dirmar continued, turning to Acrusta, 'I am here in rather more than a social capacity, Admiral. There are some matters that King Saravar wishes to discuss with you and he has suggested that you might like to attend on him at the palace directly after prayers tomorrow afternoon.'

He turned back to Ravian.

'The invitation also extends to you, Your Highness. I believe it is intended that you will meet Prince Beneen at the same time.'

'Please advise His Majesty that we will certainly be at his disposal tomorrow,' growled the Tarcun admiral.

'Very well, then – until tomorrow.'

With another winning smile and a courtly bow, Admiral Dirmar took his leave, crossed the gangway and vanished into the descending night.

'Pirates!' spat Saravar, absolute ruler of Ezreen.

Dirmar, Acrusta and Ravian stood before his throne – a jewel-encrusted couch on a raised dais.

Ravian, who had only just been introduced to the eastern king, gazed covertly about at the gilded columns and vaults of his throne room, awestruck by the fantastic opulence of Saravar's seat of power. However, if he had expected the Ezrenian ruler to be a man softened by this same wealth, he had quickly been proven wrong. Despite his fine robes and bejewelled fingers, the turbaned, grey-bearded Saravar was formidable of both appearance and manner as he descended the dais and began to pace the mirror-like floors in a state of barely suppressed fury.

'We've lost three ships to them in the last month!' he growled. 'Just yesterday, I received a message from King Baharat who admits he is having the same problem – even though he won't say how many vessels he has actually lost. If we've lost three ships though, I'll bet that Karaal has lost at least twice that! The scum are holed up somewhere in the Gertals – and you all know what that means.'

Indeed they did.

The Gertals were an archipelago of some sixty small islands in the northeast corner of the Sapphire Sea. They were close to the entrance to the Grimspot Gris, the arm of ocean that reached many days' sail into the darkness of the northern continent and, consequently, the island chain had historically been a favourite route for barbarian pirates from the north to extend their reach into the plump trade routes of the east. With no single country claiming sovereignty over them, the Gertal Islands were a lawless no man's land where the northern powers often manoeuvred to their own clandestine ends. Expeditions into the islands thus carried some political risk, especially to those countries whose trade relied on neutrality.

'Your Majesty,' said Acrusta, 'it has been many years since there was any real pirate problem in the Gertals. We cleaned out the last significant nest of them before Prince Ravian was born. I can't understand how this problem could reappear so suddenly.'

'Exactly, my friend,' agreed Dirmar. 'I have already expressed my belief to the His Majesty that there is more afoot here than some stray collection of Northerners who happen to have fallen into the pirate way. I feel the hand of one of the northern kingdoms in this.'

Acrusta looked thoughtful for a moment – the implications of Dirmar's words were serious indeed.

'Your Majesty, Admiral Dirmar,' he rumbled, 'of course the Tarcun navy is at your disposal. We will return immediately to Tarcus and I will request King Jabacus for permission to lead an expedition into the area.'

Saravar smiled.

'Admiral,' the king said, 'we never doubted that Tarcus would stand by its part of the Alliance – nor by the friendship that exists between our countries. However, I think that a full-scale operation into the area might be a mistake. It might be seen as an act of war against whichever country is behind this and neither of us wants that – even grubby little kingdoms like Graftsen still contribute to the trade coffers of both our nations. We must also remember that the Northerners can be clannish and that to buy an argument with one might be to buy an argument with many.

'No, what I suggest is this; Admiral Dirmar has one of our few war galleys in the Sapphire Sea at his disposal and he has shifted his flag to her. If the two of you were to take your ships north on a joint exercise – and you unexpectedly encountered a pocket of pirates – you would, of course, exterminate them. If it subsequently transpired that a few sailors from a northern nation had been involved...well, that would be a regrettable accident – not something that anybody would need to make an international incident over.'

Ravian was impressed. Not only did Saravar speak Chesa with the fluency of a Tarcun courtier, but he was also clearly a leader of wisdom and cunning. He was glad that Ezreen and Tarcus were allies.

'Can you sail with us tomorrow?' Dirmar asked the older admiral.

'Of course!' Acrusta bristled. 'We can sail right now if you wish. The crew has not been given leave beyond the immediate waterfront and we have been well provisioned.'

The Ezrenians exchanged knowing smiles. They were well aware of the admiral's "Old Crusty" appellation.

'Departure can wait until tomorrow morning, Admiral,' said Saravar. 'Please allow your crew to enjoy the delights of another evening in my city. I would like Prince Ravian to meet and become acquainted with my son – perhaps to spend the night here as our guest. I think that it would serve both our nations well if the princes came to know each other as well as your own king and I do. Also, if Prince Beneen might be permitted to further his education by sailing aboard your longship tomorrow, I would deem that a special favour.'

Thus it was decided, Acrusta and Dirmar returning to their ships, leaving Ravian with the Ezrenian king.

'Prince Ravian,' the monarch began when they were alone, 'your father and I are close friends. May I address you by your name only when we are in private?'

'Of course, Your Majesty,' Ravian replied. 'My father speaks of you with great warmth. May I ask how you would wish me to address you at such times?'

'Hmmm,' said Saravar, looking thoughtful. 'I believe that, if were you to address me as "Uncle", I would consider that a great honour.'

The significance of the title was not lost on Ravian. In the eastern lands, he knew, family ties were especially important. For Saravar to adopt him as a family member was an enormous honour – yet not one without its obligations.

He looked into the eyes of the older man and saw only friendship and goodness.

'You do me a great honour...Uncle.'

Saravar smiled and visibly relaxed and Ravian realised that the exchange had been important to the king.

'Wonderful! You had better come with me and meet your new cousin. He is waiting to dine with you in his quarters.'

Saravar led him from the throne room and along one vaulted hallway after another. Ravian realised that the Ezrenian palace was enormous and that, should he ever need to, it would take some time to find his way out again unaided. Everyone they passed prostrated him or herself before the king and Ravian began to appreciate the unique position enjoyed by Admiral Dirmar, who merely bowed before his monarch.

Finally, they entered a large room sumptuously decorated with rugs on floor and walls. On two sides, high, arched windows opened onto the upper parts of a lush green garden from which Ravian could faintly hear the sound of running water. A slender, olive-skinned young man of about his own age stood up from one of several luxuriously-bolstered couches and bowed as they approached.

'Ravian, Prince of Tarcus, allow me to introduce my son, Beneen, Crown Prince of Ezreen,' Saravar announced. 'You may, in the circumstances, address each other without title.'

The two youths looked shyly at each other.

Ravian had half-expected a pampered palace puppy, yet Beneen's fine featured face was intelligent and alert, his slender build tough and wiry. The Ezrenian prince's skin was considerably darker than that of the king and Ravian suspected that he had been undergoing sea training for quite some time.

'Welcome to my apartments, Ravian,' Beneen said. 'Please feel free to regard my home as your own whenever you are able to visit these shores.'

The Ezrenian prince's eyes were as deep and black as the night sky but there was a gleam in them that gave sincerity to his welcoming smile. As Ravian shook the proffered hand, he was surprised by the rough, calloused skin.

At Saravar's wave, the three royals each took a couch and, as they reclined, servants silently entered the room carrying trays of exotic and delicious food. The king addressed the two young princes as they ate.

'As you both well know, King Jabacus and I are not just allies – but also life-long friends. I first met your father, Ravian, when he and I were a similar age to that which the two of you are now. As you have, Jabacus came to this city on his first sea voyage and, just like now, my father introduced us to each other. The fact that we found it easy to become friends was a fortunate blessing from Bhana although, even had we not enjoyed each other's company, we would still have had the alliance between our two nations to honour. You hardly need me to tell you for how many generations that bond has stood – nor explain how important it is to both our countries.'

Beneen and Ravian exchanged glances. Both of them knew how vital the Alliance was.

'Unlike your father, Ravian – who was an only child – you are one of three royal princes of Tarcus,' Saravar continued. 'Bhana willing, your older brother will accede to the throne just as Beneen will one day take my place. Jeniel, is fortunate, Ravian, in that he will have the support of two full-blooded younger brothers to help him when the time comes for him to rule. It saddens me that Beneen could not have been similarly provided for.'

Ravian knew that Saravar's first wife and queen had died giving birth to Beneen and that, although Saravar had remarried many times under the Ezrenian custom allowing multiple wives, none of the children of those unions could legitimately challenge Beneen's right to the throne. It was very much in the nature of the eastern royal politics though, that his many half-brothers and half-sisters might plot to supplant the crown prince's place anyway.

'Ravian, you are being prepared for the role as commander of the forces of Tarcus,' Saravar went on. 'We will, no doubt, be seeing a lot more of you than of your older brother, although I daresay that Prince Ramus, when he completes his training in the mercantile arts, will also become a frequent visitor here. The alliance between our nations will stand more strongly if we can learn to be friends – cousins as well as allies. I don't force this on either of you, but positions of power can often be very lonely and even princes and kings need friends that they can trust. Tomorrow, you will both be sailing aboard Admiral Acrusta's flagship. I would like you to use that opportunity – and your evening here together – to learn more about each other and the ways of your peoples so that you give friendship the opportunity to grow.'

With that the king stood, waving them back to their own couches as they made to rise.

'And now, I have other affairs to attend to,' he said. 'I regret that I won't have time to see you again before you go, Ravian, but know that you will always be welcome in this city.'

There was a moment of silence between the princes as the king left the room. Outside, Ravian could see that the sky was darkening with evening and, in the far off distance, he could hear the call to prayers.

Beneen stood and Ravian also rose.

'Ravian, I must go now to offer my evening prayer to Bhana,' Beneen said. 'Before I do, I wish to say that I agree with my father and that I will also be praying for us to be friends.'

Ravian smiled.

'I thank you for your prayers but I don't think we will require the assistance of either Bhana or Delikas to be friends.'

Beneen smiled back and, placing his hands together in front of his chest, bowed his turbaned head slightly.

'Very well then, Cousin,' he said. 'I shall return in a short while. Please make yourself at home. You may wish to bathe – or even sleep. There will be a small entertainment this evening.'

Alone in Beneen's apartments, Ravian could not help feeling slightly irritated as he looked out into the deepening dusk. Tonight, while Petrus, Capernal and Billus enjoyed the exotic and legendary delights of the City of Ezreen, he would be here, saddled with the obligations of royalty.

Still, he told himself, that was his fate – his duty to Tarcus came first.

'Ravian,' the voice whispered into the black cave of his unconsciousness. 'Ravian! Cousin! Wake up!'

He opened one eye to find Beneen standing over his bed in the grey, pre-dawn light. The Ezrenian prince seemed to be shimmering slightly.

Beneen smiled.

'We have to go, or we will miss the sailing of our ships,' he said. 'I'll be back to accompany you very shortly.'

With that, Ravian was, again, alone in the palace bedroom. He pushed himself up into a sitting position against some cushions and tried to recollect the events of the evening.

It had started quietly enough.

Beneen had returned from his prayers after an hour so, and they had lounged together while servants brought additional candles, wine and more food. Beneen had insisted that he eat a small cake as a traditional start to the evening – 'hahmah', he had called the plain-looking patties. Ravian had thought them a most odd inclusion in what was an otherwise visually splendid array of food and, finding they had an oily texture and a pungent taste, he had not been at all disappointed when Beneen suggested that one would be enough.

They had sipped their wine as Beneen had told Ravian of his early life in the Ezrenian palace, and of his sea training which had now been going on for six months. Ravian had learned that his new friend had already sailed to the ends of the Spice Sea.

'And what is there at the end of the sea?' the Tarcun prince had asked.

'Why, more sea,' Beneen had replied with a laugh. 'The land keeps running to the south and east with this vast ocean widening between them. They say that it is as endless as the Western Sea.'

'How extensive are the lands to the south and east?' Ravian had wanted to know.

'I am told that they also go on forever,' Beneen had told him. 'My people have been coasting those lands since time began and we are well known among the peoples of both continents. No man from Ezreen has ever reached the end of those shores and returned to tell of it though.'

'But you must surely have charts of the parts of the coasts that are known to you?'

At this question, Beneen had looked slightly uncomfortable.

'There are charts,' he had replied, 'but they are a closely guarded treasure. Only a select few are permitted to hold them and it is death to reveal them to anyone else – even you, My Cousin. Why, I have only recently been allowed to see them myself.'

Beneen's expression had softened at the obvious disappointment on Ravian's face.

'You see, Ravian,' he had explained, 'the knowledge of the Spice Sea – and the world beyond it – is the power of my people. It is this knowledge, and the wealth that it brings, that allows us maintain our position in your world.'

For some reason, Ravian had found that he needed to consider this concept for a lot longer than he normally would have.

'I see,' he had eventually replied, more loudly and jovially than he had intended. 'Well, the Sapphire Sea is my world – and I am only just learning my way around that. Each to his own world, eh?'

Ravian remembered that, even as he had spoken, he had begun to wonder what was happening to him. He was used to strong drink and had been careful not to overindulge in the excellent wines with which Beneen's servants had been all too ready to refill his goblet, yet even then, he recalled, he had begun to feel quite thick headed and had noticed that he was starting to slur his words. The candles had also begun to flicker with a strange blurry brightness while, oddly, the rest of the room had begun to get darker and darker. He remembered that Beneen's voice had seemed to come from a long way away when he said, 'Anyway, enough of the politics, My Friend. At this stage of the evening it is the tradition to be entertained by the Halay Dance'.

With that, his friend had clapped his hands three times, each clap echoing explosively inside Ravian's head. The Tarcun prince had just been thinking what a strange and wonderful person his new cousin was when all thoughts of friendship, far-off lands and politics had been driven from his mind.

A small group of musicians – who had magically appeared in a corner of the room – had begun to play an exotic, rhythmic melody and a female dancer had entered the apartment, her hips gyrating slowly to the beat. Her pants, bodice and veil were of a diaphanous material that had given more than a hint of the undulating body beneath, and her long black hair had been held by a jewelled tiara that caught the candlelight and scattered about her like sparkling drops of water. The bracelets around her wrist and ankles – and the chains and coins around her bare, narrow waist – had jingled with her movements she had danced slowly towards the two princes.

Slowly but steadily, the tempo of the music had increased, matched by more urgent and provocative gyrations of the dancer's hips and, as band and dancer had approached a climax of rhythm, she had moved close to the Tarcun prince and he had felt himself overwhelmed by the music, the eroticism of the dance and the irresistible scent of her. Ravian remembered having been consumed by utter desire – never had he wanted a woman so much.

Then, with a final crash from the musicians, the dance had ended and the woman had spun away and pirouetted out of the room.

Ravian knew that he must have looked crest-fallen, because Beneen had taken one look at him and roared with laughter.

'Don't worry, Cousin,' the Ezrenian prince had assured him. 'That wasn't the end – it was just the beginning!'

Almost instantly, the dancer had returned – this time with two similarly attired female companions – and the band had struck up another driving rhythm. Ravian remembered a blur of whirling female bodies, pounding sound and increasingly desperate want until, after what had seemed an eternity of lust, he had lost control of himself and reached out for the first dancer as she had, once more, swayed before him. Easily avoiding his clumsy lunge, she had danced away with a laugh and, to Ravian's dismay, led the other dancers and musicians, still dancing and playing, from the room.

As the sound of the musical procession had receded, Beneen had risen to his feet, taking up a small lamp.

'Come, Ravian,' he had told his friend. 'We sail tomorrow. It is time to retire for the evening.'

Ravian recalled that, as he also rose, a dark orange mist had seemed to swirl about the room. He had meekly followed Beneen through a procession of dark halls to a sumptuous chamber lit by only one candle. There, in a large bed draped around with rich fabrics, a girl had been waiting – her eyes and smile luminous in the candle's glow.

'Estaya will help you sleep,' Beneen had told him with a smile. 'You will find her most skilled in easing that which ails you now.'

With that, he had withdrawn, closing the doors behind him and leaving the befuddled Tarcun alone with her.

At home in the White City, Ravian had enjoyed many a romp with the palace girls and, indeed, he had begun to imagine himself an experienced lover. That night in Ezreen though, Estaya had shown him just how little he actually knew about the art of love.

'I just wish I could remember it all,' he thought to himself as he pulled on his clothes in the cool morning air.

Chapter Three

Admiral Acrusta regarded the dishevelled Tarcun prince and his Ezrenian peer with a baleful, knowing eye.

'Hmmm,' he grunted. 'I see that the Palace of Ezreen hasn't lost any of its inclination to entertain royal guests royally. I seem to recall your father standing in the same spot – looking much as you do now – many years ago, Young Sir. Anyway, Admiral Dirmar has already sailed and we are about to cast off. I want you two up on the forecastle on lookout – I don't fancy having to swab whatever you've got inside you off my quarterdeck.'

Sheepishly, the two princes made their way forward.

It was a clear, bright day with a fair wind from the northeast, and *Storm Bringer* had a swift run to the harbour mouth where Acrusta altered course onto an easy reach to the northwest as the longship passed between Kaddal's legs. Outside the harbour, Admiral Dirmar's waiting galley braced its own mainsail around and took up a position on the Tarcun vessel's port quarter.

Billus joined Ravian and Beneen at the rail.

'Ravian!' he enthused. 'What a time you missed last night! Why those Ezrenian whores screw like...'

'Uh, Billus,' Ravian interrupted him, 'this is Prince Beneen, Crown Prince of Ezreen.'

'Oh,' said Billus, his face colouring as he turned to the Ezrenian prince. 'Forgive me Your Highness. I...I didn't...'

'It's all right, My Friend,' Beneen assured him. 'The hostesses of Ezreen are artists of world renown...and a very necessary and taxable function of our port. By the way, I'm here under training just as you are – so formal address is not required or, for my part, welcome.'

'Oh...ah...well, right you are then,' Billus sputtered. 'Welcome aboard.'

Then he turned back to his friend.

'But, by the beard of Delikas, Ravian,' he exclaimed. 'You should have been with us last night! We had the time of our lives!'

'I'm glad you enjoyed yourselves, Billus,' Ravian replied, straight-faced, 'but, alas, when I step off this vessel I become a mere prince again and at the mercy of the demands of state.'

'Oh, too bad,' said Billus with patent insincerity. 'I suppose that being a member of royalty isn't all it's made out to be, eh?'

'I sense he's a good man,' said Beneen, as Billus wandered happily aft.

'Yes. Very straight forward, as you can tell,' Ravian confirmed. 'There isn't a deceitful bone in his body.'

'The loyalty of such people is something to be prized,' the Ezrenian prince said – not without a touch of bitterness. 'We all need people we don't have to watch our backs around.'

'Very true,' replied Ravian, well aware of the legendary machinations of the Ezrenian court. 'By the way, Beneen, what is the story with those hahmah cakes?'

'Ah, yes – the hahmah,' his friend replied. 'The ingredients come from a range of mountains in the far northeast of Karaal.'

'But I only had one and I felt like I had drunk a tavern dry,' said Ravian. 'You had two or three – as much as I can recall anything about last night – and yet you seemed unaffected.'

'Oh, I was affected,' Beneen told him. 'But I've been taking hahmah for years and it would seem that, to a degree, one becomes accustomed to it.'

He leaned closer and put his hand on Ravian' arm.

'But you must be careful with the hahmah, my friend,' he warned in a low voice. 'Too much hahmah – like too much wine – can make a man soft in the head.'

'What about that dancer?' Ravian asked.

'Which one?' Beneen replied innocently.

'The first one, of course!' Ravian burst out. 'What an extraordinary creature! I must know her name!'

Beneen's face softened with a sympathetic smile.

'Her name is Belice,' he said, 'and she is the most celebrated Halay dancer in the land. But, My Friend, you should understand that the art of the Halay is to create desire in a man, not necessarily to satisfy it. Also, you should know that Belice belongs to my father and the penalty for any other man to touch her – as you very nearly did last night – is an amputation of a most cruel and personal nature.'

By the mid-afternoon of that day, Ravian felt that he had acquired his sea legs enough to safely join Admiral Acrusta on the quarterdeck. He found the old warrior pacing backwards and forwards, every so often glaring astern at the Ezrenian galley.

'Is there a problem with Admiral Dirmar's vessel, Sir?' Ravian asked.

Old Crusty regarded the prince from beneath a shaggy brow.

'Only that we have to sail in company with it,' he growled. 'Look at the set of our sails, Young Sir! We have our sheets so eased that I can hardly hear myself think over the luffing of the mainsail yet, even so, Dirmar can only just keep up with us. What lumbering pigs those galleys are!'

Ravian looked astern at the Ezrenian vessel. Unlike *Storm Bringer's* fore and aft sails, the Ezrenian flagship was square-rigged and seemed to be making heavy work of the moderate conditions.

'I'll wager that, if it were winter, our Ezrenian friend would not have been so keen to accompany us,' Acrusta continued. 'Just one look at that ship and you can see why the Ezrenians are so happy to pay Tarcus to carry out their naval duties in the Sapphire Sea.'

'Are they really so awful, Sir?' Ravian asked.

'They have their uses,' Acrusta conceded. 'See that ram sticking out of the bow? Get into a battle with one on a day with no wind and they'll run that into you like a spear. The only chance a longship has in such a situation is to get alongside and board them before they put a hole in you. Under oars though, a galley is faster than a longship and just as manoeuvrable – not so easy to get to grips with.'

'How many crew would she be carrying, Sir?'

'A twin-decker like that one would have over one hundred and fifty men on board,' Old Crusty replied. 'But that's another problem the Ezrenians have – all but thirty of those will be slaves. Slaves will sometimes be released and fight if they think they are going to go down or burn with their ship, but most of the time they're chained to their oars. Once you're over the rail of an eastern galley you really only have to deal with a handful of archers and armoured infantrymen.'

Ravian had no doubt that the admiral spoke from personal experience.

'But those big galleys the Northerners use are a totally different proposition,' Acrusta continued. 'They don't use slaves and, with three decks, and, sometimes, even four, that can be over two hundred men on board who will all fight like maniacs.'

Ravian considered this.

'So, why don't we have any galleys, sir?'

'Well...we used to, long before I was born – but our primary need is to protect our shipping routes from piracy and that means getting somewhere fast in all weathers.

'Take a good look at that galley, Young Sir – she's struggling to stay with us even on a gentle reach. This breeze would only have to back another point or two and Dirmar would have to drop his rigging and start rowing. And look how much leeway she is making! To keep that rowing manoeuvrability they don't have much of a keel – so they tend to crab along sideways with the wind on the beam. In rough weather, they're at risk from even a moderate storm – you can see how she's got her lower oar ports plugged for sailing now, but there's not a great deal of freeboard even to the upper ports, so a decent beam sea is real risk for her. As for running before a heavy sea – if she broaches she'll go down like a stone. The only things that a galley caught outside harbour in a strong blow can do is pull down her mast, put out a sea anchor, and pray.'

Ravian frowned.

'But, Sir, if a large fleet of Northerner galleys were to come against our own navy in calm conditions, would we not be the losers?'

Acrusta regarded the young prince with a look that was difficult to fathom.

'It hasn't happened yet, Prince Ravian – although I fancy that one day the Northerners may stop bickering amongst themselves long enough to put a fleet together. But there's lot of open water between the northern shores and Tarcus, and it would be a brave commander who risked a fleet of galleys on *that* voyage.'

Ravian looked back at the Ezrenian ship and, despite the difficulties he could see the vessel was experiencing, the sight of her ram, periodically lifting clear of the sea, filled him with foreboding.

The wind held fair and, after running up the Ezrenian coast, the two ships continued on a northwest heading within sight of the shores of Karaal. Then, early on their fifth day out from Ezreen and not long after the lands of the East had sunk below the horizon behind them, they sighted the southernmost of the Gertal Islands. They had begun to sail past this first, small island when the lookout reported a fishing boat anchored in a sheltered western cove. Acrusta immediately ordered a change of course and *Storm Bringer* tacked and headed into the bay, the galley furling her sails and running out her oars to follow them.

Acrusta was almost upon the fishing boat before bringing the longship into the wind and, as the Tarcun vessel drifted to a standstill, her gently flapping sails gave the unsuspecting fishermen their first warning of her arrival. Indeed, they stopped so close to the anchored boat that *Storm Bringer's* bowman was able to throw a line down to the four men who stood staring up, open-mouthed, from the fishing boat's stern. As they made fast to the smaller craft, Acrusta ordered the sails furled and the port anchor let go.

It was, Ravian thought, a masterful display of seamanship.

From behind them came the splash of the Ezrenian galley's anchor and Ravian looked around in surprise. The speed with which the Dirmar's ship had followed them in under oars was impressive indeed.

Acrusta Identified the fishing boat as Dalvanian and ordered its master on board. His weathered face expressionless, the old fisherman climbed over the rail even as a dinghy brought Dirmar across from his galley.

'How long have you been fishing in these islands?' Acrusta asked the skipper when the Ezrenian admiral had joined them.

The Dalvanian slowly turned and spat over the rail, evidently unimpressed at being in the company of the commanders of the two most powerful navies in the world.

'I have been fishing in these islands all my life,' he eventually replied in heavily accented Chesa.

Acrusta showed no sign of aggravation at the unhelpful reply.

'And how long have you been on this particular fishing trip, Captain?' he asked evenly.

The Dalvanian looked the older man in the eye.

'A month...maybe more.'

'We are investigating reports of pirates in these islands,' Acrusta told him. 'Have you seen any signs of them?'

The fisherman hesitated for a long time before replying.

'We are poor fishing folk,' he finally responded. 'We have eyes only for the weather and for our nets.'

'A month is a long time away from Dalvan, Captain,' Acrusta said. 'I doubt that the market in Dallana would be interested in sea produce that was so old. Perhaps you have been able to sell rather fresher catches somewhere in these islands?'

Caught out, the Dalvanian lapsed into confused silence and Acrusta pursued his advantage.

'Perhaps you have new clients here – a lot of mouths to feed?' he probed.

The fisherman remained silent, squinting out towards the entrance to the bay.

Acrusta's tone hardened.

'And perhaps these new customers have been making unwanted calls on passing trading vessels?' he growled.

The man shrugged.

'I sell my catch to whoever pays for it,' he replied sulkily. 'The squabbles of nations are not my concern.'

Dirmar and Acrusta exchanged a meaningful glance.

'But, Captain, we are making our enquiry your concern,' said Dirmar, smoothly joining the conversation. 'Believe me, now that we are here, these new customers of yours will not be buying from you for very much longer. Besides, why would you sell your catch to them – when we will give you three times the going price for whatever you have in your boat right now?'

The Dalvanian turned to the Ezrenian admiral and his face creased into a gap-toothed smile.

'Perhaps we can do business then,' he said.

'I'm sure we can,' replied Dirmar. 'But, before we do, can I repeat my friend's question and ask – again – where we might find these new customers of yours?'

Once more, the Dalvanian looked doubtful.

'We may need to hire your boat and crew for a time – top rate,' Dirmar wheedled.

The prospect brightened the old fisherman's face and he came to a sudden decision.

'Very well,' he said. 'If you buy my catch *and* hire my boat, I will take you to the island that I have been selling my fish to. I don't know anything about any interference with trading vessels but I do know that there are hard men there with fast boats.'

He looked levelly at Admiral Acrusta then.

'Perhaps more men – and harder – than you are expecting,' he said ominously.

The two admirals agreed that Dirmar would accompany the fishermen on the day's sail north to the island that seemed to be the pirates' lair. The old Dalvanian finally having talked of at least ten vessels there, it seemed prudent that they spy out the situation before making any further moves. The main force would follow more slowly, discretely anchoring in the cover of a neighbouring island to await Dirmar's return.

Thus, the following afternoon found *Storm Bringer* and Dirmar's galley anchored in a south-facing bay of the island chosen for the rendezvous. The shoreline was devoid of vegetation or any other obvious form of life – the low, black cliffs and narrow fringe of beach reflecting the fiery sun into the windless cove with a sullen intensity. In an effort to escape the stifling heat, many of the longship's crew periodically dove into the still, blue waters – frolicking heedless of the risk of sharks and temporarily forgetting the danger of their impending clash with the pirates.

Ravian, Beneen and Billus were drying in the sun on the forecastle when the lookout atop the mast called out that a boat was rounding the point into the bay. As expected, it was the fishing boat bringing Dirmar back from his reconnaissance mission. The small craft sailed smoothly up to the port side of the longship and the Ezrenian admiral – dressed in the rough garb of a Dalvanian fisherman – vaulted lithely over the rail.

As Dirmar joined Acrusta on the quarterdeck, the older admiral beckoned the watching princes.

'You two! Beneen and Ravian! Come aft and join us!' he boomed.

'Please forgive any offence that I may bring to your nostrils,' smiled Dirmar, as the two princes joined their admirals.

Indeed, there was a distinctly fishy odour about the usually impeccable Ezrenian.

'It is much as the skipper described,' he began. 'There look to be eight sea boats – fore and aft rigged – that would probably hold about twenty crew each. As well as that, there is a three-decked Dekanian galley.'

'Dekanians!' spat Acrusta. 'I might have guessed. So...maybe three hundred men in all?'

'I would think about that number,' said Dirmar. 'We didn't go into the harbour – we just trawled a net outside the heads for a while. The anchorage faces south, protected by a high headland on the western side with a lookout station on its summit. There's a permanent camp established in the bay and our Dalvanian friend tells me that most of the men are living ashore there. I couldn't see any anchor watch on the small craft but there are certainly men on the galley.'

'Any sign of the merchantmen, Admiral?' asked Ravian.

'Aye,' Dirmar replied. 'Two from Karaal and one of our own – definitely one of the vessels taken by pirates. No sign of crew from any of them though – poor devils.'

Acrusta' face darkened.

'Well,' he growled, 'we may not have been able to save them from whatever fate they've met – but at least the presence of their vessels in the harbour gives us leave to avenge them without too much concern for the political ramifications. Admiral Dirmar, how do you see our best plan of attack?'

The Ezrenian had obviously been giving the subject some thought during his return voyage.

'The key is the lookout station,' he said. 'If we can silence the guards there, then we can get in amongst the ships at anchor with surprise on our side. I suggest that we send a small party away in the fishing boat –

timing their arrival in the harbour at around dusk. The lookouts have seen that boat come and go before, so its arrival shouldn't arouse any suspicion. They can anchor just inside the headland and the men can pretend to be cleaning the catch – which is where the skipper tells me they normally do it anyway. He also thinks that it should be possible to land there so, after dark, our men can make the climb up to the lookout station and silence the guards. Once they've done that, they give us the all-clear signal. As soon as they get a reply, they return to the fishing boat and sail back to the rendezvous here.

'After sunset, we darken our vessels and bring them in close to the headland. When we see the signal from the shore party, I'll row my galley into the harbour with muffled oars and get as close as I can to the galley before I'm detected. Then I'll ram her and try to sink her. Provided the breeze is strong enough, Admiral, you can take *Storm Bringer* around the bay and fire the pirate boats at the same time. We don't have enough crew to man the merchant boats, and we don't want to leave them behind for the Dekanians, so I suggest you torch them as well. They are anchored further out in the bay, so whichever of us has disposed of his targets first will have a little more time to finish off the merchantmen.'

'A sound plan,' Acrusta rumbled. 'Since you will need your full complement of fighting men to deal with the watch-keepers on the Dekanian galley, I will provide the landing party from my own ship. Once the action begins, we'll need to swift about our business – the Dekanian pirates aren't going to stand idly ashore and watch their ships being burned.'

'Ravian and Beneen,' the old admiral continued, 'this will be a good experience for the pair of you. I want you to take a landing party of five – including the bosun – and deal with the lookout post. The all-clear signal will be three flashes of a lamp out to sea, where we'll be hove-to west of the headland. When you see our response, get back to the fishing boat and get out of there as fast as you can. Understood?'

'Aye, aye, Sir!' the princes chorused.

'Very well, report to the Bosun and get going,' Acrusta ordered them. 'It's getting late and you need to be there at dusk!'

The fishing boat reeked of its trade but it sailed well and they made it to the island with perfect timing.

Ravian, Beneen and the five crewmembers had dressed in clothes borrowed from the Dalvanians, who had prudently remained behind at the rendezvous. Despite the two princes' royal status and theoretical rank, it was immediately clear that the bosun was in charge of the mission.

Bosuns were the longship's foremen, responsible for executing the orders of the orders of the captain and his officers. Invariably, they were the toughest, most experienced seamen of the longship fleet and rigorous enforcers of its disciplines. Combus, bosun of the admiral's flagship, was at the pinnacle of his career, and appeared not at all daunted by the prospect of taking the princes of two nations into a hand-to-hand combat mission. Indeed, Ravian thought, as he surreptitiously observed the scarred, powerful figure at the helm, it was difficult to imagine anything that might disrupt the man's confident demeanour.

He looked about at the four other crewmembers on board and decided that he wouldn't want to be pitted alone against any of them without a sword in his hand. Combus had handpicked his team and Ravian could see that the bosun had chosen well.

Beneen joined him at the bow.

'This is your first time in combat, is it not, Cousin?' the Ezrenian prince asked, as they approached the headland guarding the pirate harbour in the softening evening light.

'Yes,' replied Ravian, conscious of a strange swirling feeling in the bottom of his stomach.

'Then let's keep close by each other,' Beneen said. 'I will be at your left shoulder and, being left-handed, we should make a formidable pair.'

Ravian turned and looked at his companion.

'And you?' he asked. 'Is this your first time?'

'No,' Beneen replied. 'Admiral Saravar has already sent me over the side with a boarding party in the Spice Sea.'

'Did you kill anyone?' Ravian asked.

'Yes,' Beneen replied evenly. 'I took two lives in that action.'

As the fishing boat passed under the headland, Combus blithely waved out to the sentries high above them, smiling with sinister satisfaction as they waved back.

'Looks like only half a dozen of them,' he said to his raiders. 'This should be easy but, remember, we must cut them down before they can give any sort of alarm.'

Combus anchored the boat just inside the harbour and they turned to the odorous task of cleaning the aging catch the Dalvanians had left on board, a squalling flock of seagulls materialising out of nowhere. As they worked inexpertly with their filleting knives, they surveyed the nearby shoreline, noting that the pockmarked, black volcanic rock that rose steeply from the water's edge was almost devoid of vegetation, but seemed to offer plenty of foot and handholds.

'As soon as it's dark, we'll go alongside directly across from where we are now,' Combus said, raising his voice above the noise of the gulls. 'There's a rock outcrop there that we can tie up to.'

'She looks like a steep climb right there, Bosun,' growled one of the crewmen. 'Maybe we should try a bit further along.'

'Aye, it'll be a tough climb,' Combus agreed. 'But if we pull in here, our masthead will be below the line of sight of those men up there – and that's what we want.'

As darkness fell, they silently raised anchor and, muffling the fishing boat's oars, they paddled her close to the rocky shore and made her fast. Sheltered from the breeze by the cliffs, the sea immediately beneath the headland was glassy calm.

Carefully, they removed their weapons from under cover in the stern of the boat, each man silently easing on his armour and arming himself with a short, heavy, naval sword. Then, bare-footed for agility and bareheaded to hear better, they slipped over the side of the boat and onto the rocks.

'If those sentries get one whiff of us, it will give the game away,' whispered Beneen, referring to the fishy perfume that lingered on all of them from the boat.

'Silence!' came Combus's venomous hiss from the darkness above them. 'I'll cut out the tongue of the next man who talks!'

They continued the climb in silence. There was no moon and they ascended towards the starry horizon mainly by feel. In what seemed to Ravian almost no time at all, they had arrived on top of the headland, a short distance north of the lookout post and creeping through the low, wind-stunted trees that crowned the ridge, they emerged onto a rough trail. Stealthily, they eased along the path towards the dim glow that marked the lookouts' position.

As they came closer, they saw that the sentries had gathered around a fire and were relaxing over their evening meal, their armour and weapons stacked to one side. One look at the piled equipment told the landing party that the sentries were no rough pirates, but Dekanian soldiers.

'Wait,' breathed Combus.

Ravian watched the bosun as the experienced older man scanned the campsite – assessing how far the six men were away from their weapons and whether or not there might be any others beyond the dim circle of firelight. As they watched, one of the sentries stood up and walked towards the blackness of the cliff edge at the southern end of the camp. The Dekanian spent some time scanning the velvety darkness from east to west before returning to the fireside. Ravian was certain that there were no other men and, moments later, Combus showed that he had formed the same conclusion.

'Now!' the bosun whispered and, before either Ravian or Beneen had taken more than two steps forward, Combus and his men had swarmed into the campsite like dark spirits.

The Tarcun sailors swiftly overpowered the sentries with quick, deadly thrusts – the only sound a stifled grown escaping from one of the unfortunate soldiers. Ravian and Beneen were still standing uncertainly at the camp's perimeter when they heard the sound of men approaching along the trail behind them.

'Kaddal save us!' hissed Beneen, as they spun around. 'It must be the relieving guard!'

There was no time for either youth to think as the first of the Dekanians – obviously unaware that he was arriving at a scene of slaughter – blundered towards them out of the darkness. Beneen brought his sword around in a sweeping arc that intersected below the leading man's chin, almost decapitating him and, immediately, Ravian stepped forward and thrust his blade into the throat of the next man in line. The Dekanian fell backwards with a surprised gurgle and, instinctively, the Tarcun prince stayed low as Beneen's sword whistled above his head – catching a third soldier on the side of the neck and dropping him like a felled ox. Then, two of their landing party charged past on either side of them, hacking the following guards to the ground although, beyond the dark tangle of struggling men, Ravian saw the last Dekanian turn and start running back down the trail. Knowing that he must not allow the man to escape, the prince set off in pursuit.

Burdened with full armour, helmet, and shield, the fleeing soldier soon cast the last item aside to speed his escape. He was no match in speed for the more lightly clad prince however, and, hearing Ravian closing behind him, he was forced to turn and defend himself.

Years of constant weapons drill guided the Tarcun prince's movements and he easily parried the desperate, unskilled swordsmanship of his opponent. Almost without thinking, he slipped inside the Dekanian's guard and drove his sword up under the man's armour – clamping his free hand over the doomed guard's mouth to muffle his scream. Warm blood gushed over his sword hand and he would later remember the sickening sensation of his blade grating against bone as the soldier fell away from him and his weapon pulled free.

Combus and Beneen arrived moments later to find him standing over the still twitching body of his adversary.

'Well done you two!' the bosun panted. 'A bit slow off the mark at the start but you certainly made up for it. Now, let's get back to the sentry post and give the signal.'

They trotted back to the campsite where, in the flickering firelight, Ravian saw that the ground was covered in blood. The stench of spilled guts and voided bowels made him suddenly feel ill and he breathed deeply in an effort not to disgrace himself.

One of the crewmen had already lit the signal lantern and, covering it with a cape from one of the dead guards, Combus walked to the edge of the cliff and showed it three times as he had been ordered. Immediately, three answering blinks of light came from the darkness below.

'Right!' said the bosun, extinguishing the lantern. 'We've done our job – twice over, in fact. Everybody back to the boat, and take care not to break you necks on the way down!'

The climb down was more difficult than the ascent – made all the more difficult for Ravian by his weak legs and shaking hands. Finally, though, they were all in the boat and, even as they cast off from shore, they saw the galley and the longship glide into the harbour like ghost ships. As quietly as they could, the raiding party rowed out of the headland's lee – searching for enough breeze to raise the sails. Looking back to the harbour, they saw flares of orange as Acrusta fired first one and then another of the pirate boats and cries carried faintly to them across the water. Then, by the growing light of the flames, they saw Dirmar's ship locked hard into the side of the Dekanian galley.

'Those poor bastards are pinched in,' muttered Combus, as their sails filled with breeze and the headland obscured their view of the battle. 'They'll have a fight on their hands now.'

They had not made it far out into open sea however, before the breeze eased and began to veer to the south-west, and it took the rest of the night, and numerous tacks, for them to sail back to the rendezvous.

As the sky began to lighten with the approaching dawn and they rounded the headland into the rendezvous bay, Ravian fruitlessly scanned the northern horizon for any sign of the galley or the longship to the north. Combus anchored the fishing boat close in to a small beach in a corner of the bay where, in exhausted silence, the Tarcun raiders washed off the blood of battle as they waded ashore. Without a word to the waiting fishermen, they staggered up the beach and dropped onto the black sand – sleeping where they fell as the sun eased over the horizon.

It was mid-morning when a smiling Beneen shook Ravian awake.

'Wake up, Ravian. Our ships have returned!'

Ravian sat up and looked around, rubbing the blurriness from his eyes.

He noticed straight away that the fishermen – who had prudently insisted that they be paid in advance – had slipped away with their boat while he and the raiding party had slept. The armour and weapons they had left behind on the boat had been carefully stacked close by on the beach.

Staggering to his feet, Ravian saw the longship lead the galley into the bay – both vessels under oars. As *Storm Bringer* came to anchor, he saw that her bow was smashed and splintered just above the waterline. Fire had charred the Ezrenian galley's bow and the Tarcun prince could see dark stains running down her sides that he knew were blood. For a moment, he thought that she had also lost her masts – then he remembered that galleys always removed and stowed their rigging before combat.

A boat despatched from *Storm Bringer* picked up the raiding party and rowed them back to the longship where the two admirals waited on the quarterdeck.

'Welcome back on board, Bosun, Young Sirs,' growled Acrusta. 'As you can see, we have not completed our mission entirely unscathed.'

'What happened, Sir?' Ravian asked, looking from one admiral to another.

Dirmar, a deep gash on one cheek and dark shadows of fatigue under his eyes, smiled ruefully.

'Well, after we saw your signal,' he began. 'We went in and I rowed with full speed straight at the guts of the Dekanian galley. We hit her beautifully – perhaps a little too well – because she immediately heeled over on our ram and pinched us in. Her anchor watch woke up then and, although they weren't armoured, they were armed. There we were, locked in an embrace like a whore's thighs, with twenty or so axe-swinging Dekanians storming over the bow. Into the bargain, our rowers panicked and we lost power for a time.'

Acrusta gave Ravian a quick, meaningful glance.

'Then,' Dirmar continued, 'just to add to our woes, the Dekanian somehow caught fire – so we were not only fighting hand to hand from the bow back to amidships, but we were jammed into another vessel that was both sinking and burning. While this was happening, the men onshore had launched their boats and the first of them started to come alongside and swarm up our oars. I have to say, I have been in some tight spots in my time, but I didn't think that we were going to get out of that one. Fortunately, my good friend here was able to come to our aid.'

Acrusta cleared his throat and took up the story.

'We could see that Admiral Dirmar was pinched in and – just as we fired the last of the captured merchantmen – the breeze inside the harbour dropped almost to nothing so we had to lower our sails and run out the oars. Then we aimed for the Dekanian and rammed her in the stern quarter as hard as we could. It swung the enemy galley around enough to break Admiral Dirmar's ram free and he managed to get enough oars working to back out before the Dekanian capsized on him – it looked pretty close from where I was standing. Unfortunately, by this time, we had a number of small boats full of very angry Dekanians around us and, without enough wind to sail, we had to both fight for our lives and row for the harbour mouth at the same time. We took a number of casualties.'

Behind the Admiral, Ravian could see a sail covering what was obviously a line of bodies.

'How many, Sir?' he asked.

'Eight dead,' Acrusta replied. 'Another two who will never put to sea again – if they live. Young Petrus is among those killed, I'm afraid.'

'We lost ten of our soldiers as well,' said Saravar, 'plus sixteen slaves cut down at their benches.'

'Everything seemed to go well with the raiding party, Bosun,' Acrusta said, turning to Combus.

'No casualties, Sir,' growled the sailor. 'But we had the bad luck that their relieving guard chose to turn up just as we was dealing with their first watch. Fortunately, our two Young Sirs here took care of most of 'em.'

'Indeed?' said Acrusta.

He and Dirmar regarded the two princes with interest.

'It augers well that the sons of both royal houses have distinguished themselves so early in their careers,' said Dirmar. 'Your fathers will be delighted.'

Ravian felt his chest swell with pride, his pre-battle nerves – and his revulsion at the subsequent butchery – now forgotten.

The two vessels stayed in the bay only as long as it took to make running repairs. As was the tradition of their country in such situations, the Tarcuns sewed up their dead in shrouds of weighted sailcloth and, with a short prayer to Delikas, consigned them to the blue depths of the bay. The Ezrenians however, followed their own tradition of returning home with their dead whenever they could. Both ships, the admirals agreed, would sail directly for their homeports and, thus, Beneen prepared to transfer back to the galley.

Even though they had known each other for only a few days, the events during that time had already formed a strong bond between the princes and Ravian bade his friend goodbye with real regret.

'Don't forget, My Cousin, we are one family now,' the Ezrenian prince had said as they embraced briefly.

Storm Bringer got under way on a tack to the south, Dirmar's galley soon slipping below the horizon astern of them as the Ezrenians rowed ponderously east. Billus joined Ravian at the forecastle and they spoke for the first time since the raid.

'I must say, Ravian,' he told him, 'I was absolutely green with envy when you were picked for the raiding party! I thought that we would just be rowing around the harbour burning boats while you got all the real action up on the headland. By Delikas, how wrong I was!'

Ravian smiled. His stout friend seemed to have no idea what fear was.

'Our part of the action was going according to plan,' Billus continued, his eyes shining at the memory of the battle, 'but we could see that Dirmar was in trouble, stuck fast into the Dekanian. Old Crusty is a cool customer though. He and Dirmar may be old friends but, when the first lieutenant called out to him that the galley needed a hand, he replied "We must do our duty by our country before we can do our duty by our friends" and he didn't put the ship about until we had fired the last of the three merchantmen.

'By that stage, the Dekanian had caught fire as well. I don't know how that happened, but I think one of the pirate boats we torched must have burned through her anchor warp and drifted against her. Anyway, the Dekanians still had their mast stepped and their main furled on the yard. The flames ran up the mast and set fire to the lot so, by the time we got back to Dirmar, the whole bay was lit up as if by a giant torch. What a sight!

'We could see boat after boat of pirates rowing out from the land. A couple of them had already started to board Dirmar's galley and there was a pitched battle taking place on the upper deck. Dirmar was in the thick of it, swinging that big sword of his and cutting down men faster than I could count – what a hero!

'Pieces of burning sail were raining down all around and Dirmar's ship had already caught fire at the bow. Old Crusty gave the order to row as we had never rowed in our lives and we hit the Dekanian's quarter so hard that I thought we were going to topple our own mast. We put another hole in her and she swung clear of Dirmar's ship but then started to roll towards us. Her flaming mast came down so close that it landed on the end of our last sweep on the port side. The inboard end bounced the oarsman clear off his thwart and he landed amidships. That's how he died, poor devil – it just about took his head off.

'Dirmar got his oars going and he spun his galley around and headed for the harbour mouth. They certainly move when they want to, those things – and that was with some of his slaves dead at their stations!

'We took a lot longer to come about and, by the time we were heading in the right direction, some of the boats had caught us and we began to take on boarders over the stern. I was rowing from well aft, so I had a perfect view of Old Crusty cutting them down one by one as they came over the side. The first lieutenant ordered the last five rowers on each side off their thwarts to repel the boarders and that's how I got to be on the quarterdeck with a sword in my hand. I think that I must have killed five men myself!

'Trouble was, by taking out that many oarsmen, our speed was reduced – and more and more of their boats began to catch us. Our helmsman was killed, so someone had to stand there and hold the steering oar right at the point where we were being boarded. That was

Capernal – he's a brave one, believe me. The rest of us were just trying to keep the Dekanians' swords and axes from his neck as they came over the stern rail.'

Ravian was not surprised that, while Billus had clearly been carried along by the frenzy of battle, it had been Capernal who had taken the action necessary to extricate the longship – selflessly placing himself in a position that could well have been suicidal.

'Anyway, I think that we would have been overwhelmed – but then Dirmar dropped back in line with us. He had about a dozen archers on his sterncastle and they cleared the boarders off our quarterdeck like a horse's tail swatting flies. Once that happened, Acrusta sent everybody back to their oars and we were able to leave the rest of the pirates behind – although I think they were losing interest by then anyway. What a magnificent battle!'

They expected to take four days to sail back to the White City but, towards the end of the first day, the wind started to back to the east and dark clouds began to gather on that horizon. It began to blow steadily harder and the longship, now on a reach, sailed southwards with increasing speed. Toward evening, Acrusta ordered the vessel brought up into the wind so that the mainsail could be furled and the foresail replaced with a smaller one.

'There's a bit of a blow coming,' he explained to Ravian, Billus and Capernal as the vessel got underway again – only a little more slowly than before despite the significantly shortened sail. 'My feeling is that we will have a howling northeasterly by tomorrow morning. If I'm wrong – well, we can always put more sail on again. If it comes up the way I think it will though, we don't want to be having to shorten sail in a storm in the middle of the night. That's a sure way to lose crew and we have lost too many good men already on this voyage.

'Remember lads, the time to take any action at sea is when you first think of it. By the time the sea forces you to do something – it's probably way too late.'

The three young men absorbed this gem carefully. They had no doubt that Acrusta's forecast of the weather would be borne out.

'What about Admiral Dirmar's vessel, sir?' asked Capernal. 'If there is a storm coming, won't his galley be in serious danger?'

Acrusta smiled and the boys felt a new bond with their commander – the bond of fellow veterans.

'Admiral Dirmar may be sailing a dangerous pig of a galley,' Old Crusty told them, 'but he's an experienced sea captain. He'll have seen this coming and he'll be hugging the coast during the day and looking for a safe harbour by night. I daresay it'll take him ten days at least to get back to Ezreen and, personally, with the Ezrenians' tradition of taking their dead home with them, his vessel is about the last place I would want to be by the end of that voyage. We, on the other hand, could well be back to the White City by tomorrow night.'

They drove on into the gathering darkness and, as Acrusta had predicted, the wind backed further to the north and they began to surf with the waves. To his surprise, Ravian found the motion quite comforting and, not being required for an evening watch, he slept soundly through the night.

Dawn the next day came slowly – angry and grey. The wind was now firmly in the northeast and blowing a gale.

Later in his life, Ravian would experience the terrifying sight of swells as high as hills. This day, however, as the longship ran south before the young Tarcun's first storm at sea, the grey, foam-streaked walls that marched menacingly up to the stern of the boat merely fascinated and exhilarated him. As they caught up with *Storm Bringer,* the waves would lift the vessel high and then thrust her onwards with a surge of rigging-rattling acceleration.

Ravian took two turns at the steering oar that morning – spells of about an hour each. As there was too much strain on the rudder for one man, two crewmen were detailed for the duty – with Combus standing close by to lend his experience and weight if required.

Between his spells on the tiller, Ravian talked with Acrusta.

'This is the strength of our fleet, Young Sir!' the admiral enthused. 'No other vessel in the world would risk leaving harbour today and yet, here we are, having the time of our lives!'

One look in the admiral's face was enough to tell Ravian that he meant what he said – there was a youthful gleam in the old mariner's eye that burned brighter with each downhill surge. Ravian had certainly found his time at the steering oar exhilarating and had been disappointed when taken off at the end of only an hour.

'I agree, Sir, but why was I relieved from steering so early?' he asked. 'I should have liked to continue awhile.'

'Helming a longship on a day like today is one of life's great pleasures Prince Ravian,' Old Crusty replied, 'but a man gets tired faster than he knows and starts to lose concentration. Next thing, even with a tiny foresail like this on, the stern has come around faster and further than you can catch it and the ship broaches down the face of a wave. A longship can usually survive that – I've seen longships go over so far that their masts have been level with the water – but it is a very dangerous and unpleasant experience.'

Ravian had no doubt that it would be so and was doubly cautious on his next spell at the steering oar, ending his watch without complaint or resentment.

Such was the speed of their passage that, by midday, a towering headland showed ahead on the storm-hazed horizon and, recognising The Horn, the northern extremity of Tarcus, Acrusta ordered a change in course three points to starboard. Ravian knew that he did so in order to be sure that they would weather The Tusk, the barren headland that marked the western extremity of the vast Golden Bay. With the wind squarely behind them, they just managed the leg without jibing – passing close below the steep cliffs of the headland a mere two hours' sail later. Altering course to the southeast, they gained some lee from the high cliffs that, except for the entrance to Belainus, ran unbroken all the way to the White City. The sea close to the coast was smoother, although plenty of wind still made it down from the cliff tops. Acrusta ordered a larger jib onto the forestay and the mainsail re-hoisted, although reefed down to less than half its usual area. Then, hugging the rugged coast all the way, they continued for the White City, the splintered bow hissing on the wind-rippled waters.

Ravian had never known such speed.

On and on the ship drove, faster than a horse could gallop, and the few landmarks sped down their port side – some houses of Neverius high on the cliff tops, the narrow entrance to Belainus. Then, the perpendicular headland of the Western Arm appeared ahead of them, marking the approach to the White City. The late afternoon sun was just starting to break through the clouds as they rounded the point and tacked into the harbour entrance and, as they passed between the guard towers, the White City gleamed ahead of them with a golden tinge.

It had only been twelve days since he had left the waters of this same harbour and yet Ravian felt that he had doubled in experience in that time. He looked aft to where Acrusta proudly paced his quarterdeck, while Billus worked the steering oar and Capernal studiously noted navigation marks in his journal.

Silently, the Tarcun prince thanked Delikas for his good fortune in being born into such a life.

Chapter Four

Ravian would always remember his first two years as a longshipman as a time of both intense learning and uncomplicated happiness.

Under the close tutelage of Acrusta, he rapidly absorbed the skills required of a Tarcun naval officer and, as *Storm Bringer* patrolled the Sapphire Sea and visited the kingdoms along its shores, he began to acquire a better understanding of the world and Tarcus's place in it.

He learned every mile of coast and every harbour of the Eastern Shore, the royal palace at Ezreen becoming a second home to him. *Storm Bringer* also took him to Belutius, Karaal's port on the Sapphire Sea, where Ravian briefly met King Baharat, that country's ageing potentate. From there, they had sailed north to Dalvan – a land where safe harbours and good manners were both in short supply, as Old Crusty observed. They had voyaged through the Gertal Islands to Groven, the first of the true northern countries Ravian was to visit, stopping in at the small, cliff-ringed harbour that serviced Bendim, the capital of that country. Acrusta then took *Storm Bringer* into the Grimspot Gris as far as the harbour of Canavast, the large trading port that was the capital of the kingdom of Kleeft. From there, the Tarcuns had been able to see the distant, snow-covered mountains of Graftsen, far to the north.

Turning away from the dark, brooding shores of the inland sea, the admiral had then set a course southwest for the Delenes Islands, a gentler, warmer land of small villages and fertile vineyards. The islands' ruler, King Zecretes, a good friend and significant trading partner of Tarcus, had welcomed them so warmly and entertained them so lavishly at his capital of Zedezee that they had found it difficult to leave.

By the time Ravian had gained his promotion to second lieutenant – freeing himself, at last, of the detested "Young Sir" appellation – he had coasted the Southern Shore from Ezreen to Sanja, piloted *Storm Bringer* into the shoal-ridden harbour of Beldona, and even ridden a camel train several days' south into the vast, dry continent beyond. He had seen the forbidding headlands of the Western Portal, fought another action against pirates off the coast of Saravene and weathered a violent storm off the coast of Survene.

Every day at sea bought some new experience and, while Ravian was not a particularly religious man, every now and then, an especially beautiful dawn or sunset would have him repeat his thanks to Delikas for the privilege of being there to see it.

Meanwhile, at the Tarcun palace, Jeniel seemed to have reconciled himself to his role as heir to the throne.

The crown prince had become betrothed to Kasanda, daughter of the House of Hedreel – a match with which the king and queen were well pleased. From his first meeting with the future queen of Tarcus, Ravian had also liked her very much, finding that she exuded a quiet strength and confidence that he knew would stand his brother in good stead. Kasanda also had a well-developed sense of humour which, in Ravian's case, usually displayed itself in the form of gentle teasing about his continuing bachelor status.

'Ravian, I swear that the good families of Tarcus are going to run out of comely daughters for you to sample,' she would chide him. 'You are getting quite a reputation as a heart-breaker, Young Man.'

It wasn't true, of course.

Ravian had briefly courted a few of the island's eligible maidens, but invariably found them far less exciting than some of the companions he that had enjoyed on the Eastern Shore. However, he was well aware that, as second in line to the throne, he was a prize catch in the eyes of the aspirational matrons of the land, and potential wives were thrust at him at every social and state occasion. So relentless was some of the matchmaking that the sea was often his only escape and, indeed, on one particularly pressing occasion, he had been driven to request of a bemused Acrusta that the admiral order *Storm Bringer* away on a sudden and unscheduled training voyage.

His younger brother, Ramus, had beaten both his siblings down the matrimonial path by marrying his wife, Verene, at a very young age and the couple were already expecting their first child. Verene and Jeniel's wife, Kasanda, had very similar personalities, the two young women quickly becoming firm friends – and conspirators in their harassment of their bachelor brother-in-law. Much loved by the king and queen, Verene quickly became a part of the family at the palace – which was just as well, Ravian thought, as Ramus was frequently absent for long periods on his trading missions.

His younger brother had taken to his role as Minister of Trade with an enthusiasm and energy that had surprised everybody. Indeed, Ravian saw him more often in foreign harbours than he did at the White City and he sometimes wondered where Ramus had found the time to make his young wife pregnant.

Towards the end of Ravian's second year as a longshipman, Acrusta asked to meet him on *Storm Bringer's* quarterdeck. The longship lay alongside its wharf at the naval base and, while he waited for the admiral, Ravian watched some boys skylarking out on the harbour in three small sailing dinghies.

The boats were manoeuvring about each other in the steady afternoon breeze, each young skipper trying to position his craft so that he could ram one of the others. Peals of laughter came to him across the ruffled waters as the dinghies crazily tacked and jibed.

Ravian smiled. Now there were some longship captains in the making, he thought to himself.

As he watched, one of the boats was too slow getting through a tack and one of its opponents pounced. Catching its victim on the leeward side, the attacking dinghy rode up onto the rail of its target, instantly swamping and capsizing it. As the game ended in hoots of hilarity and the boys turned to bailing the boat out, Ravian recalled *Storm Bringer's* splintered bow of after their mission against the Dekanian pirates in the Gertals.

If there was enough wind, he thought to himself, why couldn't a longship be made strong enough to use ramming as a tactic?

Acrusta arrived on the quarterdeck and Ravian immediately put the question to him.

The admiral wasn't enthusiastic about the notion.

'Well, Ravian,' he said, 'you've seen first-hand what can happen with ramming. At least a galley can usually use her oars to back out after she's rammed another vessel. If you built a longship with a ram, once you'd hit a vessel, you'd lose all your wind and you'd be stuck there to battle it out. You're much better off to come alongside with grappling lines. That way, you've still got a battle on your hands but, if you see it going against you, you can always cut and run.'

'But what if you didn't fit a ram, but strengthened the stem so that you could ram another ship and then sail off again?' Ravian asked.

Acrusta seemed to give the notion serious thought.

'To make the bow strong enough for that, you'd have put so much reinforcing into it that you'd throw the balance of the whole vessel out,' he eventually said. 'Anyway, forget such far-fetched notions for the time being, Ravian – you are not going to have time for them.'

The prince raised a quizzical eyebrow.

'You have done well, these past two years,' Acrusta continued, 'and it is my pleasure to inform you that, as of dawn tomorrow, you are to take command of *Wind Song*.'

Ravian' jaw dropped. He was still only a second lieutenant and, at barely twenty years of age, he would be at least five years younger than any other longship captain.

'I...I'm honoured, Sir, but I cannot accept. Promotion should come from experience and ability, not from any family lineage.'

The old admiral smiled.

'Noble sentiments from noble blood,' he chuckled. 'Really, Ravian, you should learn to give yourself credit for your own abilities. You're young – and I certainly envy you that – but you're no younger than Capernal, and I've just given him command of *Thunder Storm*.'

Ravian was speechless for a moment.

'Then I certainly accept with gratitude, sir,' he finally got out, 'but, surely, we are both very young and junior in rank for such honours?'

'There are precedents, Ravian,' Acrusta said. 'Experience is important, yes, but ability is even more so. Obviously, you and Capernal are very young and both of you are only second lieutenants – but the two of you are by far the most able men available for promotion to captain. Billus isn't too far behind the pair of you either – he just needs a few rough edges taken off.'

'I must say,' continued the admiral, 'that it has been a pleasure having the three of you with me these last two years. For yourself, Your Highness,' – it was unusual for Acrusta to address him by this title – 'I would like to farewell you from my immediate command with the most valuable gift that I can offer you. I am appointing Combus as *Wind Song's* bosun.'

Ravian considered this. Combus, as the most able bosun in the fleet, was a valuable gift indeed.

'But surely, Sir, you need to keep him by you?'

'Combus is a good man,' Old Crusty said, 'and the best bosun that I've ever sailed with. Nevertheless, I will be retiring when you are ready for the admiral's flag to pass to you – and that won't be long. Combus deserves to continue to be the Admiral's Bosun, so it's a well-earned reward to you both.'

Thus, the following morning, the familiar, weathered face of Combus was the first to greet Ravian as he boarded his first command.

Wind Song was brand new – the most recent product of the shipyards on the southern side of the harbour – and, at first, Ravian was thrilled by the newness of the vessel and the opportunity to take command of a fresh crew. It soon became obvious however, that both ship and crew needed considerable work if they were to become anything like the smooth machine that *Storm Bringer* was.

Wind Song sailed differently to the admiral's flagship. She was more nervous at the helm, requiring more attention from her watch officer and helmsman, and yet, from the very first, Ravian also saw that the new longship was capable of pointing higher to windward than the older vessel. The rigging needed considerable tuning though, and the crew even more so – over two-thirds of them being straight out of the Academy and dangerously inexperienced.

Ravian had learned many valuable lessons under Acrusta, and one of these was that discipline, once established, could always be relaxed – but to start things too easily was to invite trouble. Thus, he was completely ruthless with the training of his crew – relentlessly exercising *Wind Song* to harden the men and to learn the ways the longship sailed best. His first lieutenant, Godart – a young man his own age from North Cove – was a capable, loyal, second in command, but it was largely due to the efforts of Combus that things slowly began to improve.

The bosun had proved the valuable asset Ravian had expected, the raw crew quickly coming to regard the weathered senior ranker with a mixture of respect and terror. Combus seemed everywhere; hurrying the crew along with a short length of rope that he kept for the especially tardy, on hands and knees in the scuppers tracing leaks, even in the taverns of the town – extricating drunken crewmembers from trouble. At sea, when he was not drilling the men with rowing practice, boarding exercises and sail changes, Combus worked tirelessly with his captain and first lieutenant to fine-tune the rigging. Yet, even as *Wind Song* slowly began to evolve into a half-decent longship, the bosun showed little satisfaction. Nor would either of them, Ravian knew, until everything about the vessel was perfect.

Admiral Acrusta, mindful that his new captains still had a lot to learn, regularly ordered *Wind Song* and *Thunder Storm* to sea in company with his own vessel, the ships sailing in close formation, tacking and jibing in unison as ordered by flag signals from *Storm Bringer*. In the beginning, Ravian was frustrated that Capernal's vessel, five years old and with an experienced crew, always seemed to turn that much more quickly and cleanly than his own. After three months though, as *Wind Song* and her crew began to meld into a single unit, the differences between the three longships became less marked. Ravian was proud of his progress with what had been a bunch of raw recruits and he was also pleased to find that, whether sailing on or off the wind, *Wind Song* seemed to be a comfortably faster vessel than either *Storm Bringer* or *Thunder Storm*.

For a time, the Tarcun prince's whole life centred on his command. Then, one warm, late-summer afternoon, Sinur entered his world.

Wind Song lay alongside at the Naval Base, most of her crew released to a well-earned furlough after weeks of exercises. Ravian had dallied on board, loathe to exchange the autonomy of his command for the more restrictive environment of the palace. He was on his quarterdeck, enjoying the breeze and the change in the light about the harbour and city as sunset approached. The tide was at dead low and he had been gazing out over the seaward rail, so he was taken by surprise by the female voice that came from above and behind him.

'So, this is where the elusive Prince Ravian hides out!'

He spun around, less gracefully than he would have liked, and stared at the apparition above him on the quayside.

The low sun was behind her, highlighting her blond tresses and, Ravian could not help but notice, silhouetting her body enticingly through the light fabric of her summer tunic. He immediately noted the jewelled shoulder broaches that marked her as a daughter of one of the Nine Houses and wondered what a highborn woman of about his own age was doing wandering unescorted in the waterfront area.

'You have the advantage of me, Madam,' he said, rather more stiffly than he intended. 'I don't believe that I have had the pleasure of your acquaintance.'

Her smile was warm, faintly mocking.

'Why, Prince Ravian, if your reputation is to be believed, I must be just about the only daughter of the Nine Houses you *haven't* had the pleasure of. I am Sinur of the House of Kallan.'

Ravian felt himself blush at the reference to his unjustified reputation.

'Well, Sinur, how may I be of assistance?'

Her eyes flashed boldly and Ravian saw that they were as blue as the sky.

'Well, Your Highness,' she said with affected innocence, 'I suddenly realised how little we women of Tarcus know about our naval vessels and I thought that I might come and have a closer look at one.'

'And now that you have seen one, what do you think?' Ravian asked.

'I think that it is difficult to appreciate one from the quayside,' Sinur replied. 'Aren't you going to invite me aboard?'

Ravian hesitated. The deck of a naval vessel was no place for a lady, especially one so young, attractive and without a chaperone. Indeed, the only women who found their way on board longships usually did so with a strictly professional objective in mind. Nevertheless, entranced, he moved to the quayside rail and extended his hand to help her down.

Sinur's touch was cool, her smile broad and self-assured, as she stepped from the quay down to the rail and then leapt lightly to the quarterdeck. She did so with a flounce of hem and flash of leg that Ravian should have averted his eyes from but did not. Sinur allowed her hand to linger in his for some moments longer than was necessary – the spell this cast over the prince only broken by a snigger from amidships. Dropping her hand as though it had burned him, Ravian wheeled and glared forward at the crew of the duty watch – all of whom suddenly seemed to be commendably busy scrubbing the thwarts.

'It's all right, Your Highness,' Sinur said. 'I understand that men who spend a long time at sea sometimes act strangely when they re-enter the world of women.'

He turned back to face her.

'Do you ever feel strange around women, Prince Ravian?' she asked with wide-eyed innocence.

His face flaming, Ravian groped for, but failed to find, a suitable reply. What an outrageous flirt she was!

Giving him a knowing look, Sinur cast her eyes about the vessel.

'Now, Your Highness,' she said. 'Why don't you tell me all about your longship?'

Ravian was relieved at the change of subject, and launched into a description of the various features of *Wind Song*, all the while aware that Sinur was paying only slight attention. As he talked though, he felt his blush receding and he gained enough confidence to look at her directly as she pretended to study the steering oar.

What a captivating creature!

Her hair was the colour of pale gold and her flawless skin glowed with good health. Her scent came to him – a blend of freshly cut flowers and blooming womanhood – and, for the first time, Ravian began to think that Tarcus might have produced a beauty to rival those of the Eastern Shore.

Then a bellow from above cut the moment savagely short.

'Sinur! What in the name of Delikas are you doing?!'

They both wheeled to where a large, red-faced, bearded man glared down at them from the quayside. Despite the new arrival's face being contorted with rage, Ravian immediately recognised Lemalus, head of the House of Kallan and a senior member of the Citizen's Council.

'Your mother and I take our eyes off you for two seconds and you disappear!' he bellowed. 'And now, here you are on a navy ship like some waterfront floozy! What, in the name of all that is holy, are we going to do with you?!'

Sinur appeared unfazed by the verbal barrage.

'Father, please,' she said reproachfully. 'You are embarrassing yourself in front of His Highness.'

Lemalus blinked and then nodded curtly at Ravian.

'Ah, Your Highness,' he said. 'I didn't see that it was you. All the same, Sinur, I want you off this ship and back to your mother immediately! She's waiting at the end of the quay.'

Sinur turned to Ravian and smiled.

'I'm so sorry that my visit has been so brief, Prince Ravian,' she said. 'Perhaps you would care to call at our residence sometime? – My father is usually known for his courtesy to guests.'

Ravian recollected that Lemalus actually had a reputation for being a stingy, bad-tempered old bully. All the same, he took the proffered hand and assisted Sinur back up onto the jetty.

This time, with her father glowering down at him, he was careful to avert his eyes from her hem, and he found the courage to say, 'Perhaps, with your father's permission, I might be allowed to escort you out?'

Lemalus began to say something but his daughter quickly interrupted him.

'That would be wonderful, Your Highness,' she said with another dazzling smile. 'We will look forward to your call.'

With that, she turned and was gone. Lemalus lingered for a moment, looking as though he still had something to say. Then, with a low growl and a final withering glare at Ravian, he hurried after his daughter.

Ravian stared after them for some time.

Already, he was wondering how he was going to cope with Lemalus as a father in law.

Sinur, Ravian discovered, was at the hub of the White City's social world, a world that, having first been cloistered at the palace, and then wrapped up in his military training, he had no real experience of. Away from the formal state and social occasions of the city, there existed a culture of plays, musical evenings and poetry readings frequented by the crème of young Tarcun society, to many of whom the trade of the nation was simply a financial means to follow artistic or intellectual pursuits.

Two nights after his first encounter with Sinur, Ravian called at Lemalus's house to escort Sinur out for the evening. As befitted a senior and influential member of the House of Kallan, the residence was a rather grand one, sited in an established and affluent area between the theatre and the city walls. Being of a similar elevation on the crater walls to that of the palace, the sweeping view from the carefully tended grounds of the mansion was very similar to the one enjoyed by the royal family. The fragrance of summer blooms filled the warm twilight as the prince mounted a gleaming white flight of steps and knocked upon the massive, column-flanked front door. A haughty, richly liveried servant admitted him into the main reception room of the house, a vast, gleaming space flanked by two curves of sweeping stairs and filled with rich furnishings and marble statues. Sinur's mother and father awaited him amongst this display of wealth and, despite the curtsy and bow with which they acknowledged his arrival, their haughty demeanour made it clear to Ravian that neither of them was overawed by his royal presence.

'Welcome to my humble home, Your Highness,' Lemalus greeted him in a tone that was anything but welcoming. 'Allow me to introduce my wife, Deleba.'

It was immediately evident to Ravian where Sinur had got her looks from. Deleba was considerably younger than her husband, and had the confident demeanour of an outstanding beauty born into a life of wealth and privilege.

Lemalus motioned towards a large couch and Ravian sat down, Sinur's parents taking their places on a matching sofa opposite.

'Our daughter will be down shortly,' Lemalus said. 'Can I offer you a glass of wine, Your Highness?'

At Ravian's nod, a servant appeared with three glasses of red wine on a tray. Ravian took a glass, an exquisite piece of the finest crystal, and raised it to his hosts.

'To the beauty of the ladies of Kallan,' he said.

Lemalus frowned but raised his own glass before half-draining it. Deleba, however, allowed him a small, condescending smile before raising her own glass to her lips. Ravian was not surprised to find that, despite the expensive, delicate vessels in which it was served, the wine was a rough drop from Survene – and probably a year or two past its best.

A few minutes of stilted inconsequential conversation ensued until Ravian's discomfort was relieved by the arrival of Sinur at the top of one of the staircases. As she descended towards them, her golden, silky gown flowing over her body like water, Ravian was struck, not only by her beauty, but also by the complete contrast with the woman that accompanied her.

'Good evening, Your Highness,' she said, halting before him with a small curtsy. 'May I introduce Mefad – my aunt and also my chaperone?'

'Charmed,' Ravian said with a courteous bow.

Mefad responded with an artless curtsy. The middle-aged woman, her substantial girth swathed in the black garb of a widow, was as homely as her name and clearly came from Lemalus's side of the family. She said nothing, but regarded the young prince with a knowing, baleful eye.

Ravian seized the opportunity to bid good evening to Lemalus and Deleba and, offering his arm to Sinur, he escorted her from the house and out into the street – every step shadowed by the silent presence of Mefad.

'Is your aunt to accompany us everywhere?' he whispered to Sinur, as they followed the street down towards the amphitheatre and its attendant area of restaurants and taverns.

'Of course!' she replied. 'You didn't think that you were going to get me alone in the dark did you?'

It was a beautiful, warm evening and the sound of social revelry carried to them from their destination.

'But I'm of the Royal House, damn it,' Ravian seethed. 'Surely that counts for something?'

'Hah!' Sinur scoffed, the humorous gleam in her eyes taking the seriousness away from her next words. 'My parents understand that it has counted for very little with the daughters of some of their acquaintances. Don't worry, Prince Ravian, when the time is right for us to be alone, Mefad will not be an obstacle.

What an intriguing comment, Ravian thought.

What he said was, 'Please, just call me Ravian.'

At Sinur's suggestion, he had agreed to accompany her to the opening night of a new play at the amphitheatre. He had heard about such events, of course, but had never actually attended one himself. Now, as they approached the theatre, its ornate exterior glowing in the light of a many torches and thronged around by what seemed to be hundreds of Tarcuns, he had to admit to a feeling of excitement that wasn't solely due to Sinur's presence.

Passing through one of the building's tall, arched doorways, they entered a crowded, brilliantly-lit reception chamber. People recognised them now and with a flurry of bowing and curtsying, a space opened before them. Into this gap in the human press stepped the theatre manager who, after bidding them an effusive welcome, escorted them to a special box to the side of the stage, some height above the crowd. Ravian and Sinur took their seats side by side, Mefad settling contentedly on her own seat behind them.

'Do you come to the theatre often?' Ravian asked his companion.

'All the time,' she replied, 'particularly when there is a new play. Shush now – here comes Precedius.'

To wild applause from the audience, a tall, slender figure strode onto the stage. Even Ravian had heard of Tarcus's most popular actor, who now bowed deeply to his public – and again in the direction of their box – before launching into his lines.

It was from this point that the evening began to lose its charm for Ravian.

Acting, he quickly decided, consisted of a group of men and women bellowing out inane lines in support of a puerile plot. The worst part was a so-called sword fight where Precedius and another actor used toy swords to flail away at each other like children in a nursery. The lead actor's "death", when it came, was even longer and more tedious than the battle that had preceded it and, as the audience rose in its ovation, the prince breathed a sigh of relief.

'We must go back-stage and meet the actors!' Sinur announced, as Precedius took his third curtain call. 'They have such frightfully fun parties on opening nights.'

Inwardly, Ravian groaned. He had been thinking that he might be able to go somewhere quieter with Sinur and, perhaps, lose Mefad along the way. Instead, he found the crowded, noisy back stage party even more tedious than the performance itself, starting with his introduction to the leading actor.

'Welcome, Your Highness,' Precedius had said with a deep, dramatic bow. 'I don't believe that we've had the pleasure of your company before.'

'No,' Ravian had confirmed. 'This is my first night.'

'Really?' Precedius had replied tartly, turning to Sinur. 'My Dear, you have clearly taken on a grave responsibility, introducing his highness to his own kingdom's culture. I presume that you will also be guiding Prince Ravian in his appreciation of poetry and the musical arts?'

'Absolutely,' Sinur replied. 'I think that you can look forward to seeing rather a lot of Prince Ravian in the town in future.'

'When my duties allow, of course,' Ravian said quickly.

'Duties?' Precedius asked haughtily. 'And what duties might those be, Your Highness?'

'Well,' Ravian began, 'I have the command of my longship for one thing.'

'Ravian is the youngest-ever longship captain,' Sinur gushed.

'Hmmm,' replied Precedius. 'I did my basic training like everybody else, of course, but I can't say that the navy is a way of life that ever appealed to me. All that rowing and hauling on rigging and such...not exactly intellectually stimulating is it?'

Ravian felt his ears redden at the actor's rudeness.

'I think that, had you ever been involved in any real action, you would have found that stimulating enough,' he said tightly.

'Possibly,' Precedius replied in a bored tone of voice. 'Really though, I can't think of anything more ghastly than having to kill a fellow human being.'

'And yet,' Ravian replied, ' the fact that we have an army and navy of men prepared to do just that means that you and every other artist in this nation can live in peace and prosperity.'

'Each to their own, Your Highness,' Precedius responded with an airy wave of his hand. 'I do hope though, that you don't find our world as much of a bore as we find yours.'

Ravian was about to make another, angry, response when he felt Sinur's hand on his arm.

'Ravian, we are monopolising the leading actor on his opening night,' she declared tactfully. 'Let us go and meet the rest of the cast – we'll have lots of time to talk with Precedius in the future.'

'I shall look forward to that immensely,' the actor replied with smooth insincerity and, bowing deeply, he withdrew into the crowd.

'I hope the rest of the cast aren't a bunch of whoopsies,' Ravian growled.

'I count Precedius among my friends,' Sinur admonished him. 'I can also assure you that, if some of my female acquaintances are to be believed, there is nothing unmanly about him in situations of intimacy.'

Ravian was furious but he kept his silence, determined not let the actor's rudeness get in the way of winning Sinur's affections.

For the next few weeks, this was the pattern of his relationship with Sinur – evenings out at plays, poetry readings or musical recitals, crowded with people and perpetually shadowed by Aunt Mefad.

Ravian was often uncomfortable in the gay, witty conversations that were an inevitable part of these events, and the prince soon realised that it was only his royal blood, and the consummate social skills of Sinur, that saved him from summary dismissal as a military boor.

Ravian found that he did enjoy the poetry readings – if not the pretentious parties that accompanied them. He also mostly enjoyed the musical performances, despite finding the musicians themselves to be a rather detached, insular breed. The dramatic plays, however, he invariably found tedious and the actors – subsequently encountered at back-stage parties such as the one on the first night – consistently rude and egotistical.

Sinur guided him through this new world with a confident hand, introducing him as "My Gallant Sea Captain" to much eye rolling and raising of eyebrows from the regular patrons of the arts. Ravian continued to be utterly entranced by her beauty, her social skills and her attentiveness and, as his reception at her parents' home slowly warmed, from restrained hostility to cool tolerance, he made more and more time to be with her.

Their first kiss was a stolen moment in the shadows outside the theatre, having temporarily stranded Mefad in the crowd inside, and, as they became bolder, they sought the opportunity to give her the slip with increasing frequency, sometimes employing Sinur's friends to divert the dowager aunt from her dutiful attentiveness.

One particular evening, they found that their latest strategy had been so successful, that they were able to walk alone all the way from the town centre back to Sinur's parents' house. Not daring to return to the residence without Mefad, they then had to wait in the deserted street outside for her to catch up. They had both taken more wine than they should have and, seizing the moment, Ravian suddenly pulled Sinur into a darkened doorway. To his surprise and delight, Sinur embraced him with an urgency that seemed to match his own and, as her mouth hungrily sought his and she pressed against him, she allowed his hands to roam freely beneath her gown.

Suddenly they heard the footsteps that they knew signalled the approach of their chaperone and she broke away from him with a gasp.

'Tonight,' she whispered, giving his hand a final squeeze. 'Come to my balcony tonight.'

Thus, having duly bid Sinur and Mefad goodnight at the front door of Lemalus's house, Ravian circled around into an alleyway behind the property. Easily scaling the head-high, stone wall that protected its perimeter, he crept soundlessly through the immaculate garden within and, surrounded by the night chorus of crickets and the heavy scent of jasmine, he waited below the low balcony outside that which he knew to be her room.

After what seemed an eternity, the doors onto to the balcony opened and Sinur stepped into the moonlight. In an instant, Ravian was over the balustrade and they were in each other's arms, their passionate kisses igniting an irresistible fire. Staggering inside to her bed, the young couple made love until the prince crept away at the first light of dawn.

For both of them it was a moment of significant commitment.

Although virginity was not an especially prized asset amongst Tarcuns generally, society expected the daughters of the Nine Houses to be exceptions. In giving herself to him that night, Ravian knew, Sinur had contravened a strict code and it was not an act that he took lightly. At the same time, she was a passionate and exciting lover from the very first and, despite his concern for the undoubted wrath of her father should they be discovered, Ravian found himself irresistibly drawn to her balcony every evening he was not at sea.

Three months after his first tryst with Sinur, the king summoned Ravian to an audience.

The fact that his father had called him to a formal meeting filled the prince with anxiety – all Jabacus usually needed to do to talk to him when he was in the palace was to walk down a hallway and knock on his door. As he entered the audience room, it took only one look at the faces of his mother and father to confirm that his concern was not misplaced. While Beriel's face was cool and impassive – in itself a warning sign – Jabacus was clearly annoyed about something, and Ravian had barely made his bow before the king began to speak.

'I have just been speaking with Admiral Acrusta,' Jabacus announced. 'He has informed me – admittedly, after being put under some pressure – that *Wind Song* has not sailed for two out of the last six exercises.'

Ravian swallowed. He hadn't expected this.

'I am further informed,' the king went on, 'that *Wind Song* has rapidly gone from being one of the best longships in the fleet to one of the most mediocre – which is probably unavoidable with the lack of sea time the vessel is getting.'

Ravian didn't have to wait long for the approaching storm to break.

'The vessel commanded by a prince of this country must never be a mediocre performer!' thundered his father. 'And a longship commanded by the future admiral of the fleet will not sit alongside gathering barnacles while her captain flounces around town like a drunken actor!'

Ah, thought Ravian, his father's agenda was becoming clearer by the second.

'You are wasting too much time with that Kallan girl,' the queen interjected. 'She's not good for you.'

Ravian felt his temper beginning to rise. His parents had never criticised his private affairs before.

'Sinur is not to blame for my lack of attention to *Wind Song*,' he blustered, his ears burning. 'Besides, she is showing me aspects of our culture that I have not been acquainted with before.'

Now that the real topic of conversation had been engaged, the king and queen seemed to relax slightly.

'Ravian,' his father said more softly, 'it's good that you are enjoying your youth, but to do so at the expense of your training is unpardonable, almost treasonable. Your brother and this kingdom are going to need a strong, disciplined admiral.'

'And,' Beriel continued, 'neglecting your duties over someone like Sinur is simply foolish!'

'What do you mean, "someone like Sinur"?' Ravian flared. 'Is there something that I should know?'

'Not at all, Dear,' his mother replied coolly – looking away as she spoke.

'Ravian,' his father said, 'we've not interfered in your private life before, nor did we intend to up until now, but Sinur is from a powerful house of this kingdom. If you are just entertaining yourself, then you should do so with a different girl – how long do you think it is going to take for Lemalus to notice that trail wearing across his back lawn?'

Ravian felt his face turn crimson.

Of course, the royal spies had observed his night time excursions and reported them to his parents.

'It's not just a dalliance,' he mumbled. 'We...we love each other.'

'Love!' his mother snorted. 'People your ages don't understand the meaning of the word!'

Ravian locked eyes with his mother. She was a forthright, strong-willed woman who, as her three boisterous sons had been growing up, had always dealt with them with a firm but loving hand. Ravian was no longer a child though and, for a moment, he hated her.

'Look, Ravian,' his father said, interrupting the tense silence, 'I am not going to live forever and, until Jeniel produces an heir, you are still next in line to this throne. Whether your destiny is as this nation's king or as its commander in chief, you will need someone beside you who can help you carry the responsibility.'

'And for all that Sinur may be from a very good family, and for all that she may be a very nice girl,' his mother continued – in a tone that left no doubt that she didn't think Sinur was a nice girl at all, 'she is not the sort of woman who could be queen. The crown of this country may be a pretty thing, but it is no bauble and it carries an awful weight'.

Ravian looked from one of his parents to the other.

'Are you saying that I should select a more suitable wife?' he asked them. 'Is that the way it was for you?'

His parents exchanged a glance.

'No, Ravian, it wasn't,' his father said. 'I was lucky enough to meet and fall in love with someone who, from the first, I knew would be able to help me bear my responsibilities. Had I felt that your mother would not have been able to share my burden, and do so with dignity and with pride, I would never have asked her to be my wife.'

Beriel and Jabacus exchanged a loving look.

'Sinur and I haven't discussed marriage,' Ravian said, trying not to sound surly.

'Oh you will, don't worry about that!' said his mother with sudden vehemence. 'She's got her eyes on a life in the palace, that one. You are just a means to an ends, My Boy.'

Ravian was aghast – he had never seen his mother act this way.

'Ravian,' his father said in a soothing voice, 'your mother and I are only thinking about your best interests. None of us can change your royal destiny and, if Sinur is the right one for you, then so be it – but she must start to see that she needs to share you with your responsibilities. Please promise me that you will not let your social life override your duties again.'

'I don't have my own life!' Ravian protested. 'Neither does Jeniel. Nor does Ramus. None of us do!'

To his surprise, both his parents nodded sympathetically.

'That's right, Dear,' his mother said softly. 'I think that you are beginning to understand.'

Ravian said nothing to Sinur of the meeting with his parents, but he did vow to himself that he would no longer forsake his duties to be with her. It was not long before the requirements of the Tarcun navy conflicted with Sinur's social programme.

'We're sailing down to Beldona the day after tomorrow,' he told her across her pillow one evening. 'I don't expect we'll be away for much more than ten days.'

'Oh, Darling, what a bore!' she groaned. 'Precedius is opening a new play in five days – one he has written himself. There will be a wonderful party and everyone will be there. How can I possibly attend without My Gallant Sea Captain?'

Ravian grimaced inwardly. Anywhere that Sinur went without him would soon present her with a choice of handsome, attentive escorts. A crowd of eligible suitors would surround her the moment his ship was over the horizon.

Mind you, he thought to himself, it was almost worth it not to have to socialise with Precedius.

'I'm sorry, Sinur, but it really can't be helped,' he told her. 'In fact...I've been letting things slip a bit lately – because I enjoy being with you so much. I've really got to knuckle down and behave a bit more like a prince of the realm.'

Sinur paused as she considered this.

'Of course you do, Darling,' she replied. 'I keep forgetting that you are a member of the royal family. To me, you are simply a man – my man, and so much of a man – but I suppose that we have both allowed our love to obscure the fact that you have some very important things to do. Neither of us should forget that your duty must come first.'

Ravian sighed happily. He had been dreading denying Sinur her way and now he saw that the she totally understood and supported him. His parents were so wrong about her.

'Have I told you how much I love you?' he asked her.

'Of course you have, Sweetheart – just before, while we were making love. Now' – she moved against him provocatively – 'if you are going to be away for ten days, we had better make sure that you are too spent to be tempted by any of those dark-eyed witches of the South.'

Thus, their romance entered a more settled phase, Ravian happier now that he felt the balance between his responsibilities and his personal life had been restored. Within a short time, he was satisfied that *Wind Song* was once again the best ship in the Tarcun navy and, as Acrusta's retirement loomed ever nearer, he began to feel increasingly confident about taking over the old admiral's position.

His love for Sinur remained undiminished and she continued to return his affections. Inevitably, they discussed the subject of marriage.

'Sinur, we will marry,' he had told her. 'Once Acrusta retires, and I take over as Admiral of the Fleet, I'll have more control of my schedule. That will be the time for us to marry and have a family.'

'But, Darling, that's at least another year away!' Sinur had groaned. 'Why can't you make an honest woman out of me sooner?'

'It's just not the right moment,' he told her. 'Not only do I still have a lot of work to do to ready myself for the admiral's position, but I've got another project that is going to take up a lot of time.'

'As long as that "other project" is not some other woman,' she had pouted.

It wasn't.

Ravian, for the first time in his military career, shortcut the usual chain of command and went directly to his father. They met informally, seated on a sunny balcony of the palace that looked out towards the harbour.

'I have an idea, Father, to build a new sort of warship,' the prince announced.

'Ravian, I'm pleased that you are so thoroughly applying yourself to your duties, although,' his father added with a wry smile, 'they tell me that the trail across Lemalus' back lawn is now worn to dust. But don't you think that you should be speaking with Admiral Acrusta on this subject?'

'The admiral is this country's finest sailor and as loyal as any man could be,' Ravian replied. 'He has been like a second father to me and I love him dearly – but he is a man of tradition and he will never give his approval to something as revolutionary as that which I'm proposing. I have already suggested it to him informally and he showed not the slightest bit of interest.'

'I understand,' said the king. 'What did you have in mind?'

'I want to build a longship that can ram under sail,' Ravian told him. 'Not just ram, but to be able to run up and over the rail of an enemy, smashing her gunwale and, hopefully, sinking her instantly. I envisage a reinforced bow and keel of bronze, if it is technically possible. A bronze keel would be heavy, but we already put lead ballast on the keels of our longships anyway. There would be no ramming projection like the galleys use – rather, the shape of keel and stem would be like the curve of a sword.'

'And how and where would you develop such a craft?' his father asked.

'All our bronze is smelted in Belainus,' Ravian said. 'It doesn't have much of a harbour, but it will do for our purposes and secrecy will probably be easier to maintain there than in the White City. I'd like to commission a bronze worker and a shipbuilder from that city to build a half scale model to test my theory.'

His father pursed his lips.

'And at what point would you intend to inform Admiral Acrusta?' he asked.

'The admiral retires in a little over a year – and I take over his position,' Ravian reminded his father. 'If we are able to build a working model in that time – one that can be used as a template for future, full-sized construction – I would be more than satisfied. The admiral doesn't need to know that this work is going on while he is in command. In fact, the fewer people who do know about this, the better.'

'Hmmm,' his father mused. 'It sounds interesting.'

Then he smiled.

'I hope your young lady is understanding,' the king said. 'Between carrying out your captain's duties and slipping backwards and forwards to Belainus to look after your secret project, she's not going to see very much of you.'

Ravian would always suspect that his father's approval for the project had as much to do with testing his relationship with Sinur as it did with securing Tarcus's position as a dominant sea power.

Chapter Five

Ravian rode to Belainus alone, travelling most of the day on the seldom-used road that was the alternative to sea travel between the manufacturing centre and the Tarcun capital. Arriving with an hour or so of daylight left, he took lodgings at a small but comfortable inn offering a pleasant view out over the shipbuilders' yards and down the harbour. After enjoying a simple but tasty dinner at his lodgings, he decided to take a walk in the warm, golden glow of sunset.

Belainus had grown at the end of a deep fissure in the otherwise unbroken line of cliffs that made up the Lee Shore. Ravian recalled from his religious studies that this chasm, a narrow "V" that reached almost a mile inland, was where the mighty sword of Delikas himself had struck during an epic battle with Kanavas, dark god of the underworld and eternal foe of everything pure and good. The uniformly precipitous cliff sides of the inlet certainly gave some weight to the legend, he thought. It was, indeed, as if some colossal blade had sliced into the coast and, apart from an area of tumbled, broken rock at the head of the inlet where the city had been built, access to the sea was limited to a small number of steep, dangerous trails.

Ravian strolled past the city's shipyard, a collection of sheds high enough above the ocean to be safe from the crashing swells of any southwesterly storm. He had visited Belainus on many occasions and knew that, on their completion, the fishing boats and smaller transport vessels produced there would be carefully lowered down what was, reputedly, the longest slipway in the Sapphire Sea.

He lingered at the top of the white stone structure, a monument to generations of toil, and admired the way its surface, as straight and smooth as a ruler, descended over the broken shoreline before disappearing into the gold-dappled ocean below. Above him, the other landmark of the town, an even greater feat of engineering than the slipway, bisected the deepening blue of the approaching twilight.

Belainus's cargo bridge, a miracle of engineering, constructed using countless layers of hardwood, arched from one side of the cliffs to the other. Its purpose, as every Tarcun knew, was not to provide a shortcut across the chasm, but to service vessels moored in the harbour below. The truck that ran backwards and forwards along the flat deck of the bridge was immobile now, its giant hook and pulley system hanging in silhouette against the sky, but Ravian knew that it could load a waiting merchantman to capacity in less time than it took for a turn of the tide.

As he had many times before, the Tarcun prince marvelled at the amount of effort that had been invested in turning what was, at best, a barely adequate natural feature into a functional port. Certainly, the generally precipitate coastline of the island meant that it was not well endowed with harbour sites and that might well have been reason enough for Belainus to develop as a fishing settlement. An odour denoting the main reason for the settlement's existence lingered in the evening air though and burned slightly in the prince's nostrils. Not far inland, he knew, a group of low hills held large quantities of copper ore, and the open mines there supplied the bulk of the raw material for the city's main industry, the smelting of bronze.

The following morning, in a discreet corner of the inn's forecourt, Ravian met with two men whose names headed a list that had been given to him by his father. Even though the town was only just beginning its working day, the foundries' pungent smell was already strong in the still, crisp air. This blended with the aroma of wood smoke from the city's many kilns, Belainus also having become a centre for pottery. The weather was fine and the sun was already warm on the prince's back when his guests arrived.

Lederalus, the smaller of Ravian' guests, was a wiry, wizened, monkey of a man who held the reputation of being the best shipwright in the city. His diminutive figure was dwarfed by the bulk of the second man, Aphorstra, who was, by reputation, the foremost metalsmith of the land. The elephantine craftsman was clearly somewhat of an

Epicurean when he wasn't producing bronze products, Ravian thought to himself, Aphorstra's curly, black beard creating the impression that he had no neck at all.

Ravian greeted the pair over a table of light refreshments – far too light, said the look on Aphorstra's face – and outlined his idea. When he finished, Lederalus thoughtfully stroked his grizzled beard and said nothing, but Aphorstra was immediately scornful.

'Impossible, Your Highness!' he scoffed, his body quivering like a disturbed jellyfish. 'No one could cast a bronze the size you are talking about for your test model – let alone one big enough for a full-sized longship!'

'And just what would be the problem?' asked Ravian, trying not to let the obese man's negativity irk him.

'For start,' the metalsmith blustered, 'the keel for your model alone would consume almost all the tin currently in the treasury – the cost would be astronomical! The other thing is that, especially with the thickness of cross-section that you're talking about, the maximum length that we could cast in one piece would be no longer than a man's arm. We simply don't have the ability to produce anything longer.'

'As far as the tin goes,' replied Ravian, knowing that the metal had to be imported, 'if there isn't enough in the treasury you will just have to buy supplies from private holdings at market rates. Concerning the cost, this experiment is underwritten by the Royal House. As far as it being impossible goes, you must simply find a way.'

'There is no way – Your Highness!' Aphorstra reiterated.

Lederalus spoke for the first time, so quietly that both Aphorstra and Ravian had to lean towards him in order to hear.

'What about those big statues you occasionally flog off to the wealthy, Aphorstra?' he asked. 'Surely you don't cast them in one piece?'

Aphorstra rolled his eyes, and Ravian realised there was no love lost between the two men. His mission, he thought, was starting badly.

'Most of them we can cast in one piece but it's a different technique to what we are talking about here,' the big man explained impatiently. 'For those we make a very thin casting so that the molten bronze fills the mould in one, clean pour.'

'Yes, but what about that monstrosity in front of your house?' pursued the old shipbuilder, his eyes twinkling. 'Surely something that size couldn't possibly be cast in one pour, no matter how thin the casting was?'

Ravian would later get the point of Lederalus's jibe. The "monstrosity" he referred to was, in fact, a life-size statue of Aphorstra himself.

The metalsmith glared at the older man.

'Oh very funny, you little woodworm!' he snarled. 'As it happens, no, an artwork of that scale cannot be cast in one piece. As I recall, it was in five sections that were welded together – but welding won't be strong enough for the purpose His Highness is suggesting.'

'What is this welding technique?' asked Ravian.

Now it was the prince's turn to endure the smith's withering glare.

The bronze workers of Tarcus produced the best alloy in the world, the exact composition and ratios kept secret within an exclusive guild on pain of death, and Aphorstra clearly found it tedious to explain the basics of metalworking to a non-craftsman, even a royal one.

'Well, Your Highness,' he eventually began, 'after the individual sections have been cast, we assemble them into a master mould that holds them in finished position. We then introduce molten bronze into the small gap between the pieces, and this slightly melts the edges of the precast sections so that the whole becomes one after cooling. It is a process requiring great skill but, in the end, only a craftsman' – a poisonous look at Lederalus – 'can tell where the welding lines are. However – and I feel that I must repeat myself – this process will not be strong enough for your purposes.'

'But we are not dealing with an object of art here, Aphorstra,' pressed Ravian. 'We are planning a substantial device. Surely, if the keel must be caste in several pieces, then the joining surfaces could be shaped to key into each for additional strength?'

'Hmmm,' Aphorstra said, at least seeming to consider the idea, 'it may be possible, Your Highness, but I certainly couldn't guarantee the outcome'.

Ravian leaned across the table towards the two men and allowed his voice to rise.

'Gentlemen, I repeat; this experiment is underwritten by the Royal House and is undertaken with the king's authority. Let me assure both of you that it will' – he thumped his fist on the table – 'be carried out to the best of your abilities. You will be fully remunerated for the work and I expect your full' – another bang on the table – 'co-operation in return!'

Both men sat upright in surprise. The king's pup may have a bite, their expressions said.

'Now,' Ravian continued in a calmer tone, 'we have to consider the issue of secrecy. I want as few people as possible to know what we are about here. You will need to purchase land and build enclosures for casting the keel and – when we get to that point – building the ship. This will need to be as close to the slipway as possible. I don't care how you manage your workers, I just want you to understand that I will hold you both responsible if so much as a whisper of this project should reach the ears of anyone not directly involved with it. Is that understood?'

Both men nodded.

'I will return in ten days, when I shall expect you to report on the progress you've made,' Ravian continued. 'I gather that there is a traditional rivalry in this city, between those who work in metal and those who work in wood. Put that rivalry aside and work together, Gentlemen. The craft that I have in mind will combine both elements as one and you will, therefore, need to work as one to create it. Are there any questions?'

Both men shook their heads in silence.

'Until ten days time then, Gentlemen, goodbye,' he told them. 'If I leave now, I should just about get back to the White City by midnight.'

Ravian rode out of the city, leaving the two craftsmen to settle their differences and to begin the task of translating his idea into reality. He had liked the look of Lederalus but he was less impressed with Aphorstra's attitude. Still, he reminded himself, he had not expected a member of the bronze workers' guild to fall over himself to cooperate with the Royal House.

The manufacture of bronze implements, both for export and domestic consumption, was a hugely profitable business that had both required and funded the construction of the cargo bridge. The Tarcun bronze workers also made the world's finest weapons, however, they were forbidden to do so except by government contract and then only for the national armoury. Many of their number saw this regulation as an unfair denial of their right to the obscene wealth an export trade in arms would surely have brought them, and their resentment towards the Royal House had become embedded over generations.

The following evening, Ravian was, again, in Sinur's bed.

'I need to take *Wind Song* out on exercises with the fleet the day after tomorrow,' he told her after they had made love. 'We will probably be gone for seven days or so. After that, I should be back for a couple of nights before I need to return to Belainus for a few days.'

'What's the big attraction in Belainus?' Sinur asked, propping herself up on one elbow.

'My Love, I'm sorry but I can't tell you,' he said. 'In fact, I must ask you to keep my whereabouts secret whenever I ride northwest.'

'And how long do you expect this to go on?' she asked, a slight edge to her voice.

'I can't be exact, I'm afraid,' he said in a placating tone, 'but I think maybe a year – not much more.'

'All right,' Sinur sighed, putting her arm around his neck and pulling herself close to him, 'I suppose that I just have to accept the demands of the kingdom. There had better not be another woman involved, that's all.'

He looked into her eyes in the low light of the single candle in the room.

'Sinur, I love you,' he told her, meaning every word. 'You have my promise that I have eyes for no one else.'

'It's not your eyes I'm worried about,' she whispered, as she began to caress him.

Thus, Ravian began to see Sinur less frequently as he continued to perform his duties as *Wind Song's* captain, as well as journeying northwest to check on the progress of the experimental vessel. When the prince next returned to Belainus however, he was pleasantly surprised to find that Lederalus and Aphorstra had not been idle since their first meeting.

On his arrival, the pair presented him with a bronze keel section approximately the length of his forearm and about as wide. Its shape was quite different to his expectations – almost triangular in cross-section and with a deep recess in two sides while, below each recess, a groove half the depth of his thumb ran the length of the sample.

'It was Lederalus's idea,' said Aphorstra, 'to facilitate construction.'

Lederalus produced some lengths of wood and demonstrated how the ribs of the ship would fit into the recesses and the planks of the hull into the groove below, so that the lower edge of the keel projected like a blade from between the layers of timber.

'Caulking around the keel is going to be tricky,' the shipbuilder pronounced, 'but, overall, the strength of the hull should be no different to that of a conventional craft as long as the keel itself is as strong as a wooden one. Unfortunately, in comparing this moulding to a similar length of timber keel, I have found that it will be too heavy, even allowing for the ballast we usually place in a longship. I have asked Aphorstra to lighten it by removing some volume from the top centre.'

'Will that affect the strength of the construction?' Ravian asked, turning to Aphorstra.

The big man spread his hands.

'Your Highness, the question of strength will lie not in the thickness of the moulding, but at the points where the sections are welded together. As you can see, we have moulded a key into each section so that it can interlock with its neighbour. That should take some strain off the welds but, if they let go...well,' – he shrugged – 'you'll have a vessel with a keel that wriggles like a snake and leaks like a sieve.'

'That must not happen,' said Ravian, with some force.

'Please, Your Highness, don't insult us by thinking we don't understand that,' said Lederalus quietly. 'Once we've finalised the cross-section's shape and weight, we can go ahead and cast all the pieces that we will need to form a complete keel. When we've welded it together, we'll test the strength against a wooden keel for a vessel of the same dimensions.'

'Very well,' Ravian said, mollified to see that Lederalus and Aphorstra seemed to be taking the project seriously. 'When do you expect to be ready to weld?'

'It will take time, Your Highness,' said Aphorstra. 'We still have to finalise the cross-section of the sample. Once we've done that, each additional section will need to be individually moulded to give Lederalus the shape he requires – that will be about fifty different moulds. The best I can suggest is that, if I turn half my workforce to the task, we should have all the parts ready to weld two months from now.'

This was, in fact, faster than Ravian had expected. He was pleasantly surprised that Aphorstra was committing so much resource to the project.

'I saw that you had started work on the sheds and foundry as I rode in,' he said to the two men. 'When will you be able to move the operation inside?'

'In just a few days, Your Highness,' Lederalus replied. 'My boys can't really begin their work until the keel is completed, so I have turned them to building the new premises in the meantime. Have you considered what you will do if we take the project to full-scale production?'

'Not up until now,' Ravian admitted, 'but I think that it would be prudent to secure some more property handy to the slipway. We'll need enough land for three full-sized construction sheds, as well as foundry big enough to handle production of a full-sized keel. The purchase must be made discreetly, mind you – I'll let you make up your own story as to what it's for. Aphorstra, how are we going to be off for tin?'

'I calculate that there will, after all, be enough in the treasury for this project, Your Highness,' the bronze worker told him. 'I'd like to suggest though, that we begin to build up stocks for a full-sized keel – if the project is to go that far. If we slowly increase our rate of consumption it shouldn't affect the market prices in Ezreen and it might reduce the chances of anyone there becoming suspicious.'

Ravian returned to Belainus a few days later to inspect the remodelled keel section and, over the next few weeks, he rode out to the city to check on progress whenever his sea-going requirements allowed.

Lederalus' men had completed the new foundry and, as each section of the keel was finished, the casting took its place in a master mould laid out on its side on the floor. The mould hinted at the complete line of the keel from stem to stern and Ravian was excited as his idea continued to progress toward becoming reality.

Sinur continued to be supportive through his absences although Ravian had to accept that, when he was away, a number of different young, male Tarcuns escorted to her social functions. After all, he told himself, he couldn't expect her to attend unescorted and he certainly didn't expect her to abandon her social life on his account. Still, even though he loved her and trusted her, he couldn't avoid the occasional pang of jealousy. Then, one evening, a fateful breeze blew *Wind Song* into harbour fully two days before he had expected to return from a patrol about the Delenes Islands.

Ravian was aware that he had arrived on the date that a popular playwright called Crosthenes was to present a long-awaited new work. The sun was just beginning to set as he raced to the palace to quickly bathe and dress for the evening, before walking to Lemalus's house.

'She left ages ago,' Lemalus archly informed him when he got there. 'Went with some young fellow called Giogenes or something.'

The prince knew Giogenes, a young captain in the palace guard. He was a decent, likeable fellow and had escorted Sinur on more than one occasion.

Ravian walked the now familiar road down to the amphitheatre. As he arrived, he realised that the play was already over and, as was customary, the playwright, the actors and some privileged members of the audience were enjoying a celebratory wine together onstage. Loud conversation and gay laughter filled the warm evening air, as Ravian descended the stairs to look for Sinur and Giogenes. Unexpectedly, he encountered the young captain leaning against a pillar, goblet in hand and deep in conversation with another young officer he didn't know.

'How are you, Giogenes?' he began. 'Where's...?'

A burst of laughter from the stage cut his question short and, wordlessly, Giogenes rolled his eyes in that direction.

They were a group of about ten in the centre of the crowd – Sinur, Crosthenes, Precedius, some painted actors he didn't know, some citizens in gleaming white robes and...Graticus.

Ravian hadn't seen his old foe since the days of the Academy, although he was aware that Graticus had already inherited his father's house and was, from all accounts, building it into an increasingly powerful financial institution. Even though he recognised him instantly, he saw that time had already wrought some changes on his enemy. Graticus was still an impressive and powerful figure, towering above everyone else in the group, yet Ravian could see signs of excess – a slight fullness in the face, the hint of a paunch beneath the robe. It was discreetly whispered about the city that, of the many appetites that the wealthy merchant indulged in, a liking for food and wine were two of the more acceptable.

As Ravian approached the group, everybody's attention was on Graticus as he continued what was obviously a highly amusing anecdote. Sinur stood next to him, her smile broad and encouraging as the tall man made a humorous point that Ravian couldn't hear and, once again, the group roared with mirth. Laughing with the rest, Sinur put her hand on Graticus's arm and Ravian felt his intestines knot. Then she looked across and saw him, her face lighting up in a delighted smile.

'Ravian, Darling, you are home so early!' she called out. 'Come and meet an old friend of mine!'

Ravian walked forward as though in a dream, his eyes taking in every movement and detail.

The casual way that Sinur's hand dropped from Graticus's arm.

The subtle way they moved apart from each other.

The malicious smile on Precedius's painted face.

The same, malevolent, green gleam in Graticus's eyes that he remembered from his youth.

Then they were standing toe to toe, the hairs on the back of Ravian's neck lifting as if in a cold breeze.

'Graticus,' Sinur began, 'this is my Gallant Sea Captain. May I present...'

'There's no need for introductions, My Dear,' Graticus interrupted smoothly. 'Prince Ravian and I are old classmates. Isn't that right, Your Highness?'

'Well, we certainly shared some times together,' Ravian managed to get out.

Graticus was immaculately groomed and exuded a discreet scent of sandalwood. Ravian was suddenly very aware that he had barely washed and that his tussled hair was still stiff with sea salt.

'Phew!' he heard Precedius say from behind him. 'Does anyone else smell fish?'

Ravian ignored the actor.

'I understand that you have taken over your father's house,' Ravian said to Graticus. 'My congratulations.'

'Well,' replied the green-eyed man, 'someone has to make some money to pay for the navy's games.'

Ravian flushed at the blunt insult. He had been prepared to be neutral with Graticus for the sake of appearances, but he now realised that his enemy was even less in control of his animosity than he was himself.

'Now, now, Graticus,' he replied tightly, 'you know that Tarcus needs a navy so that the principles of the Nine Houses can get fat on their profits.'

At the word "fat", he let his eyes flicker meaningfully to Graticus's expanded waistline. The larger man tensed and leaned towards him and Ravian knew that – then and there, in front of the assembled citizens and actors – he and Graticus were about to do battle.

Sinur's eyes flicked disbelievingly from one man to the other and she quickly stepped between them.

'Darling, you have been away far too long,' she said, facing Ravian. 'Excuse us everybody. I want my Gallant Sea Captain all to myself for a while.'

Taking him by the arm, she gently but firmly turned him around and propelled him out of the group.

Behind them, he heard Precedius say, 'Take him, Sinur. Nobody else wants him,' followed by the sniggering of the rest of the group.

Ravian stopped and spun around to confront their vacant, laughing faces. Graticus wasn't laughing though, and his green eyes glared back at the prince as though their fight at the Academy had been only yesterday.

He felt Sinur tugging urgently on his arm and, reluctantly, followed her outside.

'Darling, what was that about?' Sinur asked as they walked towards her father's house in the moonlight.

'I'm sorry,' he replied honestly, 'but I don't really know.'

He collected himself, his blood cooling in the night air, before attempting to explain.

'It just seems that, from the first day that he and I met, Graticus and I have loathed each other. We were bitter enemies at the Academy and I haven't seen him since. Now, after all this time, it's obvious that nothing has changed. I didn't realise that you knew him.'

'Oh,' said Sinur airily, 'Graticus and I are old friends. We used to go to all the shows together.'

Again, Ravian felt his stomach knot.

'You mean that he was your boyfriend?' he asked tightly.

Sinur laughed.

'Oh, for a while,' she said. 'We were very young then and it was never serious. By the time you and I met, it was long over.'

'I would have thought it was a pretty good match,' he said harshly. 'Why did you stop seeing each other?'

She stopped and regarded him seriously in the moonlight.

'Oh, my poor, jealous Darling,' she said. 'You don't need to worry about Graticus. It very soon became obvious that the only person he cares about is himself. I don't think that he will ever marry.'

'Then can I ask that you don't see him again?' he said.

She smiled.

'You can ask all you like, My Love,' she replied. 'But the White City is such a small town that I'm bound to run into Graticus from time to time and I certainly shan't be ignoring him.'

She moved closer to him and held both his hands.

'Listen, Ravian,' she told him. 'You are the one I love and wish to marry – it's not me who is delaying our wedding. You must understand though, that, whether we are married or not, I will socialise with whomever I choose. I'm not a slave girl and I'm not a slut – but for your own sake, you must realise that everything isn't going to happen the way you want it to just because you're a member of the royal family.'

Chastened, Ravian walked her the rest of the way to her house in silence. However, by the time he had circled around and crossed the garden to her balcony, she was waiting for him with her usual ardour and they put the incident behind them.

It was becoming increasingly clear, however, that Sinur's patience regarding Ravian's absences and the delay to their marriage was wearing thin. Repeatedly, and with increasing regularity, she would raise the subject.

'Why do we have to wait so long?'

'Don't you really love me?'

'Liana is to marry Capernal and he's a sea captain too. Why can't we be married now?'

For the first time, Ravian began to have doubts about their relationship. Sinur seemed to be forgetting the priorities that lay before him and the plan that they had agreed upon.

Within the two months that he had promised, Aphorstra and his workers at Belainus had completed all the mouldings for the keel. Ravian had attended the start of the welding process and, a few days later, he returned to the shipyard for Lederalus's trial, the old shipwright having already tested two wooden keels to destruction in order to be able to make a comparison. It was the first time Ravian had seen the completed keel and, as Aphorstra had indicated, the welds were almost invisible, the outer edge running in a smooth, graceful curve.

Like an enormous sword, Ravian thought to himself, the term "swordship", coming into his mind, unbidden.

Lederalus had devised a testing apparatus that contained the rear half of the keel in a wooden casing, the bow section projecting into a massive, square frame. A system of pulleys connected the stem to the top of the frame, with a similar block and tackle running to one side. A stout cage hung from the top pulley system and, as the trial began, Lederalus's workers began to stack lead weights into this while a scribe dutifully recorded the total.

'This test is, obviously, to evaluate strength in the vertical plane,' Lederalus explained. 'We can measure the upward flex of the keel as the weight is increased, and then compare the figures with those for the wooden keel. The block and tackle exerts a force on the keel many times that of the actual weight in the baskets.'

As the workers piled more and more lead into the basket, the casing retaining the rear portion of the keel began to creak. Lederalus moved around to look over the shoulder of his scribe and whistled.

'Amazing,' he said quietly.

'What is it?' asked Ravian excitedly.

'The weight is now three quarters of that at which the wooden keel failed, Your Highness,' Lederalus said with some excitement. 'At this point, the wooden keel had flexed upwards by almost an arm's length whereas this bronze keel has barely moved at all.'

'Is a rigid keel a good thing, do you think?' asked Ravian.

'I can't be sure until we build it and sail it, Your Highness,' Lederalus replied, 'but I would imagine so.'

The workers continued loading lead until the shipbuilder halted them.

'Excellent, Your Highness,' he announced. 'At this load, the wooden keel splintered to pieces yet as you can see, the bronze keel has barely even flexed. We will now begin the test in the horizontal.'

Ravian couldn't suppress a grin of delight. He turned to Aphorstra, expecting a similar reaction, but the metalsmith's face was impassive, and Ravian realised that big man was more concerned about the horizontal test.

After unloading the vertical cage, the workers began stacking weights into the cage suspended from the horizontal block and tackle.

'This is quite remarkable,' commented Lederalus, as the test proceeded. 'On the wooden keel, flex in the horizontal was very pronounced at this point but, as you can see, the bronze keel has barely moved at all.'

Yet, even he spoke, there came a "ping" from inside the keel casing – immediately followed by a deafening "clang" as the front half of the keel slammed against the test housing. The workers scattered as keel and weight cage crashed to the ground.

Ravian' heart sank. The keel had completely sheared at the front of the casing.

With surprising composure, Lederalus looked over his scribe's shoulder at the recorded figures.

'I regret to say that the keel has failed at less than two thirds of the load of a wooden keel, Your Highness.'

'It's gone on one of the welds,' said Aphorstra. 'I told you they wouldn't be strong enough!'

Ravian stared at the ruins of the experiment – all his dreams, all the work up until now, lying in pieces on the shed floor!

'What do we do now?' he asked Lederalus.

'I don't know,' the older man quietly replied. 'We could try to thicken up the mouldings again but that would bring the weight back up and I'm not sure it will improve the strength.'

'It won't!' spat Aphorstra. 'It's letting go on the welds!'

'Or perhaps,' continued Lederalus, 'we could look at minimising the tolerances in the key shapes.'

'A waste of time,' insisted Aphorstra. 'The welds will still let go at the same point.'

Ravian took a deep breath, and controlled his inclination to lash out at the metalsmith's negativity.

'All right,' he said. 'Let's all just think about it for a while. I'll return in a couple of days and we'll see if we can't come up with a solution.'

Unable to remain a moment longer with his broken dream, Ravian rode back to the White City through that afternoon and into the night, tears blurring his vision. He had had such high expectations of the bronze keel and now it was a failure!

He immediately sought solace in Sinur's arms, but her sympathy seemed vague and it didn't take long for the source of her distraction to be revealed.

'Well, Darling,' she had said gently, 'in some ways this must be part of Delikas's plan. You are going to need more time at home anyway...because you have another responsibility on its way.'

Ravian sat up suddenly.

'You mean...?'

'Yes, Darling, I am with child.'

'Are you sure?'

'Fairly sure,' she replied. 'As sure as one can be about these things anyway. Aren't you pleased?'

'Of course I am,' he said, taking her in his arms again. 'It has just been a day of major events.'

'Humph! Well, you could at least try and be happy about this one,' she said. 'You had better go and see both our parents tomorrow.'

He better had, he thought – they would need to marry as soon as possible.

His parents were less than enthusiastic.

'I suppose she's pregnant,' his mother stated flatly.

'No,' he lied. 'We just feel that we have known each other long enough and we don't want to wait any longer to be married.'

'Well, it seems an awful rush, all of a sudden,' Beriel pursued.

'Look!' Ravian burst out. 'If Sinur were with child – which she isn't – surely that would suit you very well. She's a daughter of one of the Nine Houses and you are the ones that worry that Jeniel still hasn't produced an heir!'

'Ravian,' his father interjected calmly, 'we certainly want what is good for the kingdom but we want what is best for you as well. Are you sure that Sinur is the woman that you wish to spend the rest of your life with?'

'Absolutely,' he replied, ignoring the little twinge of doubt that his father's words had provoked.

'Well then,' Jabacus said, with a meaningful look at his queen, 'we had better set a date to welcome Sinur into our family.'

Relieved that the interview was over, Ravian stood to take his leave.

'Before you go,' his father stopped him, 'how are things progressing in Belainus?'

'Oh...ah, we've had a bit of setback,' Ravian replied, staying on his feet.

'Hmmm,' the king mused with a frown. 'That's too bad – especially when I look at the bills you are starting to accrue. Are you still confident that this new ship of yours can be built?'

'Oh yes, reasonably confident,' Ravian lied.

'Good,' Jabacus said. 'We may need such a craft if the information I'm receiving from the North is true.'

'What's going on there?' asked Ravian, settling back to his seat.

He knew that his father maintained a network of spies all around the Spice Sea, especially in the troublesome North.

'Apparently,' the Tarcun king began, 'a recent round of assassinations in Dekane has resulted in a new ruler – Bordwar, I believe his name is. He's made friends with the Geroufens and is now starting to stir up feelings against us with some of the other northern nations. I believe that, ultimately, this Bordwar fellow intends to build an alliance with which to invade Tarcus.'

'He'd have to be mad!' Ravian burst out. 'The economies of the northern nations rely on our shipping and our harbour as much as their own!'

'I don't believe that the intention would be to destroy that which makes us such an attractive acquisition,' said Jabacus. 'But the Northerners have long been jealous of our wealth and our control of the sea lanes. If Bordwar can somehow manage to stop them stabbing each other in the back for a few months, he might be able to persuade them to invade and take over.'

'But our people would never tolerate living under the rule of the Northerners!' Ravian declared.

'I agree that most of them wouldn't,' Jabacus agreed, 'but there are those in our nation who wouldn't really care who held the crown – as long as they were permitted to hold the purse strings.'

At these words, Ravian felt the hair on the back of his neck stand erect.

'Father, do you know something you're not telling me?' he asked.

'No, I don't know anything,' the king told him. 'But if this Bordwar is working towards an invasion, he might find some Tarcuns more cooperative toward the idea than you might think.'

Ravian left the audience with his head full of his father's words.

Suddenly, what had merely been a pet project had now assumed a crucial level of strategic importance, and he knew that he must overcome any obstacles to building the swordship. He returned to Belainus burdened with the responsibility of his father's revelation where, to his surprise, a surprisingly joyful Aphorstra welcomed him at the entrance to the shipyard.

'It's so good to see you back, Your Highness,' he cried. 'We have some very good news! Come and see!'

Inside the main shed, Lederalus stood by the keel-testing apparatus where, to Ravian's astonishment, the bronze keel, back in one piece, projected once more from its frame. Even more astoundingly, a full cage of lead weights dangled from the horizontal block and tackle.

'Welcome, Your Highness,' Lederalus greeted him. 'We finished the test early this morning. The weight in the cage is exactly the same as that at which the wooden test keel failed and, as you can see, there is virtually no flex in the bronze keel at all. We thought we would leave it set up for your return.'

'But what did you do?' Ravian asked.

Aphorstra smiled proudly. He looked very tired, but was obviously delighted with himself.

'I believe that the welding process somehow changes the structure of the bronze, making it weak and brittle at the joining point,' he declared. 'After you had gone, I remembered that, in most countries, they use bronze less pure than our own, and so they have to temper their weapons by reheating them and plunging them into water. That is what we did with the keel – after we had re-welded it at the break point.'

'You must have used an enormous bucket!' exclaimed Ravian.

'It wasn't easy, Your Highness,' Aphorstra agreed, 'and it will be even more difficult with a full-sized keel. We've had to build a long, open furnace, fanned by no less than ten bellows. Adjacent to this, we've constructed a water trough big enough to take the whole keel. I think I lost half my body weight in the steam bath that resulted when we rolled the keel in, but it was worth it! Isn't it beautiful?'

Ravian had to admit that the keel, with its successfully suspended load of test weights, was probably the most splendid sight he had ever beheld.

In one of the sheds, they showed him the enormous apparatuses that they had used to temper the keel, the debris of hard and urgent labour lying scattered all about the monstrous furnace and cooling trough.

'You can't have slept much since my last visit,' he said to the pair of them.

'Oh, an hour or two here and there,' replied Aphorstra, his airy tone belying the dark rings under his eyes.

'Once Aphorstra decided he had the solution, he wouldn't let any of us sleep,' said Lederalus. 'Still, now that he has finally done his job, I can get on with mine.'

'How long?' asked Ravian.

'Two months, maybe three – although this keel design does promise to take some of the labour out of construction.'

'Three months would be fine – but as soon as you can, of course,' Ravian encouraged him. 'To be honest, I had just about given up.'

'Oh no, Your Highness,' jibed Aphorstra. 'Remember, you wanted our full co-operation.'

He pounded his hand on a nearby bench for emphasis and they all laughed.

Back at the White City, Ravian reported the progress to his father.

'That's excellent, Son,' the king said. 'I look forward to seeing the finished craft.'

'Now, there's another matter I would like to discuss with you,' Jabacus continued. 'Quite a delicate issue, really.'

Ravian' heart sank. He wasn't in the mood to defend his forth-coming marriage.

'I've had some complaints from some of the citizens about your attitude,' his father began.

Ravian was genuinely astonished.

'What do they mean, "my attitude"?' he asked incredulously.

'Well, some of them have indicated that they think you have a tendency to be rather...ah...highhanded.'

'But, Father, you know me – do you believe that?'

'Ravian, I don't think that you would knowingly abuse your royal position but I also see that, when you pursue an objective, you tend do so without too much concern for the sensibilities of those who might get in your way,' the king told him gently. 'I don't think that your military career has moderated your behaviour in this respect – quite the opposite, in fact. Were you not my son, such behaviour might well be seen as forceful and decisive but, in a member of the royal family, it can just as easily be interpreted as arrogant and autocratic.'

Ravian was aghast. "Arrogant and autocratic" was certainly not how he saw himself.

'Father, are you saying that I should be careful not to tread on people's toes?' he asked.

'In a word – yes,' Jabacus replied. 'The Royal House may control the military, but it has never had to invoke its military powers against its own citizens. Sometimes, I must admit, I've been tempted to ride roughshod over the bickerings of the Citizens' Council, but the democratic freedom of our people is a precious and vital thing, Ravian, and it is what has made this country the vital nation that it is today. When the people see the second in line to the throne acting like an autocrat, it frightens them.'

'But, sometimes, there can only be one right decision,' Ravian defended himself. 'You don't see the captain of a ship stopping to consult the crew about which tack to take every time he needs to lay a new course.'

'That's true, Son,' his father replied, 'but it is not so much what you do, as much as the way you do it. I know that you are not an autocrat at heart, but I also know that you sometimes go at things like a bull at a gate and I'm warning you to be a bit more sensitive to the feelings of our citizens. It's always better to be popular if you possibly can be and, if you don't try and curb your abruptness, it will get you into trouble one day.'

Ravian left the meeting with his father in a state of confusion.

Could his father be right or was he simply the victim of some malicious whisperings?

Either way, Ravian decided, he would accept the wisdom of what the king had said – there was no point upsetting anybody if he didn't need to. He would make a point to be less abrupt in future.

Sinur and Ravian were married at the High Temple on the Western Arm. As he looked into his bride's eyes during the ceremony – eyes as blue as the ocean stretching out behind her – Ravian felt a welling up of happiness.

There would be no more creeping away through Lemalus's garden in the cold light of dawn. There would be no more pressure from his family to find a wife and produce an heir. He was in love with the most beautiful woman in the world and, even now, their child was growing within her womb.

After the wedding, any apprehensions that he might have had about Sinur moving into the palace soon seemed misplaced, Beriel appearing to embrace his wife as a daughter in the same way she had accepted Verene and Kasanda into the royal family.

As was the custom with newly wed longship crew, Ravian was given an extended period of shore leave, his old friend Billus – finally promoted from the immediate supervision of Admiral Acrusta – delighted to take temporary command of *Wind Song*. As Ravian once again set out on the road to Belainus, life seemed very good indeed and he smiled in the early morning sunshine.

Arriving at his destination, he found that progress on the ship had been swift since the successful keel test. The skeleton of the frame was now complete and Lederalus's men had half covered it with the hardwood planks that would form the hull.

'It's all pretty much conventional construction from here on,' the shipbuilder explained. 'Caulking the area around the keel was less of a problem than I thought it might be, and the structure has been a lot faster to work on than a wooden keel. We still have to complete the hull, top deck and rigging of course, but I think we should be finished in a month or so. I have it in mind to add a few more feet to the mast height – we can always trim it down if she heels too much. We are also going to have to develop some sort of carriage to get her down the slipway. Rollers aren't going to work – that keel will cut through them like a sword.'

'That's what we will call them,' said Ravian, speaking the name aloud for the first time. 'Swordships.'

'Swordships, eh?' said the old craftsman, thoughtfully stroking his chin. 'Aye, it's a good name for them.'

'What's Aphorstra up to?' asked Ravian, noting his absence.

'Well, there's not much for him to do now until the sea trial,' Lederalus replied. 'He doesn't want to start work on the full-sized moulds until then – and that's probably prudent. He's in Ezreen at present, talking to his tin suppliers. Hmmm...'

'What?' Ravian asked.

'I'm just a little concerned that he doesn't try to corner the tin market,' the shipbuilder told him.

'Ah,' Ravian said, not having considered this possibility, 'and you think that he has that much confidence in the success of the project now?'

'I have no doubt of it,' Lederalus confirmed with a chuckle. 'The crown may have bought up the land about us where the full-sized yards are to be built – so that little piece of speculation has been denied him. It hasn't stopped him buying up houses in the area like a madman though – and he has bought a large piece of land adjacent to the yards where, I believe, he is to build the biggest inn the city has ever seen.'

Ravian smiled mirthlessly.

The commercial instincts that drove, the "Golden Way", were evident in no one more so than in Aphorstra. The commencement of full-scale production would see an influx of highly paid craftsmen.

Those men would need accommodation – and they would want a meal and a drink at the end of a hard day's work.

'Well,' he said, 'I hope, for his sake, that he is being discreet. If you see him before I return next, please ask him to come and see me at the palace. I think that he and I need to have a little chat. You're not making any investments yourself, Lederalus?'

The old man's eyes twinkled.

'Yes, I believe I am, Your Highness,' he said. 'I'm too old to care much about money, but I'm more than happy to invest what time and labour I have left to me to make our country stronger. I will consider it ample return if, before I die, Tarcus is protected by a fleet of swordships.'

Back at the palace, Sinur met him with tears in her eyes, and Ravian was filled with foreboding as she led him to the balcony outside their apartment and took his hands in hers.

'Darling, I'm sorry,' she told him, 'but I'm not pregnant after all.'

It took a moment for Ravian to absorb what she was saying.

'You mean we've lost the baby?' he asked, stunned.

'Either that or I just missed a cycle,' she said. 'Really, I don't know, but we can try again. We have the rest of our lives before us.'

She was calm despite her tears and, at that moment, Ravian loved her all the more for her bravery.

'Besides,' she added brightly, 'now that you have your shore leave, we'll be able to get out and socialise a bit more together. My Gallant Sea Captain was very nice, but I didn't see much of him. It will be fun to introduce people to my new husband.'

Somehow, her words shattered the tenderness of the previous moment for Ravian. Sinur was clearly ready to move on from their grievous loss a lot faster than he was.

Chapter Six

A month after Sinur's miscarriage, Ravian travelled to Belainus for the launching of the model swordship.

It was a discreet affair – all of them still concerned with maintaining secrecy around the project. It was quieter still, because Aphorstra was still sulking after the dressing down he had received at the palace following his return from Ezreen.

'What do you mean by building that tavern at the edge of town?' Ravian had demanded. 'Don't you think that it indicates that you expect something big to happen in Belainus?'

Aphorstra, who hadn't known why he had been summoned to the palace so peremptorily, looked scared and surprised.

'But, Your Highness,' he had whined, 'what is the harm? It's only a tavern after all. It's not as though we have started building the shipyards yet.'

'I told you be discreet!' thundered Ravian, forgetting everything his father had recently said to him about the sensibilities of Tarcun citizens.

'I swear, Your Highness, that not a single word of our project has been said to any but those who need to know,' Aphorstra defended himself.

'You don't need to say anything when you begin building an inn large enough to serve the entire Tarcun navy, you idiot!' snapped Ravian. 'I hope that you were more discreet on your trip to Ezreen.'

'Of course, Your Highness,' Aphorstra replied. 'I simply increased the orders for tin as you directed.'

'And I trust,' said Ravian, 'that those orders were placed on behalf of the Tarcun treasury and not on behalf of any private enterprise?'

Aphorstra swallowed.

'Absolutely, Your Highness,' he said in a shaky voice.

'Good,' Ravian said. 'Then there shouldn't be any increase in tin prices – provided you have acted in the interests of the country.'

'Oh no, Your Highness,' Aphorstra said quickly. 'I can guarantee that there will be no price increase in the next few shipments.'

Ravian looked at the fat man, as Aphorstra gave the swordship keel one final inspection, and smiled to himself.

He had no doubt that Belainian had tried to corner the market. Nor did he doubt that, straight after their audience, the metalsmith would have sent an urgent message to his agents in Ezreen, transferring his last order from his own account to that of the Tarcun treasury. He was satisfied that the avaricious metalsmith would be forced absorb any price increases resulting from his recent manoeuvrings in the East.

Ah, Tarcun commerce, the prince sighed. Men like Aphorstra would always try for that extra penny.

Now the fat metalsmith, the old shipwright and the Tarcun prince stood by the slipway in the morning sun, the product of their labours poised for her short journey to the sea.

The harbour's exposed nature denied its shipbuilders the luxury of finishing their craft on the water as they did in the White City and, thus, the custom in Belainus was to launch new vessels fully-rigged. The completed swordship prototype was a fine looking craft, her taller than usual mast giving her an imposing appearance, despite her relatively short dimensions. From a distance, the vessel appeared conventional enough, but closer inspection revealed the gleaming bronze keel running in a menacing arc from stem to stern.

Two sets of wooden wheels on each side supported the swordship on the level, upper portion of the ramp, teams of workers standing by with block and tackle to control the speed of her descent to the ocean. A small naval crew, including Godart – whom Ravian had shamelessly stolen from Billus's command – was already on board.

'When we craned her onto the launching trucks, we could see that she's perfectly balanced fore and aft,' Lederalus said proudly. 'She's also no heavier than a wooden keeled vessel of the same size.'

'As we discussed, Your Highness,' he continued, 'there is no bowsprit so, to keep the foresail area up, we have moved the block for the jib sheets further aft than normal. The taller mast means she can carry more canvas, so it will be interesting to see how she sails.'

'Please, Lederalus, can we just get her into the water?' Ravian begged, almost beside himself with excitement.

Lederalus gave the signal and his workers hauled on their ropes to inch the new vessel forward. As the prow tilted towards the deep blue of the high tide waiting below, more men took up the slack on the stern tackle and the swordship made a smooth, graceful descent into the harbour. Everybody cheered – including Aphorstra, who seemed to have recovered his spirits somewhat.

'Look at the way she sits!' Ravian enthused, as Godart ordered the oars run out to pull the vessel clear of the shore.

Indeed, as the swordship tied up to one of the four mooring buoys beneath the cargo bridge, it was apparent that Lederalus's calculations for trim had been perfect.

'Your Highness, Citizen Aphorstra, would you care to accompany me on board?' Lederalus asked formally.

The trio walked down the ramp to a waiting boat, Ravian barely able to resist the temptation to run, and the oarsmen rowed them out to the swordship, where Godart saluted them on board.

'Well, Captain,' Ravian said, 'let's see some sail on her.'

'Aye, aye, Sir,' Godart replied, immediately ordering the foresail bent on and hoisted.

A light breeze was blowing down the harbour behind them and, as the jib filled, they cast off from the mooring. Once the swordship had made its way past some anchored fishing boats and was heading toward the open sea, Godart ordered the mainsail hoisted and the boom eased out over the beam. The vessel picked up speed, the water chattering along her hull.

'She feels good!' Ravian declared to the stern party. 'I think that she's as fast as anything else her size. What do you think, Godart?'

'Hard to say, Sir,' the new captain replied carefully. 'I don't really have any experience with craft of this size.'

Ravian turned to Lederalus and raised his eyebrows. The old shipbuilder took his time, looking around at the cliff sides moving past, before he replied to the unspoken question.

'Aye,' he finally said with a smile, 'I think she's as fast with the wind behind her as anything else I've built with the same waterline. Don't get too excited though, Your Highness. We still have to put her on a tack and try her on a reach. With this new mast and sail configuration, it's going to take us a while to find the right rigging set-up. Who knows,' – Lederalus' eyes twinkled – 'she may be faster than we think.'

They stayed out all day, only returning at twilight.

As Lederalus and his men had continued to adjust the rigging, Godart had put the vessel through her paces to the increasing delight of everybody on board. The prototype swordship ran like a dolphin on a reach and tacked higher than anything any of them had ever experienced. And she was fast – very fast.

It was as they were tacking hard towards the harbour entrance at the end of the day, that Godart made the comment that gave the scaled-down swordship her name.

'By Delikas, Your Highness,' he declared, 'she lifts to the wind like a hawk!'

'And that shall be her name, Gentlemen,' Ravian declared expansively. 'We are aboard the *Sea Hawk*!'

They celebrated well into the night at Ravian's usual inn.

Ravian and Lederalus celebrated a successful first day of sea trials, Godart celebrated his first day on his first command and, privately,

Aphorstra celebrated the astuteness of his investment in his own, yet-to-be-completed, inn.

Unable to resist the lure of the new vessel, Ravian went out on *Sea Hawk* again the following day, so that it wasn't until that evening, after another successful day's trials, that he bid farewell to Godart and Lederalus.

'I'll be back in two weeks. Keep tuning her until you've got everything out of her that she'll give. When I come back, I want to look at the ramming performance – after all, that's what the swordships will be about. See if you can find some older vessels somewhere that we can purchase cheaply to practice on. Try not to pay too much – if everything works as I hope, we'll be sending them to the bottom.'

'When do you think we'll begin full-scale production?' enquired Lederalus.

'It won't be for a while yet,' said Ravian, mindful that Admiral Acrusta was still some months away from retirement. 'In the short term, we need to keep the trials going. Once we are happy that the boat works as planned, I will invite the king to come and view the project. After that – well, it will be up to His Majesty.'

When Ravian arrived back at the palace the following afternoon, it was to be met by a furious Sinur.

'You said you'd be away two nights but you've been gone three!' she stormed. 'Did you forget your promise to take me to the new poetry reading by Aledes?'

Ravian had to admit that he had.

'Well, it's not very fair!' his wife continued. 'Now that I'm a princess, I have even less freedom than I had when I was in my father's household! It's all very well for you to just trot off to Belainus every few days – and to whatever is so important there – but I'm stuck here doing needlework with your mother and your sisters-in-law. I don't think that you consider me at all!'

'Well, why don't you find another escort you like you used to?' he tried to placate her.

'You are not listening to me!' she screeched. 'It's been made very clear to me that such things are "not done". The queen already thinks I'm the worst piece of trash ever to blow in the palace door – can you imagine how she would take it if I stepped out on the arm of a young, unmarried man?'

'Well, what about my brothers?' he tried.

'You must be joking! Ramus is never here and I think that Jeniel has an even lower opinion of me than your mother does! I hate it here! We have to move to our own place!'

His father, when Ravian broached the subject with him, was surprisingly understanding.

'I suppose that I saw this coming,' the king said wearily. 'It would probably best for everybody if you did find your own place – at least for a while. I have a house by the theatre that you could have. Once you take over as Commander in Chief, then you can move into the Admiral's Residence, if you choose not to return to the palace.'

Sinur was delighted with their new house, particularly with its location.

'Oh, Ravian, it's perfect,' she exclaimed, 'and so handy to the theatre. Everybody will be able to drop in after the shows.'

Inwardly, Ravian groaned. The admiral's position, and the more remote residency on the Western Arm that accompanied it, could not come soon enough. After two weeks, he slipped away again to Belainus where Godart and Lederalus awaited him aboard *Sea Hawk*.

'We've certainly been able to get more speed out of her,' Lederalus told him proudly, as Godart got the boat underway into a stiff, onshore breeze. 'I must say though, that she doesn't want to turn as well as she might. I'm thinking that we should take some of the profile out of the keel aft of the beam.'

'Won't that reduce her ability to point up?' asked Ravian.

'A little, perhaps, but we should be able to offset that with a bigger blade on the steering oar.'

North of the harbour entrance and out of sight of the city, they rendezvoused with two fishing boats of approximately the same length as *Sea Hawk*.

'Who's on board them?' Ravian asked, watching their targets as they tacked up the coast.

'There are three of my men on each boat,' replied Lederalus. 'They've been briefed on what to expect and they're ready for a swim. I've told them to try and make a bit of a fight of it.'

As they approached the fishing vessels, the windward one jibed and headed south while the other eased her helm and headed back towards the mainland on a reach.

'Right, Godart,' said Ravian. 'Let's go for the one on a reach!'

Godart obliged by ordering the steering oar put over, and they charged in pursuit of the second vessel. Ravian restrained himself from reminding his captain that they wanted to hit their amidships – he and *Sea Hawk's* commander had discussed the new tactics for the swordships many times already.

Easily overhauling the fishing boat on a parallel course, Godart quickly worked his vessel into a windward position ahead of her, then jibed and came at her on a port tack. The skipper of the fishing boat jibed also though, coming around onto the same tack as *Sea Hawk*. Godart hauled in, relentlessly closing in on his prey, then eased his sails and bore directly towards her.

The skipper of the fishing boat began to turn away but his vessel was too slow to escape *Sea Hawk's* charge and the swordship smashed into her target's starboard quarter. The reinforced, bronze bow cleaved into the hull and deck of the fishing boat like an axe and then, accompanied by a cacophony of squealing, splintering timbers, *Sea Hawk* began to drive upwards, heeling the stricken vessel to windward so that the sea poured in over her rail. The fishing boat's mast scraped down *Sea Hawk's* starboard side as the swordship's weight pushed the doomed boat down into the sea and, moments later, only a few pieces of wreckage and the three swimming crewmen remained bobbing in the swordship's wake.

'Well,' said Ravian, as they put about to take the volunteers aboard, 'so far, so good. You certainly wouldn't want a bowsprit when you are engaging another sailing craft. Had we had one, the rigging of that fishing boat would probably have hung up on it.'

'All the same, Sir,' said Godart, 'I think that I'll have a man stand by on either side of the bow with an axe for the next one. We should also keep a spare jib handy at all times – if the tip of that fishing boat's mast had come inboard any further, it would have gone through the sail.'

'Yes, I agree,' said Ravian. 'We need to keep working on our tactics for action against sailing vessels – although I would imagine most of our targets will be under oars.'

Godart was grimly silent at this, knowing that galleys un-stepped their masts and rigging before rowing into battle.

They recovered the swimmers and *Sea Hawk* set off on a course to intercept the other fishing boat. Lederalus, who had been clambering around in the bow to check for damage, came aft to join the captain and his prince.

'Nothing,' he reported. 'She doesn't even know she's run into another vessel.'

The other boat had made good distance to the south and it took some time to catch up to her despite the swordship's superior speed. When they finally they overhauled her though, Godart was easily able to position *Sea Hawk* to windward of his target. This time though, as Godart eased the sheets to attack, the skipper of the fishing boat turned towards them – throwing his boat onto the opposite tack in an attempt to slip past their stern. Godart jibed, but the other vessel's unexpected manoeuvre meant that the opportunity to ram her amidships had been missed.

'Take off his rudder,' ordered Ravian.

His captain gave the order to turn and *Sea Hawk's* swinging bow glanced off her target's stern, smashing the steering oar and pivot into pieces. Ravian was relieved that the helmsman of the fishing boat had seen what was coming and had ducked below the swinging, inboard end of the oar. He and the rest of his crew looked palely back at *Sea Hawk's* complement as the swordship ground past, gunwale-to-gunwale, and then sailed clear.

'What now, Sir?' asked Godart, as they tacked away.

'Well I suppose that, in a fleet battle situation, we would look to disable or sink the next available target,' said Ravian, looking back at the vessel drifting helplessly downwind. 'However, since she's the only one left, I think that we should let them know that we intend to ram them.'

They tacked close to the fishing boat and called out to the men on board to prepare themselves.

Then, as they tacked away again, Ravian said to Godart, 'Try tacking up from leeward this time and hit her just behind the bow. I want to see how much damage we can do to the stronger part of a vessel'.

Obligingly, Godart approached on a starboard tack, ordering the helm over at the last moment so that *Sea Hawk* rounded up and smashed into the fishing boat just aft of her bowsprit. There was a scream of splintering wood and the swordship stopped, her bow buried in her victim almost to the centreline.

'Back the foresail!' Godart ordered, and his crew poled the sail out against the wind.

The stout construction in the fishing boat's bow was not so ready to release *Sea Hawk* though, and their disengagement was a slow, squealing process. The bowman of the fishing boat – seeing an opportunity to avoid a soaking – stepped up onto her rail, reached up *Sea Hawk's* side and pulled himself on board. As the swordship eased back into clear water, and then tacked away from her rapidly settling victim, Ravian spoke the thoughts of all of them.

'Well, Gentlemen, we have a problem. If our cheeky bowman were thirty angry Northerners, we would now be fighting a pitched battle on the foredeck. We must try and disengage faster after ramming.'

'We could push off with the oars,' suggested Godart, turning *Sea Hawk* back to pick up the other two crewmembers on the sinking fishing boat.

'I don't think that oars are going to be long enough,' said Ravian. 'Besides, you would have to be a brave man to stick your head up over the rail while the crew of the ship you had just rammed threw everything they had at you.'

'I have some ideas, Your Highness,' said Lederalus, about to go forward to check the hull again. 'Perhaps you would care to leave it with me for a while?'

Ravian returned to the White City the next day in high spirits and, two weeks later, he was back at Belainus with his father and a small guard. He had told his team there that, if the king was impressed with the trials, it was almost certain that he would give his approval for the construction of a full-sized swordship. Thus, it was with an air of excitement and anticipation that the prince led the royal procession out to a viewpoint on the cliff tops.

There, Ravian, King Jabacus, Lederalus and Aphorstra watched approvingly as Godart, sailing *Sea Hawk* superbly, cleanly despatched two fishing boats of about the same size as the model swordship. Being aware that Lederalus had carried out his proposed alterations to the keel and rudder, the prince was delighted to see that *Sea Hawk* was even more responsive than before, while still being a superior craft when it came to making distance to windward.

Just as those in the party were about to leave their viewing position however, Lederalus spoke.

'Your Majesty and Your Highness,' the shipwright announced, 'I have prepared a special treat for this occasion.'

At his words, a half-sized facsimile of a galley rowed out from its place of concealment below the cliffs. It had only a single bank of oars but, from the lookout, its appearance – particularly with its ram punching through the light chop – was ominously authentic.

Sea Hawk immediately closed with the galley in the steady breeze but, each time Godart altered course to attack, the oar-powered boat spun and presented its ram at the swordship. Then, as the young captain sailed impotently past after his third attempt, the galley suddenly turned and shot forwards so quickly that it was almost able to ram the sailing vessel. Godart responded by veering away, before spinning *Sea Hawk* around and sending her flying back at her adversary on a tight tack. The galley slowed as its crewmen, warned of this possibility, abandoned their oars and leapt clear of their thwarts and, seconds later, *Sea Hawk* ground down her target's port side, the sound of the splintering oars clearly carrying to the ears of those on the cliff top. Godart circled the now crippled galley once, and then charged in on a reach to finish her off. It was another precise exhibition of ramming – *Sea Hawk* striking squarely in the middle of the galley's oar-less port side.

As swordship struck home, however, the galley's hull sagged inwards – the strength of its hull inherently reduced by its rowing ports. *Sea Hawk*, driving ahead under full sail, continued to ride up and over the broken, foundering vessel and, within seconds, a patch of boiling water and bobbing heads were the only sign of where she had been.

'Delikas,' breathed Lederalus. 'I hope those poor devils on the galley are all right – I never warned them to expect this.'

'I hope so too, Lederalus,' said the king. 'You seem to have created a weapon of terrifying effectiveness.'

In a sombre mood, they repaired to the slipway. There, Godart bought *Sea Hawk* in with the happy news that all the crewmembers of the galley had survived and been picked up.

'Thank all the Gods!' said Aphorstra. 'It would have been a terrible omen for the future if any of them had died.'

Ravian had to agree although, privately, he wondered if Aphorstra was not more concerned about the effect that such an omen might have on the future of his commercial investments.

They waited as *Sea Hawk* was hauled out of the tide and a short distance up the ramp. Then Lederalus detailed the prototype's recent modifications.

'It's not obvious, but we did fine down the keel aft and add some blade to the steering paddle,' he said. 'There's no real increase in strain on the helmsman and, as you saw earlier, she now turns a lot faster. The other change was the addition of these ports on either side of the bow – see how they are capped off to keep the vessel dry. If you look inside the hull, you'll see two long, stout poles. The spiked end of each pole is designed to give traction against the hull of an enemy vessel so that if, after ramming, the bow of the swordship should become trapped in the other vessel, the crew can push her off without having to expose themselves above the rail.'

'Very well,' the king announced. 'I've seen enough to give my approval for a full-sized swordship. How long until you can get one into the water?'

'About nine months, Father,' Ravian told him.

'So long?' the king asked, sounding disappointed.

'I'm afraid nine months is realistic, Father,' he replied. 'Aphorstra needs to prepare the foundry and mouldings for a full-sized keel – and Lederalus will have to build a shed big enough to house it. On top of that, we'll need a larger shed and a suitable truck to get the vessel down to the water. Nine months will be the absolute minimum.'

'I understand,' said his father. 'And once the production is set up, how long will the build time of each ship be?'

'Assuming no shortage of materials, about five to six months per vessel,' Ravian replied.

'Hmmm,' said the king. 'I want a fleet of at least ten of these swordships as soon as possible – and we can't wait five years. Didn't you say that you had acquired land for *three* shipbuilding yards?'

'Yes, Father,' Ravian replied, his heart leaping.

'Very well,' Jabacus said. 'I want the first three swordships built concurrently. Hopefully, by the time you've got your shipyards completed, you'll have attracted enough skilled labour to the city to operate them. The inn keepers and property owners of this city are going to make a fortune.'

Ravian and Lederalus both looked at Aphorstra, who blushed deep red.

If the development of the prototype swordship had kept Ravian busy, it was nothing compared to the move to full-sized production. He was in Belainus every few days – and his absences had begun to put his marriage under strain.

'You might as well move to Belainus!' Sinur wept one night when he was back at the White City. 'You don't know what it's like having you go off there all the time when you won't even tell me what for.'

Ravian realised that the he must confide in her. The project was well advanced, anyway.

'Oh, Ravian,' she cried, after he had told her all about the swordships. 'I so wish that you had told me before. I've been so miserable and there have been...well...rumours.'

'Rumours?' asked Ravian. 'What sort of rumours?'

'That you have a mistress in Belainus,' she replied tearfully. 'I've heard it now from several sources.'

'Hmmm...yes,' he said. 'And I can well imagine whom those sources might be.'

'But it's not true, is it?' his wife persisted.

Sinur was trembling and Ravian saw the tears rolling down her cheeks in the candlelight. He suddenly realised how alone she was – prey to the vicious tongues of the so-called friends in her social circle. He knew then that his marriage was in peril, but he could not relinquish his remorseless schedule in Belainus and he could not help but think that maybe Sinur wasn't suited to the life she had married into after all.

'No, Darling, the rumours aren't true,' he reassured her. 'I'll tell you what – why don't you come to Belainus with me from now on? That way we can be together and we might have a bit more luck with that baby.'

Sinur looked doubtful.

'Belainus?' she said. 'What's it like there?'

Ravian thought about the attractions that Belainus could offer someone like Sinur. There weren't many.

'Lots of pottery,' he said lamely.

'All right,' Sinur replied with an enthusiasm that took him by surprise. 'Let us travel to Belainus together!'

It was an unmitigated disaster.

A day's journey on horseback translated into at least two in horse and cart – two days of hot, dusty, juddering travel. Sinur didn't say much while they were on the road, but her expression clearly said that she was finding it a test of endurance. It was when they broke their journey at a small country inn, however, that she finally abandoned her attempts at stoicism.

'Ravian this room is filthy!'

Ravian looked about at the plain walls and swept dirt floor. He had certainly slept in worse circumstances.

'The food was disgusting,' Sinur continued, 'and this room is like an oven – but we can't open the windows because that will let the mosquitoes in!'

'Well, My Dear,' he replied, 'if you are going to accompany me on my trips to Belainus, the only alternative than I can suggest is that we teach you how to ride a horse.'

'Hmmm,' she said doubtfully, as he blew out the candle and joined her in bed.

Ravian knew that Sinur would never add horse riding to her list of skills.

They lay awake for some time – both of them restless in the stifling heat of the small room – and Ravian had just drifted off to sleep when Sinur gave a small scream that sat him bolt upright.

'Ravian, there are things in this bed that are biting me!'

He lit the candle and, in the flickering light, he saw a number of small, raised lumps on her hip.

'Bed bugs,' he said, unsure what to do.

Sinur felt no such uncertainty.

'That's it!' she declared. 'I'm not staying another second here! Tell the driver to get the horse harnessed! We are leaving!'

Thus, they arrived at Belainus rather earlier than planned the following day. Tired and short-tempered, they went to Aphorstra's recently-completed inn where, to Ravian's relief, all was to Sinur's satisfaction.

That afternoon, Ravian introduced his wife to Lederalus, Aphorstra and Godart, then gave her a tour of the production area. Charitably, he put her constant yawning down to the lack of sleep the night before although, in his heart, he could tell that metalworking and shipbuilding held no great interest for his wife.

By this stage, the three full-sized sheds approved by the king had been built, although Aphorstra and his crew had only just completed the first keel. Lederalus had recruited many extra boat builders and, while they awaited the production of the next two keels, the workforce swarmed over the first vessel's construction site like ants.

When the royal couple returned to the inn that evening, the shrewdness of Aphorstra's investment became obvious. At the end of each day, the metalsmith's tavern became the most boisterous place in the city, the well-paid workers from the boatyard thronging to it for wine, song and – not surprisingly – women. As they passed by the main courtyard on the way to their room, Sinur raked a venomous eye over the girls of the inn who were already moving brazenly among their clientele.

'It seems a lively city, does Belainus,' she commented acidly. 'I can see why a man would enjoy time here.'

'For pity's sake, Sinur,' he replied with exasperation. 'This place wasn't even open the last time I was here.'

Despite the steadily increasing noise in the inn, both of them – exhausted by the mid-night departure of the previous evening – fell quickly and soundly asleep.

Ravian, as was his habit, woke at dawn and, as the first light of sunrise crept across the ceiling, he wondered how his wife was going to cope with the return trip to the White City. Then, as Sinur began to wake and snuggled against him, he had an idea.

They could go back by sea.

Sinur was delighted at the prospect of a day at sea, instead of two more days on the road and another night at the bed bug-ridden inn en route. Ravian spoke with Godart and they agreed that the time had come for *Sea Hawk* to make its maiden voyage to the White City.

They tacked out of the harbour into a steady northeasterly later that morning and, rounding the point, Godart put on all sail for the run down to the capital. The wind having built up a long, lazy swell from astern, *Sea Hawk* surged along at high speed, her sails bellying gracefully.

Despite the gentle passage, Sinur was terribly seasick and Ravian, who knew only too well how terrible the feeling was, doubted that his wife would ever be seen in Belainus again.

Chapter Seven

Shortly after Ravian and Sinur returned to the White City, Admiral Acrusta announced his retirement and, at the age of twenty-one, Ravian assumed the title of Defender of the Nation.

'I understand that the longships are to be replaced by a whole new breed of warship,' Acrusta observed, with a knowing twinkle in his eye.

Ravian, who had gone to Acrusta's flagship to wish him farewell, struggled to find a reply. He realised that the old sailor had been aware of the swordship development long before the recent arrival of *Sea Hawk* in the White City.

'It's all right, Ravian,' the retiring admiral said with a smile. 'It seems that your new toy will give the Tarcun navy an advantage in blue-water battles it has never before had. I was wrong not to listen to your idea and that is what has told me that it is time to put myself out to pasture. You were right to pursue your idea regardless of my reservations, and it's time for you to take over as admiral.'

They were standing on the jetty beside *Storm Bringer.* Ravian felt an overwhelming sense of loss of the old admiral's experience and knowledge.

'Do you think that I'm ready for the promotion, Sir?' he asked.

'As ready as I was when I became admiral,' Acrusta replied. 'Don't worry, Ravian, I won't be far away. My wife and I are retiring to Neverius where we have bought a nice little house that looks out towards Golden Bay – it would seem that I am about to become acquainted with the challenging new skill of gardening. You will always be welcome, should you feel the need of an old sailor's advice.'

Now that he was Admiral of the Fleet, Ravian was both entitled and expected to move into the Admiral's Residence – a handsome, impressive building on the heights of the Western Arm. Traditionally, the admiral and his family resided in the upper level of the two-storey house, the lower containing the offices of the admiralty staff. Close to the residence, a long, steep flight of steps ran down the western cliffs of the harbour to the naval base.

Ravian loved the building, with its handy location to the base and its magnificent outlook. On a fine day, one could stroll about its southern balcony and take in a panoramic view that included all of the harbour and most of the city, as well as a sweeping ocean vista only interrupted by the cliff walls of the Lee Shore to the northwest. Apart from the small barracks that serviced the western guard tower, it was the southernmost building on the Western Arm and well away from the hubbub of the rest of the city. Behind it, a quiet, leafy lane meandered past a number of old, established mansions on its way to the temple where he and Sinur had married. The road then curved eastwards into the more densely housed part the city before splitting in two – one lane running up a steady incline to the palace, the other descending down to the harbour.

Much as Ravian loved the calm peacefulness of the residence's location however, he knew that Sinur was not going to be at all happy at the prospect of moving into such social isolation and, for some weeks after his promotion, he had been avoiding raising the subject with her. Even while he procrastinated though, something happened that, for a time, overrode everything else.

His father, King Jabacus, died peacefully in his sleep.

Despite his venerable forty-five years of age, Jabacus had seemed robust and vital and Ravian, like everyone in his family – indeed, like everybody in the kingdom – was shocked at his unexpected passing.

He had little time to mourn though. As the newly appointed Defender of the Nation, the responsibility for the state funeral fell directly on his shoulders. At the same time, it was also vital that he help Jeniel assume the throne as swiftly and as smoothly as possible.

The next few days were a whirl of organisation and ceremony and it was not until he was escorting his mother home from the funeral, the smoke from the dead king's pyre still hanging above the High Temple, that the loss of his father began to strike home. Beriel, for her part, had seemed remarkably composed throughout the three days since her husband's death, and had followed his funeral procession through the White City's streets with a dignity and composure that Ravian had struggled to emulate.

'Are you all right, Mother?' he asked her, as they approached the palace.

'I'm as well as can be expected, Dear,' she had replied serenely. 'How are you feeling yourself?'

'Angry,' he replied. 'Angry that father should have been taken from us so suddenly and so soon – and a little frightened, I suppose. Jeniel, Ramus and I are very young to be governing the country.'

Beriel stopped and smiled at her son, her face full of warmth and love.

'Oh, Ravian, be strong,' she told him. 'Jeniel is no younger a king than your father was – and Jabacus never had two brothers like you and Ramus to help him. Delikas has called your father to his kingdom sooner than any of us would have liked but, if you think about it, it is clear that Jabacus has fulfilled his destiny and fulfilled it well.'

'Look how well he has moulded you boys,' she continued. 'Tarcus couldn't wish for a better-structured government, a more modern navy, or a healthier trading surplus. It was time for him to leave us, Ravian – he had done everything Delikas put him on this earth to do.'

'That may be so,' Ravian replied, 'but I will miss him terribly – although not as much as you, Mother.'

Beriel looked serenely towards the heavens, her eyes far away.

'Yes, Ravian,' she agreed, 'I will miss your father more than I think you would ever imagine but, much as I grieve now and will for the rest of my days, I also have to give thanks to Delikas allowing me my life with Jabacus. He was a wonderful man, Ravian, and I have been privileged – beyond the comprehension of most – to be his wife.'

His mother was right, Ravian thought. They were all of them lucky to have had a man like his father as their family head. He wondered if Sinur, should she survive him, would feel the same way about him as Beriel did about Jabacus.

Somehow, he was not so certain that she would.

Jeniel paced the palace balcony, hands tightly clasped behind him. Even though it was only a few days since their father's funeral, Ravian saw that his brother had a lot more confidence now and seemed to have accepted his kingly destiny. Tarcus's new ruler came to a halt, took a deep breath and then turned to the Defender of the Nation. The two brothers were alone and, as Jeniel began to reveal what was on his mind, Ravian understood why he had called such a private audience.

'You know that father was worried about the rise of this Bordwar fellow in the North,' Jeniel began. 'Well, we've had an update from our people in the area and the news is not good.'

Ravian felt a fluttering in his stomach at his brother's words.

'The Northerners may be a bunch of lice-ridden, squabbling barbarians,' Tarcus's new ruler went on, 'but it looks like Bordwar has been strong enough to put together an alliance of a number of the Grimspot Gris kingdoms.'

'Which ones?' Ravian asked.

'Graftsen, of course,' the young king replied. 'And Gerouf, Kleeft and, probably, Groven.'

Ravian gave a quiet whistle.

'That's quite an achievement, if it's true,' he said grudgingly.

Jeniel grunted in agreement.

'If he has managed to put such an alliance together,' the new king said, turning to stare out over the city and harbour, 'I can only agree with father's view that an invasion of this country is inevitable. Still, it will take the Northerners at least two years to build sufficient ships and to assemble a landing force sufficiently large to make such an attempt. They're not going to declare their hand until the last moment, and we'll still have plenty of traders in their waters until then, so we will have ample opportunity to monitor developments.'

Jeniel turned back to his brother.

'Two years gives you time to get how many swordships operational?'

Ravian did some quick calculations.

'If we turn the naval yard here to swordship production, we could produce twelve swordships a year – maybe more,' he replied.

'I want production up to twenty-five swordships a year,' his brother stated flatly. 'In the next two years, all fifty longships must have been replaced by trained, battle-ready swordships.'

'You'll need funding approval from the Citizens' Council,' Ravian said, knowing additional production facilities would have to be built or acquired. 'Do you think they'll support you?'

Jeniel smiled mirthlessly.

'I think so,' he replied. 'Even now, certain influential council members are hearing of these disturbing developments in the North – I'm making damn sure they do. Give them a week or so to work themselves up into a panic, and I think that I can get the council to approve the budget without any real opposition.'

'And if the council doesn't approve?' Ravian pressed.

'Well, let's hope it doesn't come to that,' Jeniel said grimly. 'I could ask the members to declare a state of emergency of course but, to do that, the threat would need to be imminent – and then it would be too late to build enough swordships. No, if I'm wrong and they don't back me at the next meeting, I'm going to have to make things happen regardless. That's not going to look good as the first act of the new monarch and you,' – he looked meaningfully into Ravian's eyes – 'may need to mobilise the army in a way that this nation has never seen before.'

Ravian swallowed. His brother's resolve was disturbingly evident but, at the same time, he knew that the king of Tarcus would need to rule with an iron fist of to keep their nation safe through the coming years.

'Whatever your command, Your Highness,' he said with a bow.

Fortunately for the democratic sensitivities of Tarcus's citizens, Jeniel's manipulation of the Citizens' Council proved effective. At the next meeting – and with minimal objection – the august body approved the expenditure required to accelerate production of the swordship fleet.

Suddenly, Ravian found himself in charge of the biggest reformation the Tarcun navy had ever seen. Not only did he need to double the production capacity of the nation's shipyards but, with the delivery of the first swordship imminent, he also had to develop tactics and techniques for the new craft.

He quickly established a bureaucracy that included Lederalus – who agreed to move to the White City – as the overall supervisor of production. Aphorstra remained in charge of keel production at Belainus where, to no one's surprise more than the metalsmith's, Ravian also made him responsible for procurement. Godart was elevated to full captain's rank and made responsible for tactical development and training while, knowing that he would not be able to focus fully on his role as Admiral of the Fleet, as well as oversee the swordship programme, Ravian cast about for a vice admiral and quickly decided on Capernal for the post.

As the first completed swordship from Belainus arrived at the naval base, Ravian became even busier. With Capernal and Godart, he carried out tests of the new vessel, *Sea Eagle*, sailing her against both the oldest longship in the fleet as well as against a galley taken from some pirates as a prize some years before. The success of these trials indicated that the full-sized swordships were going to be every bit as effective as *Sea Hawk's* tests at Belainus had promised.

It was a time of urgency and excitement and Ravian was enjoying organising Tarcus's defences into a more effective state. Sinur, however, showed little enthusiasm for his military activities or, when he finally broached the subject, for moving to their new abode.

'Why do we have to move into the Admiral's Residence?' she demanded.

'Well, it's traditional and it's convenient,' he replied. 'The admiralty offices are in the lower storey, it's immediately above the naval base and it also has superb views all around the harbour and out to sea,'

'It may be handy to the base, but it is hardly handy to anything else,' sniffed Sinur. 'It's bad enough that I see less and less of you but, if I have to live there, I'll become a social outcast into the bargain. Can't we stay in the place we have now?'

Thus, Ravian requested of his brother that he and his wife be allowed to retain use of the residence by the theatre. To the prince's surprise, Jeniel granted his request without any further discussion, and he suddenly found himself with a choice of two homes. The demands of the prince's work though, saw him sleeping more and more often at the Admiral's Residence while, back at what he soon came to think of as "Sinur's House", his wife maintained a full social calendar regardless of his comings and goings.

If Ravian was available, Sinur attended events on his arm. If not, she now flew in the face of convention by choosing any one of a number of male companions to escort her. Bound up in his punishing schedule, Ravian found most of Sinur's social fixtures even less convenient and even more tedious than before and, knowing the ease with which his wife could summon an alternative escort, he excused himself from them with increasing frequency. He knew that Jeniel, Ramus and their wives strongly disapproved of this arrangement although, thankfully, none of them chose to raise the subject with him directly. He was also aware that he and Sinur seemed to be drifting apart but his concern was vague, overwhelmed by the greater priority of his military duties.

Once the fleet was ready, he told himself, then he would make his absences up to Sinur. Once Tarcus was protected, they could think about a family again.

More swordships began to arrive at the naval base, initially from Belainus and then from the White City's own shipyards. The number of crew that was required to man a swordship was the same as that for a longship, facilitating the transfer of complete complements from the old vessels to the new. Loath to have the retired longships broken up for firewood however, and lacking anywhere at the White City to store them, Ravian ordered boat sheds built for them at North Cove. Thus, as each longship was decommissioned, a crew under training would sail it up the coast, help to haul it out, and put it into storage there.

At the same time as he had the navy to attend to, Ravian was also responsible for the army. He made no changes at the Academy but, knowing the gentle beaches and undulating countryside in Tarcus's north to be the obvious target for an invasion from that direction, he relocated most of the standing land army to a new base at Centrus, close to Golden Bay. This was not accomplished without significant cost, but Jeniel managed to sway the council to vote its approval, even though the complaints of some members were becoming increasingly strident.

Six months after commencing the longship building programme, Ravian was able to report to Jeniel that the Tarcun Navy now boasted a dozen operational swordships.

'Excellent,' the Tarcun king declared. 'And none too soon either.'

'You've had more news from the North?' Ravian asked him.

'Yes – all bad,' his brother growled. 'Dekane and Graftsen are building extra galleys and consolidating a fleet at Durst. Gerouf and Kleeft also seem to be putting a lot more naval vessels into the water. On top of that, it would seem that the king of Groven was unwise enough to let it be known that he had second thoughts about the Northern Alliance. Well, he met with a violent accident shortly thereafter, and our friend Bordwar isn't trying too hard to deny the rumours that he was behind it. The successor to the Groven crown is, not surprisingly, utterly supportive of the damned alliance and loud in his praises of the king of Dekane. We've got a dangerous adversary in the North, Ravian.'

Ravian nodded.

'So it'll be war then,' he said. 'When, do you think?'

'I'm still saying a year at least,' Jeniel said. 'The summer after next is when they'll come.'

'That still gives us time to replace the whole fleet then,' Ravian said thankfully. 'You've the full support of the council still?'

'Near enough,' the king grunted. 'It won't hurt for them to see what they are paying for though and, for that matter, the people at large would benefit from a display of our increased naval might. I was thinking that we could have a holiday and parade the new ships – get the priests to bless them, or something like that.'

Ravian thought about it – it seemed like a good idea.

'We could get them to sail into harbour past the Southern Arm,' he said. 'The whole population could see them from there and the priests could bless them as they sail under the eastern guard tower.'

'Splendid!' Jeniel declared. 'I'll leave it in your capable hands then, shall I?'

It was a lot of extra work for Ravian and his staff but, the prince could see the benefit in boosting the population's morale. Consequently, on the duly appointed day, a line of twelve swordships, red sails filled by a steady offshore breeze, approached the city from the southeast and tacked close in along the length of the Southern Arm. Almost the entire population of the White City had packed onto the walls there, the cheers for each ship deafening as it passed the crowd before turning into the harbour mouth beneath the eastern guard tower. Atop that structure, the Priests of Delikas rained down blessings and sacred water from the Heart Lake upon each vessel. At the foot of the tower, on a raised platform built especially for the occasion, the king, accompanied by his brothers, their spouses and the heads of the Nine Houses, took the salute of each captain as his ship passed.

It was a glorious day and Ravian had every right to feel proud of his accomplishments – although the presence on the platform of his old enemy Graticus, head of the House of Palin, marred his mood slightly. Further, Sinur's dutiful attendance at his side, obliged by her royal title to attend the occasion, pricked him with a feeling of guilty discomfort.

How long had it been since they had spoken to or even seen each other, he wondered. Two months? Three?

He stole a sideways glance at his wife, watching the parade of ships pass with a vague, distracted smile. Aware of his gaze, she turned and, as their eyes met, gave him an almost imperceptible curtsy.

Ravian was shocked at how much older Sinur suddenly seemed. She was still beautiful, her face unlined and her figure youthful, but her eyes now seemed to hold a weary worldliness that was disturbing to the prince and yet, at the same time, strangely familiar.

'You have achieved a fine navy, My Lord,' she said, breaking into his thoughts. 'I trust that you consider it a good return against the investment.'

'We will need more ships,' he replied tersely, 'and there will be more cost.'

She laughed, the tinkling laughter he had once adored tinged with a cynical edge.

'I wonder if My Lord is fully aware of the real costs of his activities,' she said. 'Somehow, I doubt it. The royal family seldom seems to concern itself with petty details.'

She was almost a stranger to him now, Ravian thought with a pang of sadness.

'Sinur, I'm sorry that I haven't visited lately,' he said. 'It's just that I've been so busy, and the preparation of Tarcus's defences still has a long way to go.'

'Why, Ravian, I do believe you mean that,' she said and, for a moment, she seemed to soften and become the same girl whose balcony he had stolen to so many times.

Then the hardness returned.

'Well, don't concern yourself, My Dear,' she said in an off-hand tone. 'I've always known where to find you if I wanted to – I suppose we have both been busy. Still, you're right about one thing – you are going to need a lot more ships.'

Ravian frowned – the Sinur he had once known wouldn't have cared one way or another how many ships the navy had.

'And how many ships do you think that might be?' he asked her casually.

Sinur said nothing for a moment and Ravian sensed a conflict raging behind the deep blue eyes that had once looked into his so lovingly. Then she stepped close to him so that her scent swirled about him, placing her hand on his arm, and her lips inches from his ear.

'Ravian,' she whispered, 'not everybody in this kingdom is happy about what you and your brother are doing.'

He shrugged.

'I would imagine a few of your friends would rather their taxes were devoted to new theatres and the like,' he said. 'Such opinions are of little importance to me.'

'I'm talking about powerful people,' she hissed, her nails digging into him for emphasis. 'Have you heard about – '

Something she saw over his shoulder stopped her and Ravian turned to see the cause. On the other side of the platform, Jeniel, flanked by the leaders of the Nine Houses, was staring at them in a bemused fashion.

'We'll have to talk later,' Sinur whispered.

'Don't worry about Jeniel,' Ravian told her, desperate to know what she had been about to say.

'I'm not...' she started to say, then. 'Anyway, will you be at your residence tonight?'

'I'll be there,' he said. 'But let me come to you.'

'No,' she insisted. 'I will come to you tonight. Make sure that the sentries you have on this evening are men that you can trust, men who know to keep their mouths shut.'

Without waiting for his reply, she moved away from him and crossed the platform to strike up a conversation with some members of the Nine Houses. Ravian was about to pursue her when he realised that Graticus was in the group.

Whatever she had to say could wait until that evening, he thought. He would just have to be patient.

Remembering his wife's words earlier in the day, Ravian personally chose the guards for the Admiral's Residence that evening – two good men, trustworthy and handy with their weapons – and briefed them that he was expecting a female guest. He bathed, and then dined lightly and alone, a strange feeling of nervous anticipation fluttering inside him.

Yes, he was intrigued as to what Sinur might have to tell him – although he had little doubt she would simply be passing on the discontented grumbling of some high-placed member of Tarcun society. Indeed, it was with some surprise that he had to admit to himself that he was mostly looking forward to trying to rekindle the romance with his wife. It was, he felt, almost like the times when he had first started escorting her out – the evening was full of possibilities, but nothing was certain.

It was a warm night, and he took a glass of wine to a balcony that looked directly out upon the city, blazing with a thousand lights of festival revelry. There was no breeze and, even high on the Western

Arm, the sounds of music and laughter carried faintly to him across the black mirror of the harbour.

It was time he took more interest in society, he thought to himself, time to laugh and love again.

He finished the wine and went inside to pour another – his last, as he did not want to ruin the moment with drink. He then settled on a couch with a book of poetry that Sinur had given him long ago, thinking it would please her if she saw that he had been reading it. The words were difficult to make out in the candlelight and he had difficulty finding the rhymes. Still, he persisted as he awaited his wife's arrival.

Ravian wasn't sure what time it was when he awoke but all the candles had burned down to nothing and the room was in darkness. Staggering to his feet, he went out to the balcony overlooking the city. Only a few lights glinted across the water now and the night was still and silent – it must be well after midnight, he realised.

Sinur had not indicated the time of her visit but Ravian would not have been surprised for her to arrive at a late hour, possibly after some social fixture. This was too late even for that though, he decided, the realisation that she was not coming after all filling him with a disappointment that he could not deny. Miserably, he prepared to retire – perhaps she would come tomorrow.

He could not sleep though, tossing and turning as he wondered what Sinur's news was, and whether she also had romance on her mind. Finally, after an hour or so, he arose and dressed again.

He would go to her house and show her that he still had feelings for her, that he still wanted her in his life.

Stalking past the startled sentry at the front door, he set off up the silent lane towards the High Temple. The almost-full moon bathed the smooth cobblestones in a silvery light and he could see his way clearly. At the fork, he took the high road past the palace as the most direct route to the theatre district where Sinur's house was. The palace was dark and silent, the only sign of life being two sentries from the royal guard who snapped to surprised attention and saluted as Prince Ravian, Defender of the Nation, suddenly materialised out of the night. He marched onward, past the dark silhouette of the slumbering theatre, to Sinur's house.

At her door, he hesitated.

Was he being presumptuous?

Had he misheard Sinur or misread her intentions?

Then he made up his mind and pounded on the locked front door.

It was his house as well wasn't it?

She was his wife wasn't she?

After what seemed forever, the door slowly creaked open and a middle-aged woman, holding a dim, sputtering lamp, peered around its edge at him. Ravian recognised her as Karli, the head of Sinur's household staff.

'Your Highness,' she exclaimed, blinking at him in surprise.

'Please inform my wife that I am here,' he told her imperiously.

'Just a moment please, Your Highness,' the woman said, obviously confused by his unexpected appearance. 'I'll go and see if she's...um...in residence.'

She disappeared inside again, pulling the door to behind her.

For some moments, Ravian stared at the closed door in disbelief.

In residence?!

Where in the name of Kanavas would Sinur be at this hour of the night if not in her bed or in his? Well, he thought with a flash of temper, he was not going to be made to wait in the street outside his own house at the pleasure of his own wife!

With a surge of rage, he kicked the door open and blundered into the darkened interior. As he did so, a scream came from above him, a woman's scream that sent every hair on his body prickling. The sound came from the top of a flight of stairs ascending up out of the gloom before him. At the top of those stairs, he knew, lay the master bedroom.

His sword materialising in his hand, he bounded up the steps three at a time. A figure came running through the open bedroom door ahead of him and he barely stopped himself from cutting Karli down on the spot. At the sight of him towering over her with his sword raised, the terrified woman dropped to her knees and screamed again.

'Your Highness,' she howled. 'It is My Lady!'

The servant woman started to say something else but he was already past her and into the moonlit bedroom, flinging his sword aside as he ran to the bed and the small, still form that lay upon it.

The images in that room burned themselves into his memory forever.

Her face, beautiful and serene in the moonlight.

The coldness of her as he gathered her into his arms.

The wide black stain of her blood upon the bedclothes.

The moon beaming in through the open window to her balcony, the curtains drawn aside and hanging motionless in the still air.

Chapter Eight

'I tell you Ravian, for your own good, let it go!' King Jeniel stormed at his brother.

It was two weeks since Sinur's funeral. Two weeks that Ravian had spent locked in his apartments at the Admiral's Residence washing down cake after cake of hahmah with jug after jug of wine. Every time he had begun to come to his senses, the cold images from that terrible night had begun to fill his mind again, and he had reeled back to the numbing embrace of the only two things that could block them out. This morning though, he had woken with a mental clarity born from cold anger and, without bathing or changing, he had marched unsteadily to the palace and demanded an immediate audience with his brother. Now, thin and filthy but, at least, sober, he stared down the glare of the king.

'I will not,' he declared coldly. 'My wife's murderer is loose in this city and I will have revenge.'

'For the last time, Ravian,' Jeniel insisted. 'Sinur took her own life.'

That was what Ravian had first thought as well. The knife that had opened Sinur's veins lay beside the bed. There were no signs of a struggle and her household staff had heard nothing out of the ordinary. The expression on her face, as he would eternally remember, had been serene and peaceful.

He had wondered why she had done it though, and then it had all begun to come out – reports from Jeniel's spies, confirmation from Karli and the rest of the terrified household staff. Sinur, the Sinur that he had gone to seek reconciliation with that fateful night, had kept an open house of entertainment, hosting parties that would begin after the theatre closed and from which some attendants would only slip away at dawn. The list of names was as long as it was varied – actors, poets, musicians, successful merchants – all linked to his estranged wife. Now Ravian recognised the look in her eyes that had so surprised him the last time he had seen her alive – it was the look of a woman who expected nothing from men except their desire, the same look that he had seen in the eyes of the women he had had in Ezreen.

'I think it just all became too much for her,' Jeniel continued in a gentler tone. 'Her reputation was spreading and it was only a matter of time before news of her activities reached even your ears.'

The king stopped then, embarrassed for his brother.

Yes, thought Ravian, the cuckolded husband was always the last to know, especially when he and his wife hadn't even seen each other for months. He had been made to look a fool in front of the entire city, but that wasn't what was on his mind now.

'But she said she had something important to tell me,' he insisted. 'Why would she suddenly decide to kill herself instead?'

His brother shrugged.

'I don't know,' he replied. 'Maybe she was just making it up to get your attention.'

'No,' said Ravian. 'There was definitely something going on. She started to tell me and then...'

He stopped, remembering the way Sinur had looked at the king and his group on the platform. In his mind's eye, he kept seeing the open window to her bedroom and now an awful suspicion welled up inside him.

'Jeniel,' he said slowly, 'you wouldn't have had anything to do with it would you?'

'What!' Jeniel exploded. 'How dare you! I am your brother!'

'You are also the king!' Ravian roared back at him. 'You can't have been very pleased when you learned that your sister-in-law was a royal...'

'Whore?' his brother finished for him. 'Is that the word you're looking for?'

For a moment, the pair's heavy breathing was the only sound in the otherwise empty audience room.

'By Delikas, you're lucky we're alone, Ravian,' Jeniel finally growled. 'If you'd made that accusation in front of anyone I would have beheaded you myself.'

'I'm sorry,' Ravian said, his anger evaporating.

There was another long pause before his brother spoke.

'All right,' he finally said. 'I forgive you. It can't be easy for a man to go through what you have. Watch your tongue in future though, Brother. I need to know that you're watching my back, not looking to sink a knife into it.'

The Ravian that returned to the fleet a few days later was a different man to the one that his captains had known before, a new admiral who drove his men with a joyless intensity that demanded respect but fostered little love. Capernal and Godart would sometimes despair of Ravian ever being satisfied with their performances, Lederalus and Aphorstra came to dread his incessant demands for faster production of swordships, and every man in the Army and Navy knew that – if a disciplinary action reached the level where Prince Ravian was judge – the penalties handed down would be swift and harsh.

In the evenings, and when not at sea, Ravian would retire alone to his quarters at the Admiral's Residence, there to pore over maps, schedules, inventories and intelligence reports until the early hours. Tarcun society saw him not at all, the palace infrequently. His family had been concerned for his state of mind after Sinur's suicide but this new, cold, unapproachable Ravian was not what they had expected.

Then, after Ravian had been a recluse for almost six months, an interesting arrival in the harbour caught the attention of the entire city.

It was shortly following the peaceful death of the ageing King Saravar of Ezreen. Indeed, Jeniel, Ravian and Ramus had only recently attended the monarch's funeral and Prince Beneen's subsequent coronation. The three brothers had been sorry to see the passing of Saravar – a good man and a good friend to Tarcus – but they knew that the throne of Ezreen was safe with their likeable "cousin".

Ravian was working in his office at the Admiral's Residence the day the unusual ship arrived. Normally, he would not have been aware of anything out of the ordinary, but a blast of horns from the harbour below caught his ear and he strode out onto a cliff-edge parapet that looked down into the bay.

A curvaceous, high-stemmed, Eastern-style vessel was rowing slowly into the harbour. In the mid-afternoon sun, it seemed that the entire craft was made of gold as her gilded top decks sparkling against the deep blue water. A group of musicians clustered at the bow, the sound of their horns ringing around the crater and ensuring that every citizen of the White City was conscious of the arrival.

How odd, Ravian thought. Jeniel usually let him know if he was to expect any foreign dignitaries in order that he could pay the appropriate marks of respect from the navy. Clearly, this was an important arrival, yet his brother had given him no warning.

Ravian shrugged.

If Jeniel had slipped up on this one, that was his concern, he thought. All the same, he summoned one of his guards.

'Go down and see what all that noise is about,' he ordered his man.

The man doubled off and Ravian returned to the intelligence report he had just received from the North.

It was more of the same. Bordwar and his allies were continuing their build-up of warships in the far north of the Grimspot Gris. The Dekanian king continued to maintain a vicelike grip on his alliance though, thankfully, no new members had joined. Everything continued to point to an invasion of Tarcus in the next year.

Ravian was deep in thought, considering at what point he would recommend to Jeniel that he generally mobilise, when his guard returned. The prince had quite forgotten the golden ship and the mission he had sent the man on.

'A most wonderful sight, Sir,' the wide-eyed man reported. 'The whole boat is covered in gold leaf.'

'I could see that from my balcony, you numbskull,' growled Ravian. 'Where is she from? Who is on board?'

In his excitement, the young guard was not as cowed by his admiral's irritability as he might normally have been.

'She's come from Ezreen, Sir,' he said excitedly. 'After she had come alongside, they craned across a gangway you could ride a chariot over and then this procession started – giant Southerners blowing their horns, dancing girls – quite a sight as I said, Sir. Then, this covered litter comes down the gangway on the shoulders of four of the biggest, blackest Southerners I've ever seen. Those men were wearing so much gold that, had they fallen into the tide, they would have gone straight to the bottom. Anyway, I could only see the silhouette of the occupant of the litter but it was certainly that of a woman. A queen or a princess of some sort, I suppose.'

'What do you mean, you suppose? You were supposed to find out!' Ravian barked.

The guard had been in the Admiral's Residence for over a year and was more used to Ravian than most. He knew that, as long as he had done his job to the best of his ability, he had no need to fear the admiral's bark.

'That's the thing, Sir,' he replied. 'Nobody knows.'

'Did you not think to ask anyone at the palace?' Ravian asked acidly.

'They didn't go to the palace, Sir,' the guard said, trying not to smirk. 'The whole procession marched up to the big house just up the road from here – the place they call the House of Palms. They are still unloading the vessel and everything is being hauled up the hill and taken there.'

Ravian knew the house, a handsome residence standing amidst beautiful, landscaped gardens. Named for the towering palm trees that framed it so gracefully, it was one of the most imposing buildings on the Western Arm, but it had stood empty for some months.

'Surely someone must know something about it?' he growled.

'Well, Sir, I did spot a well-to-do citizen waiting at the door to hand over the keys,' said the guard, looking pleased with himself. 'Once he came out of the gate, I approached him and told him on whose business I was. He said that he was just an agent and didn't know who the woman was either. All he knew was that he had sold the house to a representative of King Saravar a few months ago and that, as part of the deal, he was to maintain the house and grounds until the resident turned up. He received a message last week to say that the new owner was on her way and that he would certainly know when she arrived.'

'He would have to be deaf and blind not to,' grumbled Ravian. 'I'm sure that even Kanavas heard her entrance.'

Gruffly commending the guard for his initiative, Ravian sent him back to his post. Ambassador, wealthy relative or businesswoman, it made no difference to Ravian who his new neighbour was. He returned to his work and forgot about her.

Two days later, he met with Jeniel at the palace to discuss the further developments in the North and the rate of preparation of their defences. As Ravian was about to leave, his brother casually enquired if he had made the acquaintance of the House of Palms' new owner.

'No,' replied Ravian. 'All I know is that the building was acquired by Saravar some time ago.'

'That's all anyone seems to know,' said Jeniel. 'I can't understand why the old boy was so secretive about it. Anyway, Ravian, if you bothered to indulge in society, you would realise that the whole city is abuzz with rumours and gossip about your new neighbour. I must confess that, under savage pressure from your sisters-in-law, I've had to send a message off to Beneen to ask just who this woman is.'

Ravian smiled, something he did rarely these days.

It was typical of Tarcus that even its ruler didn't know who the new arrival was, the trading nation having a respect for capital that sometimes seemed to transcend its sovereign interests. The house had been bought and paid for with solid gold, taxes had, no doubt, been collected on the importation of the new owner's possessions and her vessel lay in the harbour generating mooring fees. As far as anyone knew, a squad of Ezrenian assassins might well be training within the walls of the House of Palms but, as long as the owner had paid her dues, not even the king was prepared to make an overt invasion of her privacy.

'Oh well,' he replied, without any real interest, 'I suppose we'll all know in a week or so then.'

Ravian didn't have to wait that long however. That evening, as he prepared to dine – alone, as was his habit – one of his servants came to him with a bemused expression on his face.

'Your Highness,' his man announced. 'There is an Ezrenian gentleman at the door who has requested that he be allowed to hand you a message. He says that he has come from the House of Palms.'

'Very well,' said Ravian, slightly irritated that his dinner was to be delayed. 'Show him in, please.'

The Ezrenian was an impressive character. Dressed in a white turban, vest and loose pants, he towered over the Tarcun prince and, as he bowed, Ravian had the thought that the man's massive shoulders could easily rip an enemy in two.

'Good evening, Your Highness,' he rumbled in a deep, bass voice. 'My mistress has asked that I deliver this to you personally.'

He handed over a parchment note, folded and sealed with wax. Ravian turned his back on the man, broke the seal and read the elegant handwriting inside, a pleasant scent of sandalwood wafting to his nostrils as he did so.

'Your Highness,

Please forgive the lateness of this invitation but I have only just now finished getting my new household in order.

It would please me greatly if you were able to dine with me tonight.

If you are unable to attend, please advise Terim. If you are inclined to share a meal with me, please return with him.

B'

'And you are Terim?' Ravian asked, turning back to the messenger.

The big man bowed again.

'Indeed I am, Sir,' he replied in flawless Chesa. 'Will you be accompanying me?'

Why not, thought Ravian. At least he would be the first person in the kingdom to know who the mysterious lady of the house was. He followed the huge Ezrenian past the mystified guard at his door and out into the lane.

'And your mistress's name is...?' Ravian probed.

Terim smiled, his teeth very white in the warm twilight.

'I believe that my mistress wishes to introduce herself,' was all he said.

It was only a short walk to the house.

At the property's gate, two Ezrenian sentries, both fully as large as Terim, bowed deeply. Ravian and his escort followed a torch-lit path to the house's front entrance, also guarded by two turbaned guards, where Terim rapped on the door, the sound booming in the still air. It was opened almost immediately by a girl dressed in a veil and a flowing silk robe.

'His Highness, Prince Ravian,' announced Terim, bowing Ravian into the house, but remaining where he was.

The girl also bowed deeply, hands together in front of her, and stepped aside as he entered.

Inside, what would once have been the entrance hall to the home of a wealthy Tarcun merchant had been transformed into an eastern palace. Beautiful carpets hung from the walls and covered the floors, huge mirrors gleamed in a blaze of torchlight, and the hall was filled with graceful potted plants, stands of peacock feathers and the like. Ravian was particularly intrigued by a stuffed and mounted cheetah that stood guarding the stairs to the upper level.

'The mistress's pet,' the girl explained, as she led him past the beautifully preserved animal. 'She was heart-broken when he died.'

Ravian smelled the spicy aroma of eastern cooking and, as his mind went back to the sumptuous meals he had enjoyed as a guest of the palace at Ezreen, his stomach rumbled. A year of simple meals at the Admiral's Residence had seen him forget the pleasure of eating.

The girl opened some ornate double doors and ushered him into what was obviously the dining room. Here, the wall hangings and carpets were even more sumptuous than those in the entrance hall, large and luxuriously bolstered couches filled the room with their massive presence, and he could faintly hear a small band playing the exciting, pulsating music of the East.

'His Highness, Prince Ravian, Mistress,' said the girl from behind him and he heard the door close as she left.

A veiled woman rose gracefully from one of the couches and, as she crossed the floor to him, the prince sensed something familiar about her – something in the way her hips undulated as she flowed towards him.

'Your Highness,' the voice was pure velvet – lightly accented. 'Welcome to my home. I hope that you will make it yours whenever you choose.'

It was, Ravian knew, a traditional Ezrenian welcome. The way the woman said it though – and the knowing boldness of her dark eyes above the veil –seemed to give it special meaning. She extended a hand to him and, as he took it, he thrilled involuntarily at the warm softness of her touch.

'And whom do I have the honour of addressing?' he asked.

'My name is Belice,' she replied. 'Please, do come and sit down. We have a little while before the meal is served. Perhaps you would like some wine?'

He sat down self-consciously on a couch opposite hers. She reclined easily, tucking her feet beneath her, clearly not overawed by the presence of royalty in her dining room.

'Surely we have met before?' he asked, raising his glass to her and taking a careful sip. The wine was excellent.

Her head tilted back and she laughed musically, the points of her breasts dancing distractingly beneath the sheer fabric of her gown.

'Indeed we have, Your Highness – at King Saravar's palace. I should have been quite heart-broken had you forgotten me, even if we were never formally introduced.'

Ravian' jaw dropped.

'Of course! Belice!' he exclaimed. 'You're the king's dancer!'

He had never since wanted a woman in the same way as he had wanted her that magical night.

'Well done, Your Highness,' she said with slightly mocking tone.

She took a sip of her wine.

'Mind you,' she said, her eyes big and knowing over the top of the veil, 'I would have thought that, considering your condition that evening, one veiled woman would have looked the same as another.'

They both knew that nothing could be further from the truth, yet the mildly flirtatious remark disturbed Ravian. He had been celibate since Sinur's death and, having largely avoided the company of women, his confidence in their presence had diminished considerably.

'Not at all,' he said, and then brusquely changed the subject. 'May I ask what brings you to the White City, Belice?'

Again, her knowing look disturbed him. She was well aware of how ill at ease he was, he thought, and of the effect that she was having on him.

'Why – you, Your Highness,' she said.

Ravian was dumbfounded for a moment.

'I...beg your pardon?' he finally sputtered.

'No one told me you were hard of hearing, Your Highness – but I'll repeat myself. I...' she spoke very slowly and deliberately, pointing first to herself and then to him, 'have...come...here...for...you!'

'What on earth do you mean?' Ravian demanded, knowing, even as he said the words, precisely what she meant.

'I am here as a final gift from your uncle, King Saravar, who has taken his place in the halls of Bhana,' she announced. 'He must have loved you very much, because I was his most treasured possession.'

Ravian was on his feet, blushing furiously.

'Then Saravar has made a mistake,' he said angrily. 'I do not keep slaves – and I do not retain concubines!'

Belice remained seated.

'No, Your Highness,' she replied calmly. 'There is no mistake and I am no slave – the king gave me my freedom before his death. Not only that, but he presented me with the title to this house, the ship in the harbour, my own slaves, and all the pretty things that you see about you. He has bequeathed me a fortune beyond the wildest dreams of most mortals and I am free to go wherever in the world I choose. As for being a concubine – ha! I was never a mere concubine, as you saw yourself.'

'But, if you are free, how can you be given as a gift?' asked Ravian, still struggling to understand what she was telling him.

'You must understand, Your Highness,' she said, 'that as the king's favourite...um... companion, things would not have been comfortable for me in the palace after his death. King Beneen is a wonderful man, but that gang of harpies who are his stepmothers bears the most spiteful feelings for me and, really, who can blame them. King Saravar knew that he was dying and that I would be at risk after his passing, so he made sure that I was provided for. He summoned me to his deathbed, told me of his gifts to me and then asked, as a final favour to him, if I would consider the possibility of becoming your mistress.'

'What?!' exploded Ravian, sitting down heavily.

'Why, Prince Ravian,' Belice laughed. 'I really am becoming most concerned about your hearing. Do I have to repeat everything I say?'

'King Saravar,' she continued, 'was a wonderful man and he loved me very much. He wanted to see me cared for once he had gone and he was just as concerned about you. "My agents have bought a house in Tarcus", he told me, "right next door to young Ravian's residence". He felt that you needed a woman in your life again – and he understood that I would need a man in mine. "Go and have a look at him", he told me. "He's a good man, if a little hot-tempered and impetuous at times. If you don't like the look of him, you can always sell up and move on".'

'You...discussed...my circumstances?' Ravian asked incredulously. He still could not believe his ears.

'Oh yes,' she admitted. 'And don't forget that I saw a little of you when you visited the palace – possibly more than you realised on most occasions.'

Ravian gaped.

'I was always close by the king's side,' she explained. 'All those secret meetings and conversations – my ears and eyes were never too far away. Anyway, I didn't find what I saw or heard of you too off-putting, so here I am – although I am beginning to wonder about my judgement now.'

Ravian rose to his feet again.

'Well, your judgement has, indeed, let you down, Madam,' he said haughtily. 'Whatever the norm may be in Ezreen, I can assure you that I am not going to be appraised and found a mate for like some prize bull! I suggest that you market this property immediately and move on to your next destination at your earliest convenience!'

Belice remained reclining on the couch, her eyes dancing with humour.

'How fiery! How noble! How passionate!' she exclaimed. 'No, I think that my judgement was right, after all – you just need a bit of that stiffness taken out of you. I believe that I'll stay here for a while and give you the chance to reconsider the situation.'

'There is nothing to consider in the first place, let alone reconsider!' Ravian stormed as he wheeled to leave the room. 'You will be on your way in two days!'

'Oh no, Your Highness,' she called after him. 'I think that I'm going to be here a lot longer than that.'

We'll see about that, he thought, as he marched back to his residence. He would see Jeniel tomorrow and have the woman expelled!

Despite the tears rolling down his cheeks, Jeniel was far from sympathetic to Ravian's plight.

The tears were tears of laughter, accompanied by roars of mirth.

'Now, let me get this right, Brother,' he said when he had controlled himself enough to speak. 'King Saravar's favourite consort, endowed now with freedom, wealth and property, approaches you to make her your mistress and you take offence?'

Ravian didn't reply. His brother's laughter would have drowned out anything he said anyway.

'By Delikas,' the king chortled, 'I always knew that old Uncle Saravar had a soft spot for you, but I didn't realise he loved you that much!'

'I saw her dance once myself, you know,' he continued, conspiratorially lowering his voice out of respect to Queen Kasanda, who was in the next room. 'There isn't a normal man alive who wouldn't cut off one of his hands just to touch her with the other. Tell me, what does she look like without that veil?'

'I don't know and I don't care,' said Ravian. 'I want you to pack her on her way!'

Jeniel sobered slightly.

'Actually, Ravian, I don't think that I can do that. She has legal title to the property and she isn't breaking any laws that I am aware of, so there is no good reason that I can think of for her residency to be terminated. Besides...' the king leaned closer to his brother and lowered his voice, '...if word got out that you had turned down one of the most famous beauties in the Sapphire Sea, it might give credence to some of those rumours.'

'What rumours?' Ravian demanded.

'You know...'

Jeniel jerked his thumb rudely upwards.

'What!?!' Ravian exploded.

'I'm afraid so, Old Boy,' the king confirmed. 'You can't live out on the Western Arm for a year, with no one but a bunch of young sailors for company, without someone starting to spread malicious stories.'

Ravian returned to the Admiral's Residence in a daze.

On the one hand, Belice was assessing him like some stud animal and, on the other, he was apparently suspected of being a homosexual!

That evening, Terim again brought a note to his door.

'Dear Prince Ravian,

A sumptuous feast awaits you at my house.

If you would do me the honour of dining with me, please accompany Terim as you did last night.

Your servant,

Belice'

'Please tell your mistress...' began Ravian and then thought better of it.

Instead, he scribbled a note of his own for the Ezrenian to return to Belice.

'Madam,

I will not be attending any of your dinners.

I recommend that you seek a more social climate.

Ravian'

Despite Ravian's repeated refusals, Terim returned each night with a similar invitation. Even when the prince escaped to sea for a week, on the first night of his return, the big Ezrenian was, again, at his door.

'I wonder if I could talk Jeniel into having her expelled for this harassment?' he wondered, as he headed to another meeting with the king the next day.

He was just leaving the palace after the meeting when he saw Princess Verene bearing down on him.

'All right, Brother-in-law, tell me everything,' Ramus's wife demanded.

Ravian, who had always liked and trusted his sister-in-law, gave her the facts of the matter.

'And now,' he raged, 'it seems that I can't do anything about it without confirming some suspicions that I might be inclined to "polish the golden boom"!'

Verene was silent for a moment, then, a mischievous gleam appeared in her eye.

'There is one thing you could do,' she said.

'Yes?'

'You could let her have her way, make sure that everyone knows, and then be such a bore that she loses interest and leaves. That shouldn't be too hard for you, My Dear.'

Despite himself, Ravian smiled. It had taken a while, but his sense of humour was slowly returning.

'That would take far too long,' he said. 'Besides, who's to say she wouldn't like a man who behaved badly?'

'Oh well,' said Verene off-handedly, 'it's certainly up to you. I must say that, if I was a man who had spent the amount of time on my own that you have, I'd be scared of a woman like Belice too.'

'You think I'm scared of her?' Ravian bridled.

Verene looked at him affectionately and placed a caring hand on his arm.

'I don't know what to think of you, My Pet,' she said, 'but Belice isn't the only one who is playing a game here. After all, if you really wanted to stop this, you could just have her servant – and these invitations – barred from your residence.'

On his way back to the Admiral's Residence, Ravian decided that Verene was right. Well then, he would just order the guards to keep Terim off his property!

Yet, he never gave the order and, disturbingly, he realised that he would be disappointed if Belice's man did not come.

That evening though, Terim arrived with a note quite different from the previous invitations.

'Dear Prince Ravian,

I am sorry if I have offended you.
I assure you that my respect for you has only increased with each day that I have been in your country.
As a mark of this respect, I will follow your wishes. I will be leaving Tarcus tomorrow and my property here will be sold. You need never see me again.
However, there is something that I must show you before I leave. If you would return to my house with Terim tonight, I would be most grateful.
Your servant,
Belice'

The note aroused a storm of conflicting emotions in Ravian.

'Your mistress is really leaving Tarcus?' he asked Terim.

'You can come back with me and see for yourself, Your Highness,' the man replied. 'Most of her effects are already boxed up and ready to go aboard her ship.'

'Very well, then,' Ravian decided. 'I will return with you.'

As they walked the lane to the House of Palms, Ravian was, again, struck by the powerful aura of the huge man beside him.

'You look like you would be a handy man in a fight,' he remarked conversationally. 'How does a soldier like you wind up as a bodyguard for someone like your mistress? Surely you are not her slave?'

'I, like the rest of her bodyguard, was freed by my mistress, Your Highness,' Terim said proudly. 'All of us consider it an honour to stay in her service and, if necessary, to lay our lives down for her. In that respect, I suppose we are, indeed, still our lady's slaves.'

'Well said,' Ravian commended him, 'but surely you realise that you have effectively followed her into exile. What about your families back home?'

Terim stopped and turned to him just short of the hearing of the sentries at Belice's gate.

'Your Highness, may I speak frankly?' he rumbled in smooth Chesa.

Ravian nodded.

'I think that you do my lady a disservice,' Terim told him. 'When she was the companion of King Saravar, she was a lot more than just his dancer. As long as she had his ear, she never allowed him to forget the plight of the poor, the sick, or the other needy of Ezreen – particularly the children – and the orphanages and hospitals that the king built were because of her. The people of my country knew that and they loved her for her intercessions on their behalf, which is yet another reason why the queens were all so jealous of her. I, and all her staff here, have family who have benefited, nay, who have been saved, by her good work. So, you see, we have a duty to our families to look after her now that she is alone.'

'Hmmm, I begin to see why you have such loyalty to her,' said Ravian thoughtfully.

'Indeed, Your Highness,' Terim declared, towering above Ravian in the night. 'I have more respect for her than any *man* I ever served. There have been some who have not shared my respect – and I have helped a good many of them on their way to Heaven. Of course, sometimes the lady herself extends her protection to disrespectful persons who would, otherwise, know the edge of my sword.'

'Yes, I think I see,' said Ravian, too distracted by Terim's revelation of the other side of Belice to take any real offence at his implied threat.

They walked to the door of the house and, once more, the household maid showed Ravian alone into the dining room. Certainly, all the wall hangings and effects in the entrance hall had disappeared, apparently into the large boxes that were stacked along its walls. The dining room, however, was exactly as he had last seen it.

Belice rose and approached him across the floor, her silk robe caressing her body in the soft light.

'Prince Ravian,' she said demurely, taking him by the hand and leading him to a couch. 'I must thank you for coming. As you can see, I have respected your wishes and will depart tomorrow.'

Sitting down beside her, Ravian suddenly realised that he wasn't ready for her to leave.

'Where will you go?' he asked. 'Surely you are better off here than anywhere else?'

She looked down, her eyes sad above the veil.

'I must admit, Your Highness, that the White City is lovely,' she said, 'and that it suits me very well. But there was really only one reason for me to be here and, as that is not to be, then I really need to move on.'

'It's your decision, I suppose,' said Ravian carefully, 'but don't let this silly business between you and I be too much of a factor in it. I...uh...I could become used to having you as a neighbour.'

She looked at him directly then, and he thought he saw laughter dancing in her dark eyes.

'Your Highness is too kind,' she said, 'but, no, I think that my mind is made up.'

'Please stay.'

The words were out before Ravian even realised that he was going to say them. Belice's eyes became soft and shiny and he was sure that she smiled behind the veil.

'You are most forgiving, Your Highness,' she said, 'and I will consider your invitation carefully, really I will. But I forget myself. You have come here at my request so that I can show you something you need to see.'

'Oh...ah...yes,' Ravian said stupidly.

Damn, he thought to himself. What could he possibly do to change her mind about leaving?

'Your Highness,' she said, leaning confidentially towards him so that she filled his senses, 'what I have to show you is a great secret that has been known by none bar King Saravar for the last ten years. His last request to me was that I reveal it to you. Would you like to see?'

Ravian nodded.

Slowly, deliberately, Belice reached up and, detaching one side of her veil, let it swing aside.

The Tarcun prince found himself staring into the most beautiful face he had ever seen.

Chapter Nine

Ravian did not leave the House of Palms for two days and, when he did so, it was with a spring in his step and a smile on his face.

He would have had one of his sailors severely beaten for such an absence from duty, he reflected, as he returned the salute of his guard salute at the Admiral's Residence. On the other hand, he rationalised, what was the point of being a prince if one didn't indulge oneself every once in a while?

'Every once in a while,' he chuckled aloud, as he entered his private quarters and threw himself on the bed. 'Try once in almost a year!'

To his surprise and relief, Belice had been a gentle and understanding lover – the first time. After that, and as he regained his confidence, her passion seemed to become increasingly aroused and they had made love in so many ways that he had difficulty recalling all of them. Between their bouts of lovemaking they had eaten, sipped wine and talked, going over the maps of each other's lives.

What a woman!

She was intelligent, caring, sensual, beautiful, educated – and she was his!

Ravian couldn't recall ever being so happy.

Jeniel, when they next met, contrived to cloud his happiness.

'I understand that you recently disappeared for a couple of days, Ravian?' he enquired innocently.

'Uh...yes, I wasn't feeling so well,' Ravian said, feeling his ears beginning to redden.

'All better now?' asked his brother, solicitously.

'Oh yes, much better, thank you,' Ravian replied, unable to suppress a smile.

'Oh Delikas, save me,' Jeniel groaned with a wry grin. 'I presume that we are getting on a lot better with our neighbour then? No need for me to set the palace guard on her?'

'No,' Ravian said. 'She is probably the most wonderful woman I have ever met.'

Jeniel's grin vanished and he shot his brother a sharp look.

'I'm sure she is, Ravian,' he said seriously, 'but don't forget *what* she is. Don't fall in love with her. She can never fully be a part of your life.'

'Oh, don't worry about me,' said Ravian, airily. 'I'm just enjoying myself.'

'Hmmm,' was all that Jeniel said.

As the intelligence reports from the North became increasingly alarming, Ravian continued his vigorous drive of Tarcus's defensive preparations. Now though, those evenings that he was in the city belonged to Belice – as did the occasional moment during the day.

She rarely left her property and Ravian could arrive there unannounced at any time, the guards and servants bowing him into the house as though he was its master. Belice was always ready for him – their lovemaking a varied and exciting delight he had never known before. Sometimes she would dance for him, driving him to that same frenzy of desire he had known when he first saw her at Saravar's palace.

As entranced as he was by Belice sexually, it wasn't long before her full nature began to weave a spell on him. As well as a passionate lover, he discovered in her a gentle and understanding companion with whom, to his surprise, he frequently found himself discussing the problems of a difficult day. While her very presence soothed him, he also found that she was often able to suggest solutions that he had been unable to see, and he began to understand why she had been so close to Saravar. Belice had a canny political mind, a solid grasp of tactics and an acute intuition regarding people.

She expanded his knowledge of Ezreen – its culture, its politics, and its economy – as well as the countries to the north and south of that kingdom. She intrigued him with her empathy for the plight of the downtrodden and, as she told him of her early life, he began to understand why she felt so.

'My parents were poor folk who lived in the mountains of Karaal,' she told him. 'There was a particularly harsh winter and the following springtime brought nothing but famine. We were all starving – my brothers and sisters and I – and, as the oldest girl, my parents had little choice but to sell me to a passing Ezrenian trader. I cannot have been more than eight years old.

'I was taken to the slave market in Ezreen, where the best fate I could have hoped for would have been a life of domestic servitude, but, being pretty enough to attract attention even at that age, I was purchased by a wealthy Ezrenian widow who specialised in producing Halay dancers. I loved to dance – it made me feel free – and I excelled in the art. As I became older though, and my body began to blossom into womanhood, my owner saw the opportunity for an even greater return on her investment than she had first hoped. In addition to my Halay skills, she had me instructed in Sulee, the scriptures of erotic congress, all the time guarding my virginity like a tigress. When I reached the age of fourteen, the widow made contact with the king's agents and, thus, I was sold to the palace.'

Ravian soon learned that the slavery was a subject on which Belice was extremely sensitive.

'You have no idea what it is like to be a slave,' she went on. 'You Tarcuns don't even have slaves – which I think is one of the reasons I like it here so much, one of the reasons that I like *you* so much.'

'It's not your fault, my love,' Belice continued, 'but, unless you have been a slave yourself, you cannot possibly imagine what it is like. There I was, a fourteen-year-old virgin child, made to dance for the king and then picked out from among the other dancers and ordered to his bed to await his pleasure. I was terrified!

'Saravar, as you know, had a good heart and he treated me gently and kindly – but how different it could have been. He could have done anything with me. He might have abused me and then thrown me to his guards for their sport, or worse – and I have certainly heard of worse!

'Yes! I have had a lucky life – for a slave. A charmed and happy life, if the truth be known – but I was still a slave!'

Ravian was silent. He remembered his thoughtless, youthful romps with the girls of Saravar's palace and was ashamed of himself. He had never considered the side of slavery that Belice now described.

She looked at him and her eyes softened.

'Darling, I know what you are thinking, but the past is the past – or can be for you anyway. Just promise me that you will never sleep with a slave or a prostitute again.'

He had solemnly promised, without reservation. After all, Belice was the only woman he would ever want for the rest of his life.

Two weeks after he had spent that first night at the House of Palms, Ravian stood upon the quarterdeck of *Sea Eagle* as she led a growing fleet of twenty-seven swordships out to sea.

Despite the dead calm of the previous evening, it was an inclement morning, a warm but strong south-easterly driving sheets of rain that periodically obscured the coast, as the single file of ships began its run up to Belainus. As he looked up at the Western Arm through a momentary break in the weather, Ravian caught a glimpse of the waving palms above Belice's house.

She would still be asleep in the bed he had left that morning, he thought, remembering the smell of her as he had kissed her goodbye and the warmth of her body as she, only half-waking, had arched against his embrace. Despite the rain and the increasingly uncomfortable motion of the ship, he smiled.

Old Lederalus, who had elected to sail with the fleet this day, saw the smile and the direction of the prince's gaze, and an impish grin lit his face.

'I say, Vice admiral,' he said, addressing Capernal just loudly enough for Ravian to hear, 'the Commander in Chief seems to be in a good mood these days.'

Capernal looked nervous. So did Godart, who was now *Sea Eagle's* captain. Combus, who generally took the tiller when entering or leaving harbour – or for battle stations – stared straight ahead impassively. After half a year of cold black rages, the re-emerging sense of humour of their commander was something none of them was in a hurry to test.

'I'm sure that we are all glad to be back to sea,' Capernal said neutrally, declining to follow the old shipbuilder's mischievous lead.

Lederalus rubbed his chin thoughtfully and decided that there was sport to be had, even if his colleagues were reluctant to play.

'Tell me, Vice admiral. Did you notice any of this breeze last night?' he asked.

'No,' Capernal replied nervously, unsure where Lederalus was heading. 'It was flat calm until just before dawn. Why do you ask?'

'Well,' said Lederalus, 'it was the oddest thing, but I was out for an after-dinner stroll last night and I passed by that House of Palms place. I didn't think there was any wind but those palm trees around that house were waving and tossing as though there was a hurricane amongst them.'

The two younger men grinned.

'I daresay there probably was,' Godart chuckled.

'What in the name of Kanavas do you two think are doing?!' Ravian bellowed, wheeling around from where he stood at the rail. 'Is this a warship or a hen house?!'

Capernal and Godart jumped and then snapped to attention.

'Vice admiral Capernal!' Ravian roared. 'Your fleet is strung out behind us like a bunch of drunken sailors! Have them signalled to tighten the line and close to proper formation distance!

'Captain Godart! If you are so concerned about weather conditions, why have you not trimmed your sails properly since we rounded the point? The main is luffing so loudly I can hardly hear myself think!'

The two men leapt to their tasks with expressionless faces, and Ravian turned his back on them. He became aware of Lederalus beside him at the rail.

'And what do you want, you old gossip?' he growled.

Lederalus grinned. He was too old to fear either admirals or princes.

'I just wanted to say that it's good to see you back to your old self, Your Highness,' he said. 'You had us all quite concerned for a while.'

'Hmmm,' grunted Ravian. 'I imagined that I had been rather more discreet.'

Lederalus rolled his eyes.

'It's a small island, Your Highness – and the lady and yourself are its biggest story at the moment. Why, if you were in the habit of frequenting the taverns of the city, you would realise that your love life is now celebrated in a very popular drinking song.'

'Oh...er...how do I stop that?' Ravian asked, appalled at the very idea.

'You don't, Your Highness,' said the old man. 'If you understood your men a little better, you'd realise that they're proud of you. Their commander, sleeping with the most beautiful woman in the world? – They love you for it. Somehow, it gives them pride in themselves.'

If Ravian had been surprised at this revelation about the psychology of his men, an even greater surprise was in store for him when the fleet returned to the White City a few days later.

Eager to see Belice, he had left *Sea Eagle* as soon as the ship had tied up, and bounded up the long flight of steps clinging to the cliff side between the naval base and the Admiral's Residence. Bypassing his own home at the top, he had headed up the lane towards the House of Palms. Somewhere ahead of him, a din that sounded like a large number of children disrupted the usual quiet of the Western Arm, and Ravian had thought it odd that he had never noticed a school or nursery in the area before.

Then he had stopped, open-mouthed, at the gates to Sinur's home.

As always, two of Belice's men were on guard duty there. Today though, they smiled even more broadly than usual at the arrival of the prince while, behind them, at least forty children frolicked with the house servants and the rest of the guards on the residence's immaculate lawns. It seemed that they were playing some sort of game of tag, and the air was filled with piercing shrieks of delight.

Feeling as though he was in some odd sort of dream, Ravian walked towards the house. Belice, barefaced and bare-footed, danced up to him and kissed him on the cheek.

'Welcome back, My Darling!' she yelled above the noise. 'Aren't they wonderful?'

Ravian noticed a grinning Terim in the middle of the melee, carrying one ecstatic child on his shoulders and another under each arm.

'Um...what...?' he asked stupidly.

'It would seem that, even in Tarcus, there are children with no one to care for them,' she said. 'My people have rescued these little waifs from the streets of the White City.'

'But...what are you going to do with them?' he asked, still having difficulty believing his eyes.

'They are going to live here,' she replied, her chin lifting defiantly.

'An orphanage?' he asked.

'Precisely.'

Ravian stared at the scene about him.

What was going to happen to their nights and days of passion?

How did one enjoy the delight of Halay and Sulee with a pack of screaming children charging about the place?

Belice gave him a searching look and seemed to read his mind.

'Look, My Love,' she said, 'someone has to care for these children – and I've more room and servants than I need. I thought that, if it suited you, maybe I could move into your residence.'

Ravian couldn't restrain his sigh of relief and, taking his eyes off the chaos before them, he looked at Belice closely for the first time since his return. Her hair was unbound and tousled, her face flushed from the children's games. Her eyes were shining happily and he thought that she had never looked more beautiful. The House of Palms was pleasant enough, but he had missed the sea views of the Admiral's Residence.

'Yes,' he said. 'What a wonderful idea!'

'What, in the name of the blue balls of Kanavas, were you thinking?!' King Jeniel bellowed at him.

It had taken two days from the time that Belice had moved in to his residence for his summons from the palace to arrive. The brothers stood facing each other on the wide balcony outside Jeniel's private apartments – the king didn't want any witnesses to this discussion.

'I fail to see what the problem is,' Ravian replied loftily.

'Oh you do, do you?' Jeniel ground through clenched teeth. 'Well, let me spell it out for you, you moron.'

'Have you even remotely considered the implications of your setting up house with this woman?' his brother continued. 'She's an ex-slave! A celebrated concubine! A harlot! How can you possibly allow yourself to be seen to live with her like husband and wife? – and in the Admiral's Residence?!'

'She is a truly good person,' Ravian defended. 'She's done more good work in the short time she's been here than most of our civil servants have in a lifetime!'

'I'm not denying that, you idiot,' his brother snapped, 'but I don't care if she single-handedly saves every poor soul in the world and sinks the Northern battle fleet into the bargain! The issue is you, and who you are!'

Ravian was silent as the king stormed on.

'You can't attend any civic function with her – in fact, I forbid you to be seen with her in public. She can never enter the palace, you certainly can't marry her and, while you are playing happy families with her and her orphan brood, no respectable girl is going to even look at you. And don't you *dare* have any children by her!'

'I'm in love with her,' Ravian said simply – the first time he had admitted it even to himself.

'No, you're not,' his brother snapped. 'She's just the first woman that's come along since Sinur and you've let your testicles get the better of you.'

'That's not true!' Ravian snarled, his suspicions about Sinur's death suddenly welling up again.

Had she really killed herself? Had his brother had anything to do with it?

Jeniel was silent for a moment, as Sinur's ghost floated between the two brothers, unacknowledged. Then the king sighed.

'All right, Ravian – maybe you are in love with her – but that doesn't matter. Kasanda and I are still childless. What do you think would happen if I were to die tomorrow? Do you think that the citizens of the country would accept a new king on their throne with someone like Belice as his consort? How much chance do you think any issue from your union with this woman would have of making it to the throne after your death? It's a recipe for civil war.'

Ravian was silent, knowing that Jeniel was right.

'All I'm asking you to do, Dear Brother,' Jeniel continued in a more reasonable tone, 'is to face up to your responsibilities and get her out of the Admiral's Residence. Have your fun, but be discreet, for heaven's sake – and find a respectable girl to marry and continue the line with.'

They locked eyes.

'No,' said Ravian.

Jeniel glared at him, and Ravian waited for his brother's next move. Neither of them were children anymore, he thought with a touch of sadness. The games they played now were serious.

'Very well,' the king finally said. 'I'll leave it for the time being but, sooner or later, you are going to have to realise that your duty to this kingdom goes beyond your military activities. Enjoy your time with Belice, Ravian – it won't last forever.'

Ravian turned Jeniel's words over in his mind as he stalked back to his residence, the wound of Sinur's death torn open again.

He still believed that his wife had been murdered but, over the preceding months, he had more or less decided that his brother had not been involved. But if not his brother, then whom and why? What had Sinur been about to tell him that was so important that it had cost her her life?

And if he was wrong about Jeniel not being so ruthless, was Belice's life under threat even now?

Despite Ravian's efforts to conceal his feelings, Belice quickly deduced at least a part of the reason for the king's summons and, as they lay together that night, she tenderly put her hand to his cheek and brought his eyes to meet hers in the moonlight.

'Darling,' she said gently, 'you do realise that we are not meant to be together forever, don't you?'

'But we will be,' he replied stubbornly.

Her smile was sad.

'No,' she shook her head. 'There will come a time when we will both have to go our own ways. You are a prince and I was a slave and a concubine. Our time together is wonderful – will always be wonderful – but it will end.'

'But you're free now,' he said.

'No I'm not, my love,' she said, and kissed him gently. 'Once a slave – always a slave.'

And, with that, their love was changed. As the months passed, their feelings for each other grew even stronger – but, now, they were tinged with the poignant knowledge that their time together would have an end.

Chapter Ten

'Damn!'

Ravian was standing on the balcony of the Admiral's Residence.

The prince had noticed the sail coming out the northwest an hour beforehand and, even when it was just a small triangle on the horizon, he had had a strong feeling of foreboding. Now, as it closed with the land, he identified it as one of his spy boats and, observing how hard its skipper drove it – its mast carrying every available inch of straining canvas – he could guess at the news that it carried.

Their two years were up.

The wind was steady from the north and the enemy battle fleet would soon follow the boat over the horizon.

Through their spies, Jeniel and Ravian had followed the build-up of the enemy fleet in the far north of the Grimspot Gris and, two months earlier, they had learned that the fleet of Geroufen and Dekanian warships assembled at Durst had moved south to a new anchorage at Canavast, the capital of Kleeft. Kleeften ships, as well as vessels from Graftsen and Groven, had joined them there and, even though the enemy fleet now numbered over one hundred and fifty, the build-up had continued.

The reports indicated that the enemy force was almost entirely composed of war galleys – mainly two and three-deckers, with perhaps ten massive four-deckers – a fact that intrigued the Tarcun king and prince.

Where were the transports for the thousands of warriors they would need for a landing at Golden Bay?

Regardless of this anomaly however, the enemy fleet still represented over twenty-five thousand warriors and King Jeniel had had no difficulty in persuading the Citizen's Council to declare the state of emergency that had recalled every Tarcun male under the age of thirty to active service in the military, the same declaration also requiring the nation's older men to present themselves for weapons muster and the allocation of battle stations.

As trade with the North had continued, the merchant vessels that visited Kleeft had nervously reported the growing forest of masts there, and every Tarcun now knew that the looming invasion was inevitable and its launch only a matter of time. Jeniel and Ravian had lived with the prospect of the attack for longer than anyone had and there were no surprises for the prince as the skipper of the spy boat made his final report on the enemy's disposition.

Approximately two hundred vessels were due to have sailed from Kleeft that morning. The final tally of transport vessels remained small, however – only ten ships carrying less than two thousand men.

Ravian immediately ordered one of his swordships north to locate the approaching enemy, although he had already calculated that, if the wind held, the Northern fleet would be off the White City within two days.

'Damn!' he swore again – only a few days previously, he had given Capernal permission to take a week of leave with his wife, Liana.

Still, it had been hard to decline the vice admiral, his friend having worked tirelessly through the previous two years to help build the swordship fleet up to full strength. To his knowledge, Liana, daughter and sole heir to the House of Dadicaeus, had dutifully borne her husband's long and frequent absences without complaint. Indeed, Ravian had always thought them a good match, and he was pleased that Capernal, the son of a Belainian coppersmith, had shown that, with ability and a sense of duty, anyone could rise to a position of wealth and power within Tarcun society.

Now though, after only two days of blissful rest at an inland retreat, Capernal would have to be recalled. Ravian ordered a messenger to summon the vice admiral, before going to the palace to advise Jeniel of the spy boat's news.

'Well, at least we have time to stand our defences to in an orderly manner,' the king said, after Ravian had made his report. 'Do you believe the wind will hold?'

'I hope so,' Ravian replied. 'If it does, we'll have time to engage them north of the Tusk. Although this northerly breeze theoretically gives them the weather gauge, it also puts us in the position of being able to tack into them.'

'Any further thoughts on tactics?' Jeniel enquired, even though they had exhaustively discussed every possibility in the previous months.

'I'll brief the captains at midday,' Ravian said. 'We'll sail before dark so that we can hit them as far to the north as possible, and the first priority will be to locate and sink the troop transports if we can. Their four-deckers worry me because their sides are too high to ram over, but I'll be ordering ten of my captains to concentrate on disabling them – one swordship for each four-decker. That leaves the other one hundred and eighty-odd galleys to the remaining forty swordships – which means they will be busy. I'll be stressing to everybody to disable and move on – we will only have a day and a night in which to cripple or sink them all.

'Frankly, considering how long he's had, I can't give Bordwar much credit for his battle plan,' Ravian continued. 'He must be hoping to win the battle at sea and then back up his troop landing at Golden Bay with some of his galley crews. In his place, I would have gone for more transports – he would only have needed a hundred galleys or so to keep our navy occupied and, while they were, he could have put twenty thousand men ashore.'

'I don't think that he is targeting Golden Bay,' replied his brother. 'It looks to me as though he intends a direct assault on the White City.'

'He must be mad then,' Ravian said matter-of-factly. 'Even without our fleet to worry about, his ships won't be able to enter the harbour with the guard chain up. What's he going to do – put his galleys up against the seawall and throw siege ladders across?'

The king looked thoughtful for a moment. With the chain raised between the two guard towers, the White City was virtually impregnable to a sea-borne attack.

'All the same,' Jeniel eventually decided. 'I want you to pull two of the divisions at Centrus back to Dalvin. Wherever Bordwar decides to make his landing, they'll be able to get there in support within a day.'

Ravian nodded his agreement – Dalvin was almost halfway between Centrus and the White City.

'I'll make a general address to the citizenry mid-afternoon,' the king continued. 'I want you and Ramus to attend with me.'

'Certainly,' said Ravian. 'My meeting with the captains will be over by then.'

'And I would like to address the fleet before you sail,' his brother continued.

'Of course,' replied Ravian. 'As long as it is before sunset.'

Inwardly, Ravian cursed the rift that had developed between his brother and him over Belice. Their conversations ever since – even now, at this eleventh hour – were always so stilted and formal.

He returned to the upper storey of the Admiral's Residence to bid Belice farewell.

'You know that you are going to win, don't you?' she told him, although she had tears in her eyes.

'I believe we will,' he replied, 'even though the swordships haven't been tried in a real battle.'

'Then why do you look so grim?' she asked.

'This country has never been in a conflict like the one coming,' he replied. 'I passed so many of our people on our way back here, all looking so staunch and brave, but they have no idea what a real war is like and, in a few days from now, most of them will have lost fathers, sons and brothers. We have no choice in this war – for which I curse

Bordwar – but, whether Tarcus survives or not, her citizens will pay a high cost in blood.'

'I'll be praying for a mighty victory,' she said, 'and I'll be praying that you come home to me.'

'Then pray that the wind holds, My Love,' he told her. 'Pray the wind holds.'

Ravian couldn't quell his feelings as he briefed his captains on the battle plan. His commanding officers were grimly resolute but they, at least, he thought, had some notion of the odds they faced. Later though, as the king addressed his people from the palace steps, every sentence of his inspired oratory bringing frenzied roars of approval from the massed audience, Ravian couldn't help but wonder how many of them would still be alive and still be cheering by the time the forthcoming battle was over.

Jeniel's subsequent speech to the thirty-five hundred crewmen of the swordship fleet was, if anything, even more stirring and powerful. Ravian, however, was distracted somewhat from his morose inner thoughts as he looked in vain for any sign of his vice admiral's return. He was going to have to sail without Capernal he realised – at least able to take some comfort in the knowledge that his friend would survive what he knew was going to be a bloody conflict at sea.

The Tarcun fleet sailed immediately following the king's address and tacked up the Lee Shore in the gathering darkness. Tacking against the northerly meant maddeningly slow progress through the night and, by the following dawn, they were still only just west of Neverius. By midday though, they had left the Tusk well behind them, when the lookouts reported the sail of their reconnaissance vessel ahead on the northern horizon. The captain of the swordship quickly closed with *Sea Eagle* and, putting his vessel on a course close beside her, hailed across the water to his admiral.

'They are still well over the horizon, Sir,' he called out. 'If you adjust your course two points to port you should intercept them about an hour before sunset.'

An hour before sunset would suit them well, Ravian thought, as the scout ship dropped back into formation. It would give them time to assess the enemy before darkness fell, make an initial strike, and then fight a running battle down the coast during the night. He was also pleased that Bordwar's fleet seemed to be on a heading that would take them well west of Tarcus – a battle too close in to the lee of the land might have given the oar-driven galleys a crucial advantage.

'Alter course two points to port, if you please, Captain,' he said calmly to Godart.

The Tusk had almost disappeared below the horizon astern of them when they saw the first enemy sails.

As the scout had reported, Bordwar had made a lot more way to leeward than Ravian could have hoped for, the enemy fleet being considerably further west than the Dekanian king could possibly have intended. Ravian ordered Godart to ease the sheets and, as they ran northwest to meet the Northerners, more and more galleys hauled into view so that the enemy sails covered the horizon as far as the eye could see. Bordwar had assembled the biggest fleet in the world and, as his foe's overwhelming numerical superiority came on full display, Ravian felt his courage falter.

Could the Tarcun swordships and their brave crews possibly prevail against such odds, he asked himself?

Then he shook the feelings of foreboding away, knowing that, at this moment more than any other, his men were looking to him for courage and leadership. Also, he reminded himself, Bordwar had sent no emissaries ahead demanding their surrender. The leader of the Northern Alliance had given them no other choice but to fight.

The galleys, seeing the approaching threat from the southeast, began to drop their sails and masts, the transition rippling across the horizon like a forest suddenly shedding its leaves. Now the enemy ships were close enough for the Tarcuns to see the banks of oars swinging backwards and forwards in unison, and the splash of foam as they dipped. Godart ordered his own men to their battle stations, and the spray from the sail-soakers began to drift over the Tarcun crewmembers.

The sail-soakers had been an ingenious development by Lederalus who, concerned at the risk posed by fire arrows, had developed a device that pumped water up a leather tube on the side of the mast to two men in a protected crow's nest. From that vantage point, the men were able to keep the sails doused during battle, as well as being able to extinguish any fire arrows that might lodge in the rigging. Ravian was sure that the Northerners knew nothing of the sail-soakers and that they would be surprised to find their fire arrows ineffective in the coming battle.

'Can you see any of the transports?' he asked Godart.

'I can see one on the other side of that four-decker, Sir,' his captain replied.

'Very well,' Ravian declared, 'that's our first target. Please signal the fleet to engage.'

Ravian could hear the pounding of the Northerners' timing drums and the chanting of their rowers. In contrast to this commotion, the Tarcun fleet swept into battle in menacing silence.

Suddenly, *Sea Eagle* was confronted by a three-decker galley at the forefront of the enemy formation.

'Take his oars!' Ravian ordered his captain.

Godart allowed his ship to pay off slightly before the wind – dancing away from the thrust of the enemy's ram – before hardening up again and sending her grinding along the galley's side. The noise was enormous – the squeal of the vessels' hulls against each other, the splintering of the oars and the screams from the galley's starboard rowing bank as the shafts flailed about inside, ripping and smashing flesh. From the stricken enemy's stern, a small group of archers fired an accurate but ineffective stream of fire arrows into *Sea Eagle's* sails and rigging, and the swordship's crew responded with a deadly hail of return fire. As the two opponents drew apart, only the dead and the dying remained on the galley's quarterdeck.

Now, *Sea Eagle* quickly accelerated back up to speed, more fire arrows from a two-decker, fifty yards off her port side, falling impotently about her. There was a tremendous noise and Ravian saw that, all around him, the two navies were fully engaged in battle.

'Watch your starboard bow,' he warned Godart, as another three-decker came at them on an intercepting course.

Coolly, Godart held his own heading for a few moments, committing the Northerner to his line of attack. Then he bellowed at Combus, 'Haul in! Bring her up as high as she'll point!' and, as the bosun swung *Sea Eagle's* bow back towards the northwest, they tacked clear of their assailant.

Looking across at the enemy galley, Ravian saw furious bewilderment on her captain's face. Nothing else under sail pointed as high as a swordship and they had taken their foe completely by surprise. After a brief exchange of arrows, the two ships were out of each other's range and Godart continued west in search of the transport vessel. The sound of a crash came from starboard and Ravian saw one of his swordships rip through the oars of a four-decker – the screams from the galley carrying clearly across the water.

'There they are!' Godart exclaimed beside him, pointing ahead.

The transports had kept their sails up, maintaining their southeasterly course behind the screen of the galleys. Now though, as the Tarcun ships began to burst through the Northerners' protective screen, they bore away to the southwest in panic.

'I can only see five, Sir,' Godart reported, confirming Ravian's count.

'Well, let's dispose of them first, and then look for the others,' the prince replied.

A two-decker on their starboard bow made a brave attempt to head them off, presenting *Sea Eagle* with a tempting target as she did so. Godart did not need to be reminded of their priority though and skirted around the galley in pursuit of the transports. Looking about him, Ravian saw that at least ten swordships had broken through the Northerners' line and were joining in the chase of the terrified enemy troop carriers. Astern of them, a swordship suddenly reared up over the beam of a two-decker and Ravian watched with grim satisfaction as the galley's back broke and she disappeared below the waves.

Now, the first of the Tarcun ships – *Sea Lion*, Ravian saw, under Billus's command – was upon the transports. A dark cloud of arrows leaped at his old friend's vessel but to no avail, as Billus brought his ship smashing into the beam of the transport in a perfect ramming manoeuvre. As *Sea Eagle* sailed past, *Sea Lion* was already polling herself out from the gaping chasm she had made in her victim's side, the sea flooding into the mortally wounded enemy.

Sea Eagle was the first swordship to the next troop carrier.

The Northerner skipper, having witnessed the fate his fellow, put his helm over as they approached, thereby denying the swordship a beam attack. Nevertheless, amidst a furious exchange of arrows between the vessels, Godart drove hard at the transport's stern so that *Sea Eagle* glanced off the enemy with a mighty crash, tearing away her steering oar before bearing away again as the crippled vessel fell off the wind. Beside Ravian, Combus suddenly grunted and pitched forward onto the deck, an arrow protruding between his shoulder blades. Instantly, Godart stepped astride his body, seized the tiller and put the ship about to run headlong at the helpless transport's starboard beam. As the range swiftly closed again, Ravian could see the pale faces and wide eyes of the enemy troops crowded amidships in the doomed craft – two hundred men watching certain death bear down on them.

They struck just aft of the transport's mast, *Sea Eagle's* bow kicking high and her sails shivering with the impact. The troop carrier's sides caved in for twenty feet either side of the point of impact, and the swordship squealed to a halt with her bow protruding out beyond her target's port side. As the sea hungrily rushed into the breach, Ravian saw scores of Northern soldiers disappear beneath the water in moments, dragged under by the weight of their armour and drowning inside a vessel that was, itself, about to slip below the surface.

However, having overrun their target by so much, it was impossible to pole off and, despite Godart's order to back the sails, the two ships remained firmly locked together. Ignoring the arrows from *Sea Eagle's* crew, desperate Northerners began clambering up over the swordship's bow and a deadly battle ensued on her forecastle. Then, with a roaring surge of foam, the sea claimed the transport, her mast plummeted beneath the waves, and *Sea Eagle* was left floating on a boiling patch of ocean dotted with floating debris and terrified, swimming men. The remaining Northerners on the forecastle were swiftly despatched or pitched overboard and Godart got the swordship underway again – just avoiding the thrust of a Northern three-decker seeking revenge.

'Take her out to the west if you would be so kind, Godart,' said Ravian, wanting to take stock of the situation before it became dark.

As a replacement helmsman took the steering oar and Combus's body was carried below, they tacked clear of the battle and towards the setting sun while Ravian looked, in vain, for the sails of any further troop ships in the melee behind them.

'I don't see how there could have been ten transports,' he said to Godart. 'Maybe our information was wrong.'

'Perhaps they are heading to Tarcus in a separate formation, Sir,' Godart suggested.

'Well,' said Ravian, looking south to the silhouette of the Tusk, rapidly merging into the gathering darkness, 'if they are, then the army shouldn't have any problem dealing with a landing by such a small force. Let's get back to the action here while there is still some light left.'

They ran back towards east but the light was fading quickly. In the distance ahead, Ravian saw a swordship pinched into a three-decker she had just rammed. Despite desperately polling out and backing her sails, she appeared stuck fast and Ravian could see the galley's crew swarming up over her bow to do battle. Another Northern three-decker seized the opportunity to charge down on the swordship – ramming her so hard that the Tarcun's mast toppled. Then, as the second galley hauled on her oars and pulled her ram free, both wounded vessels swiftly settled beneath the waves in a mortal embrace. It was dark by the time *Sea Eagle* reached the scene and there was no sign of any survivors in the moonless night.

Darkness, however, worked to the Tarcuns' advantage.

The galleys continued to sail southeast, marshalled by a beacon on a massive four-decker that Ravian assumed to be Bordwar's flagship. But the flickering light also marked the general location of the enemy fleet for the circling swordship pack while, at the same time, the noise of each galley's oars gave away its position more specifically.

Ravian could not communicate with his captains but he had briefed them well and, independently, they harried the Northerners throughout the night. The wind had eased at sunset and, while it was not strong enough for the swordships to risk making ramming attacks, there was still enough breeze for them to ghost suddenly and silently in out of the dark, and shear off a bank of Northern oars.

When the wind picked up for a spell about midnight, Godart was able to catch a three-decker beam-on, the galley's captain having imprudently allowed himself to drift a short distance away from the rest of the Northern fleet. *Sea Eagle* smashed into her starboard side before her crew even knew she was upon them and, without her archers having time to fire even a single arrow in her defence, the galley rolled over and went down like a stone.

As dawn came to the ocean, Ravian was able to assess the situation.

Despite the night's attacks, the Northern fleet's commander had held his course for the White City, and the Western Arm was now faintly visible some ten miles ahead. Ravian estimated there were approximately one hundred and thirty enemy vessels remaining on the water, and he thought that he could still count six four-deckers among them. Having herded closer and closer together in the night though, the Northerners had chanced upon an effective defensive tactic and now they continued to row in as close a proximity to one another as they could. Ravian knew that, for a swordship to ram one of the galleys with several of his fellows only a boat length away would be suicidal, and he was fully aware that his fleet had neither the time, nor the numerical advantage, to engage in such a battle of attrition.

Despite the elimination of the transports and the loss of a quarter of the Northerners' galleys, the prince knew that the invading fleet still posed a significant threat to the White City. Even allowing for some casualties aboard the surviving warships, over twenty thousand enemy warriors remained afloat and on course for Tarcus where, if Bordwar could commit even a third of them to a landing, the defence of the White City would be a desperate one. Even now, he knew, Jeniel and his commanders would be watching the approach of the Northerners from the cliff-tops of the Western Arm and, soon, the king would withdraw to his headquarters at the palace from where he would direct the city's defence. Belice would be watching too – praying for his safety and for that of the children of the orphanage.

Ravian asked Godart to signal a recall of the swordships and, as the Northerners ground on towards the Western Arm, the red sails of Tarcus began to converge upon *Sea Eagle* in the freshening breeze.

They had lost nine ships since the start of the battle, one of which, Ravian was distressed to learn, had crossed the bows of a sister swordship in the darkness and been fatally rammed by one of her own. Still, he thought, nine Tarcun ships in exchange for perhaps seventy of the enemy sent to the bottom was a gratifying ratio – if it could only be maintained.

He ordered the fleet to heave to in the lee of *Sea Eagle* and gave his orders.

'Pass the word to concentrate on disabling the Northerners,' he instructed Godart. 'Tell the captains to attack from astern of the enemy formation and take off their steering gear and rowing oars. This wind will take any disabled vessels past the harbour entrance and we can finish them off at our leisure once the White City is safe. No one is to attempt to engage by ramming until I show the signal flag.'

As he waited for his orders to be passed, Ravian cast his eye over his fleet. The bows of many of the swordships showed scars from the night's action and one of them, he saw, had a blackened deck and scorched mainsail where fire had almost taken a fatal hold. Enemy arrows bristled from the hull, sails and masts of all of them, but their crews looked back at him resolutely and he knew that they were ready to follow his orders to the last. Despite the knowledge that next few hours would decide the fate of their homeland, Ravian's chest swelled with pride.

The Tarcun fleet got underway again, sweeping down from astern of the Northerners. Arrows from the vessels of both sides darkened the sky as the swordships harried the rear of the formation, smashing through oars and steering gear. Within an hour, at least fifty Northern galleys had dropped out of the battle, wallowing downwind helplessly or so damaged that they were unable to keep up with their fleet. Obedient to their admiral's orders, none of the swordships had attempted to ram and, to Ravian's delight, they had lost no further ships.

The battle was turning in the favour of the Tarcuns and Bordwar responded with a desperate move.

Abruptly, all the remaining Northern two-deckers – some forty in number – wheeled about and charged towards Ravian's force in a close-spaced line. With dismay, he watched as one of his captains tried to breach the line – running down the side of a galley and shearing off her oars – but the neighbouring galley instantly spun towards the Tarcun vessel and she was caught between the two foes. Ravian watched helplessly as the crews of both galleys poured on board the swordship, slaughtering her crew.

'Do we give the signal to ram, Sir?' Godart asked, as another two swordships attempted to break through the line.

One broke through cleanly in an explosion of shattered oars. The other was caught by the enemy and, again, her crew was quickly overwhelmed.

'Not yet,' Ravian ordered, knowing that to attempt to break the line would deplete his fleet too badly to make an impact on the main body of the Northerners. 'Bring her around on a course to the Northeast and signal the fleet to follow in line astern.'

Godart seemed surprised by the order and opened his mouth to say something before, obviously thinking better of it, he swiftly obeyed his commander's directive. As *Sea Eagle* led the rest of the fleet away from the advancing line of galleys, Ravian was painfully aware that they were sailing in the opposite direction to the White City. Steadily, however, they began to put distance between themselves and the line of two-deckers struggling upwind after them.

'As soon as we can run past their eastern flank, put the ship about,' Ravian ordered Godart.

Each minute that they held their course was agonizing, but Ravian took some comfort from the poor tactical understanding of whoever was in charge of the two-decker squadron. If the enemy commander possessed any knowledge of sailing strategy at all, the Tarcun prince thought, he would realise that he was about to be outflanked and, instead of vainly pursuing the Tarcuns to the north, the Northerners should be rowing east to block them. The two-deckers continued to hold their course though and, after what seemed like an eternity,

Godart finally ordered his ship turned to starboard. Ravian watched with satisfaction as each of his remaining swordships came up to the same mark before putting their helms over. The months of training were paying off – and now his captains could see what he intended.

Too late, the commander of the two-decker squadron realised the Tarcuns' tactics. Too late, he altered his own course to starboard in an attempt to impose his formation between the swordships and the rest of the Northerner fleet.

Sea Eagle, her sails filled with the following wind, passed well clear of the easternmost galley and, looking astern, Ravian was exulted to see most of his swordship fleet do the same. Only the last ship of the line was unable to avoid the easternmost galley of the enemy formation, but her captain was in no mood to be delayed. To a mighty roar of approval from the Tarcun fleet, he drove his vessel straight up and over the galley, rolling and sinking her with barely a pause.

'Take that captain's name!' Ravian growled to Godart. 'I haven't given the order to ram yet!'

Godart looked around in disbelief, and then saw that his admiral was smiling.

'Aye, aye, Sir!' he said with a laugh and a salute.

Both men knew that day was within their grasp but, ahead of them, Ravian could see that the rest of the Northern fleet was now very close to the Western Arm. They still numbered over fifty vessels – including five four-deckers. That meant about ten thousand enemy crew, he calculated, with perhaps another five thousand in the two-decker squadron struggling along in their wake. He also judged that the swordships wouldn't be able to overhaul the enemy before they rounded the point – but they would be close!

Tensely, the Tarcuns ran down on the enemy, but they were still half a mile away when the first of the four-deckers disappeared behind the cliff edge of the Western Arm. As *Sea Eag*le rounded the point on the tail of the last of the galleys and the White City hove into sight however, Ravian saw that the Northerners' formation had unravelled, presenting the perfect opportunity for the swordships to attack freely.

'Order the fleet to ram!' he roared.

Godart ordered the signal pennant hoisted and then sent *Sea Eagle* smashing into the laggard three-decker with all the force of the north wind. They stuck into her for a time, the swordship's sails towering over the stricken Northerner and driving both ships past the harbour entrance. Although the galley slowly began to sink, at least fifty of her crew made it up onto *Sea Eagle's* forecastle.

'Repel boarders!' Ravian bellowed and, drawing his sword, charged the length of his flagship to join the battle.

Quarter was neither asked nor given, the Northerners fighting with berserk bravery even as their own vessel foundered beneath the swordship's keel. They were tired though, having rowed at action stations since sunset the previous evening, and Ravian despatched three of their number with relative ease. Within moments, all the Northerners who had boarded them were dead.

As his men threw the bodies of the slain enemy over the side, Ravian rejoined Godart on the quarterdeck. All about them, it was ship-to-ship and hand-to-hand outside the harbour walls.

'Look at that!' exclaimed Godart, pointing toward the harbour entrance.

One of the four-deckers, harried by a swordship, had rowed at full speed between the watchtowers and ripped her bottom out on the chain. Now she was sinking rapidly by the stern, her crew throwing off their armour and stampeding into the water like cattle.

'By Delikas!' exclaimed Ravian. 'I thought that everyone in the world knew that the harbour was guarded by a chain!'

Another four-decker – Bordwar's flagship, the prince thought – had gone alongside the harbour wall. Arrows flew thick between the galley and the Tarcun defenders, as a horde of Northern warriors clambered down off her to mass at the base of the breakwater.

'They're suicidal!' gasped Godart.

'Let's give them a helping hand then,' Ravian snarled. 'Put *Sea Eagle* into her starboard side, Captain!'

The massive Northerner's crew were so busy giving battle to the defenders on the wall that they didn't notice the swordship's approach, and not a single arrow flew to meet them. As *Sea Eagle's* bow drove into the immobile galley's hull, it was, as Ravian would later recall, rather like crushing an eggshell – the extra row of oar ports in the four-decker's sides seeming to make her even weaker than the lesser-decked vessels. So deeply did they penetrate below the enemy's gunwale however, that the swordship's forestay stretched and then snapped, collapsing the foresail and causing her mast to sag sternward.

'Pole Out!' bellowed Godart, as the sea began to flood into the galley and the giant ship began to roll ponderously toward them.

They came free easily and, as they pushed clear, Godart ordered the mainsail dropped and his crew to their oars. As the swordship backed out to sea, the galley, her port side grinding against the sea wall, continued to roll to seaward, capsizing with a mighty splash. Perhaps a hundred Northerners were trapped inside her hull, Ravian guessed, the rest mercilessly cut down by Tarcun arrows as they continued to mill at the base of the sea wall.

As *Sea Eagle's* crew frantically tried to rig a new forestay, and the swordship turned to do further battle, Ravian looked about the battle scene and placed a hand on the Godart's shoulder.

'It's all right, Captain,' he said. 'I think that your men can leave this repair to the shipyard.'

They had won.

The only Northern vessels still floating were obviously crippled or in full flight. Debris littered the sea outside the harbour entrance and they could hear a mighty cheering from the harbour walls.

'Call the fleet in,' Ravian ordered Godart.

There were twenty-seven swordships still floating, but the close-in fighting had been costly. Including *Sea Eagle*, eleven of them had either lost too many crew, or were too badly damaged, to pursue the remnants of the Northerner fleet.

'I want those swordships that are still seaworthy to finish off the crippled enemy vessels,' Ravian ordered the remaining sixteen vessels' captains. 'After that, if this northerly holds, you should be able to overhaul and sink those that have fled. I don't want a single Northerner to make it home.'

As the able members of the fleet sailed on their mission to pursue and despatch, the harbour chain was lowered and Ravian led the balance of his fleet into harbour. All along the sea walls and from the guard towers, the land-based defenders of the White City roared their cheers, the noise continuing unabated, as they rowed into the naval base. The jetties there were thronged with a joyous press of victorious Tarcuns, led by Jeniel, who leaped across to their gunwale as *Sea Eagle* tied up.

'A great victory!' the king exclaimed as he bounding up to the quarterdeck and embraced his brother. 'It was even closer than even you think though.'

'How so?' asked Ravian, certain that none of the invasion fleet had made it over the walls or into the harbour.

'The Northerners landed a force at the South Gate,' the young monarch explained. 'While the rest of us were watching the battle outside the harbour, they somehow got over the walls and wiped out the guard there. They'd actually opened the gates and were entering the city, but Graticus got there with a small force and held them long enough for the alarm to be raised. He's the hero of the moment!'

'Well, that was fortunate,' Ravian said charitably, privately irritated that, even in his finest moment, Graticus had stolen some of his glory. 'What about Bordwar?'

'He was on the four-decker that you rammed against the sea wall,' Jeniel said. 'He's dead – I've just seen his body.'

'There's another thing you should know,' his brother continued more soberly. 'Capernal's been killed. He was at the South Gate when the enemy took it.'

Ravian was stunned.

'What was he doing at the South Gate?' he asked.

'From what I can understand – and things are still fairly chaotic – your messenger didn't find him for some time,' Jeniel said. 'He and Liana were coming back on the Mount Perios Road when they saw the enemy transports sailing down the coast below them – the Northerners must come down the Weather Shore and passed Land's End during the night. Apparently, Capernal rode on ahead at full speed to warn the commander of the South Gate guard and he must still have been there when the enemy attacked.'

'We've lost a good man...we've lost too many good men,' said Ravian, the death of his friend, and that of Combus, throwing a pall over the swordships' success.

'Nevertheless, a great victory!' Jeniel exalted, seizing his hand and raising it to the wildly cheering crowd. 'Those Northerners won't try that again!'

It was a great victory, Ravian would later reflect.

Bordwar had been killed, and not one of his followers had made it back to his homeland. Indeed, the remaining, able, swordships had run down and despatched the last surviving galley at the very threshold of the Grimspot Gris, ramming and sinking the hapless enemy vessel within sight of the shores of Gerouf. Thirty-four thousand northern warriors and over two hundred vessels had perished in Bordwar's attempt to take Tarcus, whereas the cost to the island kingdom had been relatively small – twenty-three swordships sunk and the loss of just over two thousand men, including the guard at the South Gate.

The action at the South Gate gnawed at Ravian though.

That a thousand of the enemy should have taken the heavily-guarded portal so easily was a concern in itself but, of even greater significance, was the close proximity of their breakthrough to the eastern guard tower. A thousand northern warriors coming upon the Tarcun defenders, unexpectedly and from behind, would have wreaked havoc along the sea wall, Ravian knew, and, had the Northerners then been able to take the guard tower and lower the chain guarding the harbour, Bordwar's galleys would have been able to row directly into the port and disgorge their crews into the heart of the White City. Had that happened, the prince suspected, the outcome of what had, inevitably, become known as, "The Great Sea War", would have been very different.

Ravian knew that he should join with the rest of Tarcus in lauding Graticus and his men – who were now hailed as the Heroic One Hundred. It seemed to him though, that Bordwar had been utterly confident that the harbour chain would have been lowered by the time his forces arrived off the White City, and this explained the milling confusion of Northerner fleet when it became apparent that it had not. What had appeared to be a senseless battle strategy on the part of the Dekanian king had, in fact, been a well-coordinated plan that had come so close to success that it made the Tarcun prince's blood run cold just to think about it.

Was it the fact that it was his old rival that had saved the day that made him suspicious, Ravian wondered?

Or was it because he could not shake off the feeling that Bordwar would never have left such a crucial part of his battle plan to chance?

Ravian couldn't shake the feeling that something wasn't quite right in the kingdom of Tarcus.

Still, ahead of him lay the task of rebuilding the navy as swiftly as possible – the threat from the North may have been put paid to, but the pirates of the Sapphire Sea would see the depletion of the Tarcun fleet as an opportunity. Tarcus must continue to prosper – and he must ensure that she continued to be protected by her swords in the sea.

THE END

Thank you for reading

THE SWORD IN THE SEA

If you enjoyed the book, please consider posting a review on the site you downloaded this book from and, please, tell your friends.

I'm always interested in hearing from readers and I welcome any comments and feedback.

Email: jerry.carpenter@clear.net.nz

Website: www.jerrycarpenter.co.nz[1]

1. http://www.jerrycarpenter.co.nz

Bonus Material

Ravian's Quest (The Second Chronicle of Tarcus)

Available Now

Chapter One

'The woman is a whore and you will put her aside!'

Jeniel, King of Tarcus, had gone very red in the face.

Hardly a soul in the kingdom who would dare confront the monarch when he was this angry, but the subject of his rage stood his ground and glared back at him.

'I shall not!' snarled Prince Ravian, his younger brother, Defender of the Nation and hero of the Great Sea War. 'Belice has stood beside me more loyally than any daughter of the Nine Houses.'

'*One* daughter of the Nine Houses!' Jeniel roared. 'And you virtually ignored the woman the whole time you were married to her!'

There was a tense silence.

They were alone in the palace's Hunting Room, their only witnesses the animals' heads that decorated its walls. As their father had before him, the king preferred this particular sanctuary for private meetings, and his brother had immediately become suspicious when Jeniel had summoned him there.

His marriage to Sinur had been a disastrous mistake, Ravian admitted to himself, but he had never entirely exorcised his suspicion that Jeniel had somehow been involved in her murder. Now, it was as though his dead wife's ghost floated between them, her cold presence powerful enough to quench the flaming tempers of both brothers.

'You won't be seeing much of your Ezrenian harlot for a while anyway,' Jeniel continued, in the tight tone of one who has just wrestled himself back under control. 'It is time to repair our relations with the nations of the North and rebuild some of the trade that the Great Sea War has cost us. In my name, you will head a mission to the countries on this list and attempt to re-establish formal diplomatic ties.'

Jeniel handed Ravian a parchment scroll which the prince snatched and immediately unrolled. The prince's eyes widened as he began to read out the formidable tally inscribed upon it.

'Groven, Gerouf, Dekane, Graftsen... Survene? Saravene? Grenwain?!' Ravian exclaimed. 'This is more like a list of the whole world west of Dalvan! Most of these countries did not even take up arms against us!'

'True,' his brother replied, 'but while you're carrying out your mission, you might as well cement ties with the friendlies and try and bring some neutrals onto our side as well. Some monarchs might be upset if they thought they had been bypassed.'

There was an odd smile on Jeniel's face now, and Ravian decided he didn't like the look of it one bit.

'Needless to say,' the king continued, 'your legendary diplomatic skills – or lack thereof – will make this mission a challenge for you. With this in mind, I have decided that the good Citizen Lectus will accompany you as your mentor and advisor.'

'Lectus!' Ravian exploded. 'Surely you jest! Do you really expect me to represent Tarcus to the world in the company of some...some pederastic whale?!'

'I'm not joking at all, Ravian,' his brother replied evenly. 'Citizen Lectus may be on the large side, and he may well prefer the company of men, but I don't believe that his tastes extend to boys. More relevantly, he has an extensive knowledge of foreign customs and diplomatic protocol, which you will find invaluable in carrying out your mission.'

'But it will take a year to voyage around the countries on this list,' Ravian said angrily.

'Oh, at least – probably longer,' the king agreed smugly.

'Send Ramus then, if you're so worried about my lack of diplomacy.'

The king's smile widened and Ravian realised he had stepped into a trap.

'Alas,' Jeniel sighed. 'Would that I could, but our little brother is increasingly busy with our trading partners in the East. Besides, he has a wife and family to think about...a *royal* wife and three wonderful princesses.'

Ravian knew that there was more to come.

'In fact,' the king continued, 'Ramus's eminently suitable marriage and abundant issue are precisely what make him unsuitable for the *other* part of your mission.'

'Oh yes...?' Ravian coaxed his older brother suspiciously.

'Well...,' Jeniel said, 'there is this other list that I want you to consider.'

He handed his brother a second scroll.

'Princess Veletia, daughter of King Paxim,' Ravian read. 'Princess Flamina, daughter of King Zecretes. Princess...Is this what I think it is?'

'If what you think it is, is a list of young women of noble birth whose parents would consider a marriage alliance with the royal family of Tarcus, then you are correct,' his brother replied.

Don't miss out!

Visit the website below and you can sign up to receive emails whenever Jerry Carpenter publishes a new book. There's no charge and no obligation.

https://books2read.com/r/B-A-NREPB-CZUMD

BOOKS 2 READ

Connecting independent readers to independent writers.

www.ingramcontent.com/pod-product-compliance
Lightning Source LLC
LaVergne TN
LVHW041204150826
845673LV00001B/280

* 9 7 9 8 2 3 0 8 2 0 9 9 4 *